Breaking Butterflies

M. Anjelais

Chicken House

SCHOLASTIC INC. * NEW YORK

Library of Congress Cataloging-in-Publication Data Available
ISBN 978-0-545-66766-1

10 9 8 7 6 5 4 3 2 1   14 15 16 17 18

Printed in the U.S.A.   23
First American edition, September 2014

The text type was set in Adobe Garamond.
Interior book design by Abby Kuperstock

To all those who chose to live when they felt like dying,
to 29:11,
and to RRRK, who was not afraid.

1

When my mother was a little girl, she walked to the playground by herself every day after school. I can picture it easily; photos of her as a child are almost indistinguishable from photos of me when I was little. I used to look at her old yellow-edged school photographs a lot. My mother had a shy, quiet look, a round face, and the same straight brown hair I used to have, though in every picture hers was pulled back from her forehead in two tight little pigtails.

She was lonely when she was little. No one ever asked her to play; she was the clumsy one whom nobody sensible wanted on their team, the timid one who was too chicken to climb on top of the monkey bars. It was the same for me. While other children swirled over the jungle gym and slides in a frenzy of make-believe and hide-and-seek, I would sit by the swings on my own, kicking at the dust. We were two of a kind when we were really young, I can tell. But that was before she met Leigh, and long before I learned how to be strong.

I don't know much about what happened before Leigh, about the lonely time. All that was just a vague prologue; meeting Leigh, and what happened after that, was the real story. That was what I'd grown up listening to my mother tell and retell, until I'd heard it so many times that I had the dialogue memorized and could whisper the whole thing to myself if I wanted to. Not only was it about my mother, but it was about me, too. In a way, it was the beginning of both of us. And I treasured that story so much that I used to let it own me. Looking back now, two years gone by since everything that happened when I was sixteen, I think perhaps that was my first mistake.

My mother's part of the story started on a Tuesday, a week or so before her seventh birthday. She'd arrived at the playground and found her usual swing occupied by a girl wearing a pink tutu over her clothes. The girl had a pair of rhinestone-studded sunglasses perched on her head, and from her feet dangled her mother's shoes, red and high-heeled. She was swinging her legs back and forth contentedly, admiring the shoes, but she looked up when my mother drew near. Her hair was blonde and wavy, and reached down to her waist. My mother never mentioned being jealous of it, but I had a feeling she must've been.

"What's your name?" the girl said.

"Sarah," whispered my mother. I used to move my mouth along with my mother's as she told this part of the story, echoing her lines.

"Last name?" prompted the girl.

"Quinn," said my mother hesitantly.

"Sarah Quinn," repeated the girl. She looked up at the sky, and back down at her pumps. "That sounds like a superhero's name. The name they have when they're not doing hero stuff, I mean. Like Clark Kent is Superman's regular name, you know?"

"Yeah," said my mother. "What's your name?"

"Leigh Latoire," answered the girl.

My mother said she was in a state of faint awe. "That sounds like a movie star's name," she said, which was exactly what I always thought whenever I heard this part.

"Thank you," said Leigh graciously. "But I don't want to be a movie star when I grow up. I want to be a pirate queen."

"I want to be a vet for horses," said my mother, who was currently in The Horse Phase, which is an important part of growing up (I myself have gone through The Horse Phase, meaning that I am definitely a normal girl).

"That's nice," said Leigh politely. She had not gone and would never go through The Horse Phase, because she was out of the ordinary. My mother understood this right away. She stood leaning against the frame of the swing, and looked at Leigh — at the rhinestone sunglasses, at the red high-heeled shoes, at the tutu, at her long, flowing blonde hair, at her eyes, which were a pale, pale blue. And as she looked, she began to feel like she really was in the presence of a queen. Perhaps even a pirate queen.

"Hey," my mother said, "do you want to come to my birthday party? I invited everyone in my class at school."

"Sure," said Leigh. "Sure, I'll come to your party, Sarah."

She was the only one who did.

"Where are all the kids from your class?" she asked as she came into my mother's backyard, which had been festooned with cheap streamers and wilting balloons. My mother was sitting on her back porch steps, a ridiculous cone-shaped party hat on her head, feeling terribly ashamed of her empty party. When she told me this part, I could feel her embarrassment in my own chest, heavy and pressing down toward my stomach; there had been parties like that for me, too.

"They didn't come," muttered my mother, and wiped her nose on the back of her hand.

"Well, I came," said Leigh, handing my mother a present wrapped in pink sparkly paper. "Go on, open it."

I always imagined the pink paper unfolding and falling away as though I were opening it with my own hands. Leigh had given my mother toy horses, a set of four of them — matching mothers and foals, one pair of palominos and one pair of bays.

"Do you like them?" asked Leigh eagerly.

"I love them," my mother said. The horses were flocked and soft. I knew because the first time that my mother had ever told me the story, she had taken the horses down from where she kept them on her dresser and let me touch them.

"I thought you would," said Leigh. "Let's play the party games now!"

She and my mother played egg-and-spoon race, pin-the-tail-on-the-donkey, and scavenger hunt. They beat the piñata into a rainbow assortment of torn pieces. They had two pieces of birthday cake each, and they divided the contents of all the unclaimed goodie bags between themselves. They made a fort out of two lawn chairs and an old sheet, and carried all of the candy from the piñata into it, where they devoured it in secret. My mother said it hadn't mattered that there were only the two of them, with no other guests around. Whenever my mother described it, she made it sound like the best party there ever was. I imagined it in extra-saturated color, a rainbow bursting out from a backdrop of muted vintage tones.

It was during this party that Leigh, as her little fingers unfolded the comic wrapper from a piece of Bazooka gum, had asked my mother to be her best friend.

"Really?" my mother asked.

"Well, don't you want to?" Leigh's eyes were large.

"Of course," my mother said. They had both laughed. When I was really little, I used to like this part. It was the beginning of a lifelong friendship, the end of my mother's childhood loneliness — a good thing, I always thought. But there would come a time, when I was older, that I wondered how differently my life would have turned out if Leigh had never been on the swing that day, if she had not been the sole guest at my mother's party. And I wished, sometimes, in a dark place in the back of my head, that my mother's answer to Leigh's offer of friendship had not been a happy agreement.

Leigh had instructed my mother to run inside and get a pin, saying eagerly, "We have to become blood sisters!" And my mother dutifully went into her house and brought out a pin.

Leigh took it from her with the utmost ceremony and stabbed her thumb, squeezing it to bring the blood to the surface before handing the pin back to my mother, who bit her lip nervously. She used to feel the same way about blood as I do: beyond queasy.

"Go on," urged Leigh. "You can do it. It doesn't hurt that bad."

My mother pricked her thumb, and when a little drop of crimson welled up on the tip, she was terribly proud of it, even though she tried not to look at it for too long. Leigh pressed her thumb against my mother's.

"There," she said, pulling her hand away and sucking on her thumb. "We're blood sisters now, and best friends forever." She had paused thoughtfully before finishing, "Let's plan out our lives."

"What do you mean?" my mother asked, wiping her own thumb on the fort sheet. At seven years old, she hadn't known that the most important part of the story was coming next. But as a grown woman, telling it to me, she knew, and she always dropped her voice at this point and leaned in toward me, her eyes sparkling.

"Let's just make a plan, all right?" Leigh had said. "I'll go first." She took a deep breath, and began, "When I grow up, I want to be a pirate queen, but if that doesn't happen, I want to be a fashion designer and make fancy clothes. I'm going to have two houses, one in the United States and one in England — if I end up being a fashion designer anyway. If I'm a pirate queen, I'll live on a ship. No matter what I am, though, I'm going to have a kid — one kid, and it'll be a boy, and I'll name him Cadence, the most beautiful name I have ever thought of. And of course, all through my life, I'll be best friends with my blood sister, Sarah Quinn." She stopped in order to breathe, and said, "There, see? That's my life. Now plan yours."

"Okay," my mother said, and she thought for a moment. "Well, when I grow up, I want to be a vet for horses. If that doesn't happen, I want to work in advertising, just like my mommy does. I just want one house, and it'll be in the United States. I'm going to have a kid too, just one — a girl. And I'll name her . . . Sphinx. I learned that word in history class, but I think it's pretty. I can call her Sphinxie as a nickname. Oh, and all through my life, I'll be best friends with my blood sister, Leigh Latoire."

The other spoken lines in the story were half-guesses, what my mother thought that she and Leigh had said, but the plans were exact quotes. My mother had never forgotten the words, and after years of hearing them repeated to me, neither would I. They were written on the inside of my mind forever, like an internal tattoo.

"Since you're having a girl, can she marry Cadence?" cried Leigh excitedly. "Then when they have kids, we'll be grandmothers together!"

"Yeah," agreed my mother. "Yeah, they'll be best friends, and then" — here was the part she didn't tell me until much later — "they'll get married."

She left the fort for a minute and returned with the set of four horses. "Look, Leigh," she said. "It's me and you and Cadence and Sphinx. You and Cadence are the palominos, and me and Sphinxie are the bays." She opened the box and took the horses out. "Here," she said, handing Leigh the palominos. "They're friendship ponies."

"And reminders," said Leigh, stroking the palominos. "They'll remind us to follow our plans, for always." She picked up the bay foal and held it in one hand, the palomino foal in the other. Slowly, she touched their noses together in a kiss. "Cadence and Sphinx," she whispered.

I learned in health class at school that when a little girl is born, she already has all of the eggs she will ever have inside her. So, in a way, I had experienced the story firsthand. Cadence and I were there as our mothers made their plans, as they named us, as they betrothed us. As Leigh touched the foals' noses together, we were dormant and sleeping inside. And perhaps we stirred slightly, knowing somehow that the plan would hold and we would some-day burst out into the world as red-faced newborns, ready to grow. We, under the old sheet of the fort, two eggs out of millions.

We were there.

2

My mother went into advertising. She prepared layouts for magazine and newspaper ads, and her lettering was beautiful. She met my father at work, and they dated for a very long time before he asked her to marry him. Her wedding dress was white and puffy. She and my father moved into a house in Connecticut, a house with an extra bedroom for a baby, with a nice backyard for a set of kiddie swings that would become my favorite place to play.

Leigh became a fashion designer. She had clothes with her name on them in the high-end malls, and she sat in the front row at glitzy runway shows, watching girls with high cheekbones slope down the catwalk wearing dresses she'd created. She bought a house that was bigger than my mother's house, in a wealthier neighborhood several miles away; a year later, she bought her house in England, and flew back and forth between the two. She met her husband at a fashion show, and they dated on and off for a very long time before he asked her to marry him. Her wedding dress was a viridian green — she made it herself. I saw photos of it once and couldn't decide how it made me feel because, though it was beautiful, it made my mother's dress look old-fashioned and fussy. It was in a class all its own.

Even after they got married, my mother and Leigh remained best friends; they met for coffee, shopped together, talked on the phone, sent cards, and invited each other to one thing and another. Leigh designed a dress inspired by one that my mother had worn as a little girl, and named the design after her. My mother worked on advertisements for Leigh's clothes. She cut them out of magazines when they were printed and kept them in a box, carefully saved. Every so often, I looked through them, leafing through the glossy pages. And always, the palominos stood behind a glass pane in a china cabinet in Leigh's England house, and the bays were on my mother's dresser.

Leigh was the first to find out that she was pregnant. She teased my mother about it, saying that she'd beaten her to it and urging her to hurry up. My mother caught up quickly: Only two months later, she received the news that she was pregnant too. She'd gone with Leigh to her ultrasound appointments, and had been there when the technician asked Leigh if she wanted to know what sex the baby was. Leigh had squeezed my mother's hand nervously; she was afraid that she was going to have a girl and the plan would be spoiled. But the technician pressed down on Leigh's stomach and informed her that it was a boy, and my mother laughed out loud. It was all going according to plan.

"It'll be my turn soon," my mother had told the technician. "You'll be looking at my little girl." She patted her stomach. When her turn came, the same technician brought my image up on the ultrasound screen and announced that, yes, she was looking at my mother's little girl. Leigh and my mother set aside dates for baby showers.

My parents decorated the extra bedroom for me, all in pastel pink. I would end up leaving it that way. The furniture changed as I grew, of course, and when I hit my preteens I started putting up posters and photographs of my own, but even now I'm still pretty happy with my soft pink walls.

Leigh hired someone to come in and do Cadence's room, but she didn't have them do it in blue. Light blue for a baby boy was too ordinary for Leigh. She created a color scheme based around a swatch of green fabric, the same fabric used to make her wedding gown. She had someone paint trees on the walls, and a night sky on the ceiling. When the lights were turned out, the stars glowed in the dark.

At the baby showers, my mother's friends brought pink onesies and footie pajamas, rattles shaped like flowers, a mobile with plush butterflies hanging from it, soft baby blankets with roses embroidered on them, cards that welcomed a little girl. Leigh brought me a gigantic stuffed zebra with a purple ribbon tied around its neck. *Made out of all organic fibers,* the tag said. *Tag made out of 100% recycled material.* It's still at the end of my bed, a formidable presence that new friends always ask about when they enter my room for the first time. Leigh's friends brought Cadence things like that:

eccentric stuffed animals and rattles made of wood, classy in their simplicity. My mother brought him a huge teddy bear and a set of blue onesies with little trucks on the front.

Then suddenly, we were born, pushed out into the air and bright lights, the cords connecting us to our mothers severed. My mother went over to Leigh's house and they sat in the airy living room, spinning an Enya CD in Leigh's stereo system, nursing us on the wide sofa. And soon enough, watching us crawl over the wooden floor. Lying on our plump stomachs, reaching for the toys scattered over the living-room rug. Standing. Stumbling forward. Growing like weeds, from two eggs to two babies to two toddlers to two children.

There was nothing particularly remarkable about me as a little kid. I looked a lot like my mother had; I was not as shy as she had been, but I was not particularly outgoing, either. I never initiated the games when my friends came over; I politely said hello and showed them where my toys were and waited for them to tell me what to do. If there was ever a disagreement, I'd flee to my mother, pressing my head into her chest to avoid dealing with the conflict. While my peers busied themselves grabbing each other's toys and giving each other experimental whacks across the face, I already understood that certain things made people feel badly, or made their bodies hurt. Empathy, perhaps, was my only talent — I never showed very much promise in any other areas.

Cadence, on the other hand, was one of those children everyone was stunned by. He was an excellent artist even when he was little. While I was just beginning to draw stick figures, he was drawing amazing pictures of people, like some child prodigy. It was like that in almost every part of life: While I still stuttered and baby-talked, he amazed people with his long sentences and perfect speech; while I clung to my mother, he was totally independent, and he always got what he wanted. And while I was a slightly pudgy, brown-haired child, indistinguishable from the masses of little girls in the world, he was a striking little wisp of a kid, his face a sharp white angle surrounded by wavy blond hair like Leigh's, his eyes a fierce shade of ice blue.

I always felt vaguely stupid when I was around him. I was simply too ordinary, while he was this vision of talent and good looks, whirling through life and dazzling everyone with his greatness. I never really hated him for making me feel less than him; I was just in awe of him, like my mother had been in awe of Leigh when she had met her at the playground all those years ago. I thought of him as shining, always shining. But light can be blinding; it can shine so hard into your eyes that you don't realize what's behind it — and then, like a car hidden behind glaring headlights, it hits you at full speed.

It was my father who saw it first, when we were five. Cadence and I were out in my backyard, while Leigh and my mother were inside, having tea. My father had volunteered to take us outside and watch us play. I don't quite remember what we were doing, only that at some point a brilliantly colored butterfly appeared and began to dance over the grass, up and down, up and down. It paused on a flower, and then it fluttered off again, darting this way and that, iridescent blue wings catching the sunlight. It was the most beautiful thing I had ever seen. I ran for my butterfly net, but when I came back, Cadence had caught it in his bare hands. When I saw him do it, I was delighted. I didn't know what was about to happen.

"Look at that, Sphinx, I don't think we've seen one of those before," my father said. "Isn't it lovely? Cadence, open your hands a little so Sphinxie can see."

I leaned eagerly over Cadence's cupped hands. He opened his fingers slightly. The butterfly was calm between his palms, its little sticky feet splayed out, its curly proboscis tasting Cadence's skin. The wings were shimmering, making me think of stories about fairies. I reached a finger out to touch it.

Cadence looked up, and the blue of his eyes was so bright. Then he closed his hands together, and I heard the soft sound of the butterfly being crushed. Being broken.

"Cadence!" my father said, astonished, and I burst into tears.

At five years old, this was the most terrible act of violence I had ever seen. I'd never been so shocked in my whole life. Cadence just stared at us, at the way I was sobbing into my father's pant leg, at my father's wide-eyed face, the mouth turned down in disgust. He opened his hands, and the mess of the butterfly's body was spread all over his palms. The crumpled wings fell away. Cadence stared at us for a moment longer, his eyes narrowed, as though he were reading a difficult paragraph in a book. And then, all of a sudden, he looked down at his hands and burst into tears, just exactly like I had.

My father carried us both into the house. Our mothers picked us up and comforted us while my father explained what had happened out in the backyard. I put my hands over my ears. The thought of the crushed butterfly was making me sick.

"Well, he didn't mean to kill it, did you, Cadence?" said Leigh, wiping the tears from his face with her shirtsleeve.

"No," said Cadence. The tears that Leigh had wiped away were not replaced; while I sobbed on in earnest, he seemed to have run out of sobs. He was as carefree as if nothing had ever happened. "I didn't know what would happen," he said. "I was just seeing what would happen."

Leigh held him up so he could wash his hands in our kitchen sink. "Now you know what happens," she said. "Don't do that again."

"Okay," he said. Leigh handed him a towel to dry his hands on. He dried his hands and dropped the towel on the floor. I was still crying, my face buried in my mother's neck.

After they went home, I was watching a cartoon on television when I heard my parents talking in the kitchen. Our kitchen was open, and right next to our living room, so I could hear everything that they were saying — they just thought that I was busy with the cartoon and wasn't paying attention.

"There's something wrong with that kid," my father said.

"He didn't mean to smash the bug," my mother said dismissively. She was doing the dishes, clinking plates together in the sink.

"You didn't see him, Sarah. He *meant* it. He wanted to kill that butterfly, and he did."

"He's only five years old," my mother said.

"So is Sphinx. Does she go around killing butterflies?"

"No, but she's sensitive, and she's a girl. Little boys are odd. I wouldn't put it past a little boy to smash a butterfly just to see what would happen."

"He knew what would happen," said my father insistently.

"Did you see how he was crying afterward?" my mother asked. "He felt bad about it."

"I don't think so. When we were outside, Sphinxie started crying first, then he started. It was like he realized from seeing her that he was supposed to cry. Otherwise, I don't think he would've cried at all. Just do me a favor, Sarah — watch Sphinxie when Leigh's over with him, okay? Can you just do that for me? Don't let them play alone."

I turned slowly back toward the television, fixing my eyes on the bright moving shapes. Even though I was only five, I knew what my father was talking about; I had seen it too. It was something about Cadence's eyes. They had been burning, shining bright, so bright, and so cold, like sun reflecting on an icy landscape. Everyone loved Cadence's eyes, people were always saying how beautiful they were, how unusual. How completely out of the ordinary. *Sometimes,* I thought, *ordinary is better.* It was the first time in my life that I realized something could be so unusual that it was broken, so out of the ordinary that something was wrong with it.

3

Cadence never killed another butterfly, and my mother said that he had learned his lesson. Nevertheless, she watched us carefully, as my father had requested. For a while, it set me on edge; I remember being unable to think of anything but the butterfly incident when I saw her standing near, her eyes fixed on us. It upset me so much that Cadence stopped being my shining friend for a while.

But before long, the memory began to fade. Slowly, new days pushed the images to the back of my brain like old clothes shoved into the back of a closet, dusty and forgotten. I decided my mother watched me only because mothers were silly like that. And Cadence shone once more — brighter than ever. He had an intensity about him: He wasn't hyperactive like some little children, he simply had an energy that was alive with some kind of fire. Leigh said the teachers at his school told her that Cadence was definitely going to do something great one day in the future.

But there was still something wrong, even if I didn't really understand what it was. It most likely had something to do with my personality, I thought at the time; I tended to follow anyone who wanted to lead. And Cadence was an excellent leader even at six. He always knew exactly what games to play, and they were always the most exciting games, the best games I had ever played, the most thrilling times that I'd ever had. When I left Cadence's house, I always left feeling exhilarated, as though he had taken me into his own shining world.

"Cadence," I would declare, "is my best friend!"

"I knew he would be," my mother would answer happily, thinking, I suppose, of her life's plan. Cadence and I had grown up hearing the story of how our mothers had planned their lives at seven under a fort in a backyard, but we only knew the first parts at that point. I suppose they didn't tell us the marriage part because they thought it would be too strange. Perhaps she and Leigh even had secret visions of revealing the final part of the story one Thanksgiving, while Cadence's and my children ran circles around their feet. Maybe.

He wasn't always a good best friend, though. There were days when I made a mistake, didn't play the game according to his rules, didn't feel like playing at all. On those days the bright eyes would come out, the fierce sun would rise over the icy wasteland of blue, and he seemed so much taller than me, so much bigger. He was powerful and frightening and demanding. And at the same time, he was still my shining friend: I so wanted to please him. I had to do it his way, and only his way. And if I didn't, that startling intelligence that everyone admired was deadly. He could lie like an undercover agent, get me in trouble, and escape totally blameless.

"I hate you!" I screamed at him once. Something he'd done had unfolded before my eyes, and I had seen for the umpteenth time how he had used or insulted me. He only stared at me, icy and unmoved.

"Cadence," I cried to my mother later that day, "is absolutely *not* my best friend."

"Sometimes we have disagreements with our friends," she said reasonably. "You'll work it out." And we always did, in a way. The next playdate would come, and the memories of the lies and the way he seemed to tower over me would fade away like the memory of the butterfly, just as soon as he opened the front door of Leigh's elegant house and stepped out eagerly onto the porch, waving and calling my name.

We had a shared seventh birthday party, set in between the dates of our real birthdays. It was our mothers' idea (they meant it to honor the seventh birthday party that my mother had had, when Leigh had given her the horses), but we didn't mind it — or at least, I certainly didn't. I don't know what Cadence really thought, only that he smiled and hugged me, saying he couldn't wait for his and Sphinxie's birthday party. He wanted a real artist's easel, he said. I wanted Barbie dolls.

The party took place at Leigh's house, and stayed with me forever. Even years later, I could remember every detail: the bright colors of the wrapping paper on the stack of gifts by the back door, the huge cake that was half vanilla and half chocolate, the smiles of my mother and Leigh, who stood by and watched us with proud, knowing eyes. Balloons were everywhere, all the colors of the rainbow, bobbing up and down in a soft breeze. Our party guests were swarming over the swings in the backyard, countless boys and girls from school. But when I wandered over to them, clumsily trying to join in the fun, I could see only one person.

Cadence was on one of the swings, swinging higher than the boy on the swing next to him, higher than I had ever seen anyone swing before. He was glowing from behind, looking as though the sunlight were drawn to him. In that moment, he was ethereal to me, a fairy prince. I marveled at the fact that this was *our* party, that this day belonged to me as much as it belonged to the illuminated child on the swing. He looked down and saw me standing there, with my head tilted slightly backward, gazing up at him. And then he jumped from the swing, and for a moment, I really thought he was flying, hovering above my head, magic.

"Let's go, Sphinxie," he said when he'd somehow touched down on the ground in front of me. He reached out and grabbed my hand. "I only want to play with *you*." And I was led away from the swings, away from the mass of children, and into Cadence's imagination for the rest of the party, following him around the edge of the yard on a make-believe adventure until our mothers called us over to return to our guests and open our gifts.

It was shortly after our party that Leigh's marriage began to dissolve. It hadn't been very good from the beginning, I don't think, and it only went downhill from there. They saw a counselor, who helped them stay together for a while, but it didn't make any difference in the end. They kept fighting, kept struggling, and eventually they filed for divorce. When Cadence and I were ten, Leigh's husband finally bought a house of his own and began to pack up his things. Leigh came over to our house and sat in our kitchen, which was so much smaller than her own, and she cried into my mother's shoulder. All her years of struggle and spitfire had led to an ugly, ugly divorce; Cadence would not be visiting his father.

One day, in the midst of their family chaos, I went over to his house to play. We went up to his bedroom, which was still painted with trees and sky, just as it was when he was born. My mother had by then dismissed the idea of needing to watch us too closely. Cadence sat on his bed, and I sat on the floor. That was a rule he had insisted upon for several weeks: I was not allowed on his bed, I could not even touch the duvet. And somehow, that seemed okay to me at the time, even though now I can look back and see that his rules were just a way of showing his power over me.

"My dad is moving away," he informed me matter-of-factly, and swung his legs back and forth. His feet were bare and slender. The subject of his father made me feel awkward. My mother had explained the divorce to me earlier, but I was still leery of the idea. I love my father, I always have, and at ten years old, the thought that fathers could just go away creeped me out.

"I'm sorry," I said.

He watched his own feet go back and forth. Then he looked up, and his eyes were burning. "I'm not," he told me.

He did that every so often, looked you right in the eye and blurted out something that sounded absolutely awful. He had told me once before that he wished a boy at his school would die, that a girl who'd taken one of his pencils during art class would get her fingers cut off. And it always made me shiver slightly when he said things like that, but I never told on him, because wishes were different from something real. Sometimes, I too wished for someone to leave and never come back, for something bad to happen to a child who'd wronged me. Was that any different from the things that Cadence said? I didn't know.

"You're not?" I asked quietly. "I'd really miss my dad if he moved away."

"I won't miss mine," he said, and hopped lightly off the bed. "He yelled at me one time." That was another thing about Cadence: He never forgot, and never forgave. Your trespasses against him were written in permanent ink inside his head, never to be washed away, not in a million years.

"Oh," I said, unsure of myself. Cadence was over at his desk, rummaging around in one of the drawers. "So, Cadence," I piped up, eager to change the subject. "What are we going to do today?"

Cadence turned from his desk and faced me. "I'll tell you later," he said. "Right now just look at this." He had something in his hand. When he pressed a button on the side, a silver blade flicked out. *Click.*

"Are you allowed to have that?" I asked, staring at the knife.

He returned to his bed and sat again, swinging his legs just as before. I should have run away at that point, but suddenly my body wasn't under my command. My limbs felt heavy. I remember feeling glued to the floor of his bedroom, as though he'd paralyzed me by whipping out that blade.

"It's my dad's," he said.

"Does he know you have it?"

He cocked his head to one side. "Yes."

I knew he was lying, but I also knew from experience that it was better not to argue with him. He pressed the button again and the blade disappeared. *Click.*

"What are you going to do with it?" I asked him. I wasn't scared right away. I was a pretty sheltered kid: I wasn't allowed to watch violent shows on TV and my father didn't leave the news on when I was around. I couldn't imagine Cadence really doing anything bad with that knife. It was just a heavy feeling of something being wrong that had me frozen, a discomfort brewing in my gut.

"I don't know," he said carelessly.

"You should give it back to your daddy before he notices it's missing," I blurted, then realized — too late — that this particular sentence revealed that I thought he was lying. He looked up from the blade, and the blue of his eyes contracted, tighter and tighter, brighter and brighter. They were like a camera flashbulb going off, bright enough to hurt your eyes.

"It's not missing, Sphinxie," he said. "My dad knows that I have it."

"I —" I tried to begin, but he cut me off abruptly.

"You're so stupid, Sphinx," said Cadence firmly. "You're so dumb. That's the only reason you think I'm lying, because you're too stupid to know any better. You're too stupid to even think up games for your own party." His perfect little face was suddenly ugly. This, too, I had experienced before: his sudden rants, insults, and put-downs hurtling down on my head like missiles. "Nobody likes you, Sphinx, because nobody could ever like someone like you. Not even your daddy likes you, Sphinx. Not even your mommy likes you."

I was frozen, stinging all over, stunned as always that such horrible things could spew forth from someone . . . someone who I still somehow managed to think was absolutely perfect. Then suddenly, I remembered something from school: A woman had come into our classroom to talk to us about the dangers of bullying. Bullies, she had said, might hurt you by hitting you — or they might do it by saying bad things. They might lie to get you in trouble. They might make you feel like you weren't worth anything. You had to stand up to a bully in order to make them stop.

"And this knife, Sphinx," Cadence went on, "it doesn't matter if I took it. I deserve to have it. I'm better than you, Sphinx. That's why. I'm better than you. I can do anything I want. I can do anything to you. You're mine, Sphinx."

He was talking quickly, so quickly, and leaning forward toward me. Growing every minute, taller and taller, like a skyscraper rising over a rural countryside. I shrank backward from him, my head spinning. *You're mine, Sphinx.*

The most important thing about bullying, said the woman who came to my classroom, was to tell an adult. An adult would make the bullying stop, and so the most important thing was to tell an adult. I got up from the floor and stood under the skyscraper.

"I'm telling," I said, my voice shaking. "I'm telling you have that knife."

His eyes flashed. He clenched his hands, the slim fingers curling in anger. He leaped from the bed, and the fury left his face, to be replaced by a stony blankness like the face of a statue. *Click.* The switchblade popped open, and for a split second I saw the reflection of his bedroom wall in the blade's shiny surface, gleaming in the sunlight that streamed in through the window.

I did not move when he came forward, did not move when he grabbed a fistful of my hair, holding my head captive. I did not move when the icy coldness of the blade was dragged across my cheek, barely an inch down from my eye.

It didn't hurt at first, and in that void of nothing before the searing pain took hold, I was looking up into Cadence's eyes, into his blank and beautiful and terrible eyes. He was staring at me like he never had before, and his fingers were gripping my hair so tightly that it felt like he would never let go. I could hear my own heartbeat in my ears. I thought he was going to hold on to me forever.

Then the blade was lifted, and his hand let go of my hair, and agony ripped its way across my face, as though it had been brought on by the release of his grip. As though it all would have remained painless if he had only held on a little longer, if he had only kept looking at me. *You're mine, Sphinx,* his voice said again in my head.

And then all I know is that I was screaming and screaming, and the blood was dripping down my face and onto my hands, while he stood, still stony, still with the knife in his hand. Our mothers' footsteps pounded on the stairs. They flung open the door to his bedroom and I saw them briefly framed in the doorway, their blurred faces white; my mother came forward and picked me up, and I felt the fabric of her shirt underneath my fingers. When I clung to her, blood smeared over her shirt and I couldn't believe that it was coming from me. I felt sick. My heart was pounding so fast that it felt like it was going to rip itself from my chest. I know because if I think about this part too long, my heart still does that.

Leigh grabbed Cadence's arm and he dropped the knife on the floor, struggling in her grip, pulling his arm this way and that.

"You're hurting my arm, Mommy!" he shrieked, his voice high with pained innocence.

"What did you do?" she screamed hoarsely, and shook him back and forth. "Cadence, what did you do?" Tears sprang to her eyes and streamed down her face like rivers.

"You're going to be fine, Sphinxie." My mother's voice shook as she pressed her hand over my cheek, which was covered in warm, wet crimson. "You're going to be fine, okay? It's fine. You'll be all better soon." Her voice sounded far away to me, like an echo.

I stared over her shoulder at Cadence jerking back and forth with Leigh's frenzied shakes, as though she could somehow pull him back in time and undo what he'd done to me. His eyes locked onto mine, and I thought desperately, *He's not sorry.* My slashed cheek was throbbing.

And I saw the butterfly smashed into nothing in his hand, and I couldn't believe I'd ever thought that was bad. I couldn't believe I'd never known that people could slice open other people's skin like this, I couldn't believe how much my face could hurt. I couldn't believe how tightly he had held on to me, and how he had looked at me like I was the only person on the face of the earth. And I heard the switchblade opening and closing, over and over again.

Click. Click. Click.

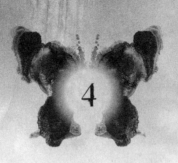

4

I needed stitches — fifteen of them — in my upper cheek, just under my eye. I was supposed to be thankful that Cadence hadn't aimed a little higher, because then I wouldn't have had an eye, but I wasn't. How was I supposed to be thankful when my face felt like it was splitting apart? The doctor said it was a deep cut; there would be a scar, and there was nothing that could be done about it. And even when the bleeding had stopped and the stitches were done, the cut was a brutal streak of red-hot pain, searing its way across my cheek. And that wasn't all.

There was something else, too, a feeling blooming in my chest that I didn't understand. I knew that I had been hurt, that I should be angry at Cadence for what he had done. And I suppose I was, but underneath that thin layer of typical emotion, there was a terrible twisted excitement for the fact that I would always have the scar. He'd said I was his, and now there would be a mark on me forever to prove it. A mark right smack across my face, to remind everyone of what had happened to me — and to remind me that I was linked to Cadence, that he'd practically signed his name on me like I was one of his drawings. I didn't really understand what that meant at the time. I was still young, after all.

When we came home from the emergency room that day, my mother looked so old. She had aged somehow between the whiteness of the examination room and our doorstep. She kissed my forehead and apologized, over and over, for what had happened to me. Her tears dripped into my hair.

"I should have known better, Sphinxie," she sobbed, clutching me to her chest. "Your daddy was always right, your daddy knows better than me."

My father had hugged me for a long time when we came home from the emergency room, but he didn't seem able to look at my face. He left the house, slamming the door behind him, a once-in-a-lifetime event. I'd never seen him act that way before, and I never have since. My father is not the type of man given to storming off.

"It's not your fault, Mom," I told her faintly after the headlights of my father's car receded down the driveway and into the darkness. "Cadence is so good."

"What do you mean?" she asked me.

"He's just so good," I said. "You can't tell . . ." I trailed off, unable to articulate what I wanted to say.

My mother put me to bed, read me my favorite storybook three times over, even though I should have outgrown my love for it by then, even though earlier that year I'd decided I was too old to be read to at bedtime. It was something about a princess, something corny with lots of pink in the illustrations. After that night, it ceased to be my favorite and we never read it again, although it remained on my bookshelf for a few years afterward until one day I boxed up and donated a bunch of things I thought I was too old for, storybooks included.

When my mother finished reading, she asked me if I wanted her to sleep with me, if I was still feeling scared. I politely refused her offer and told her that I wasn't scared. And I wasn't really, not at first. I was just stunned. I still didn't quite know what had happened to me, or what was happening inside my head.

"Is Dad mad at me?" I blurted when my mother reached the doorway of my room.

"No, sweetie, never! What made you think of that?" she asked, stepping a little way back into my room in concern.

"He left when he saw me," I pointed out.

"That's not because he's angry at you," my mother explained. "He's just angry that something happened to the little girl he loves so much and he couldn't do anything to stop it. When your father's angry, he likes to go off by himself to cool down. He'll be back soon." She came back into the room and kissed me again. "Are you sure you don't need me to stay with you?"

"Yeah," I said. Her need to comfort me had begun to scare me, because it meant that something truly horrifying had happened. "Good night, Mom. I love you."

"I love you too," she said, and she left.

If I could go back in time and hold my little-girl self, I would, because I know now that I really did need someone to stay in my room with me. But by then I was scared. Needing to be held is scary sometimes.

So there I was. I just lay in bed alone with my eyes open and stared at my ceiling. I listened to the sounds of my mother moving around downstairs. She opened and closed the fridge. She washed the dishes. I heard her crying again. Then the phone rang, just as she blew her nose. She answered it, and I heard her voice faintly.

"Leigh," she said, her voice muffled by distance and the walls of the house. I sat up in bed. I wanted so badly to know what she would say to Leigh. Would she be angry with her? Would they yell? And what had happened to Cadence? Was he being punished for what he did to me?

On a show I had watched on television, a girl had eavesdropped on her teenage sister's phone conversations by picking up the other line and listening, staying so quiet that her sister didn't even know she was there. I got out of bed, and crept down the hall. There was a phone in my parents' bedroom, on their nightstand. Slowly, I picked it up and pressed the receiver to my ear.

It was the first time I had ever purposely done something that I knew I shouldn't. Whenever I got in trouble when I was younger, it was for things like accidentally talking back to my mother because I was overtired or hungry. I was never the type of kid to willfully do so-called naughty things. I'm still not. But that night, everything was off-kilter, and I eavesdropped in spite of the feelings of guilt that began to creep into my stomach the moment that my little fingers reached for the phone.

"I'm so sorry, Sarah," Leigh was sobbing into the phone. "Oh my God, I'm so sorry. I should have known. I should have taken him to a doctor or something . . . oh God! Is Sphinxie okay?"

"She'll have a scar," my mother said.

"Oh God!" Leigh's sobs intensified. They were both crying now, and I half expected water to drip from the receiver onto my shoulder.

"How did I not know?" Leigh asked, and her voice was pulled taut across the phone line. "How did I not see this coming?" For a moment, the line was silent, save for a few echoing sniffles on both sides. Then Leigh said tearfully, "Sarah, please, tell me what I did wrong. What did I do wrong?"

"You didn't do anything wrong," my mother said as steadily as she could manage. "Some things aren't anyone's fault." I could almost hear her biting her lip, to keep herself from saying that my father had seen it years ago. My father had seen it when the butterfly died.

"But it *has* to be me, Sarah!" Leigh went on, almost wailing now. "When a kid is messed up, it's the mother's fault . . . it's the mother's fault for not raising him right . . . it's my fault . . ." Her voice caught raggedly in her throat. "What the hell did I do? Tell me what I did, Sarah, you have to know . . . you know so much better. You did everything right with Sphinxie, she's such a good kid. But I messed up, Sarah . . . I messed up."

"No, okay? Just no," my mother said. She'd stopped crying now. "Listen to me: You might feel like it's your fault, but it's not, okay? You did everything right, okay? Now you have to help him, Leigh. You can do it."

I could hear Leigh breathing, in and out, hoarse, sounding like wind blowing rough against rough. "I love you," my mother said.

"You can't mean that," Leigh said. "You're angry, Sarah, you have to be angry."

"Angry? All right, a little. Angry at myself, though, for not watching my kid."

That was confusing, because suddenly I wasn't sure who was truly responsible for what had happened. Previously, it had been easy: Cadence was the one with the knife. But wasn't my mother supposed to protect me? Wasn't that what parents were for? If she had been watching us, I wouldn't have needed to be saved in the first place, would I? There was a cold lump in my throat now.

Leigh laughed, that sort of little, weak, spindly laugh that people let out when everything is at its least humorous. "I messed up, Sarah," she whispered. "I messed up the plan." She laughed again.

"Oh, Leigh," my mother said, and her voice was so soft.

I hung up the phone. My cheek seemed tight and stretched with the stitches in it, and my mind felt the same way, full to bursting with all of these things that I didn't understand. The cut on my face, the scar I would always have, the boy who had given it to me, the way that he'd looked at me when he'd opened me up. I walked back into my room and climbed back into bed. My chest was starting to feel heavy with guilt for listening in on my mother's phone conversation. What I had heard was so private, so raw. I knew that she would never have wanted me to hear them talking how they were, crying and frightened and small.

A few minutes later, my mother came upstairs. She came into my room to check on me, and of course, I was still awake, my eyes wide. And I was both glad that she was there and entirely unsure of myself. When I looked at her, I didn't know what to think. She loved me and I loved her, but she had chosen to be friends with Leigh in the first place, she was the one who had left me alone with Cadence. And now here I was, with fresh stitches crisscrossing my face, burdened with so many conflicting feelings that I couldn't work out what had happened to me. Feelings that were going back and forth between terror and something like exhilaration as I slowly lifted a hand to my face and touched the cut lightly with my fingertip, checking to make sure that it was all real and not some kind of dream. I had never been more confused.

"Are you having trouble sleeping, sweetie?" asked my mother, sitting down on the edge of my bed.

"Mom," I said, my voice quivering. "I did something I shouldn't have." I had to confess, of course. I couldn't let the night go on getting any stranger. Things had to be set right.

"What?"

"I listened to you and Leigh on the phone," I whispered, feeling shrunken with shame. My mother closed her eyes. She rubbed her temples with her fingers.

"It's okay, sweetie," she said finally. "Just don't do that again. It's rude."

"I know," I said. My chest was sour on the inside. I licked my dry lips. "Mom," I said, in such a tiny, tiny voice. "How did she mess up the plan? Cadence and I are still here, you still have your jobs, just like you said. How did she mess it up?"

"Oh, Sphinxie," my mother said, her eyes welling up for what seemed the thousandth time that day. "It's just silly. Don't think about it. It's just silly." Years later, she would end up telling me that we were supposed to be married, but at that moment she only bit her lip.

A week later, after we'd recovered somewhat from the initial shock, my mother and I ventured outside to meet one of my other friends at a playground. She hung upside down from the jungle gym and pointed at my cheek. "What happened?" she asked me, swinging back and forth by her knees.

"Got cut," I mumbled, looking away from her and hoping she wouldn't ask any more questions. I didn't feel capable of explaining how I'd been cut. I didn't want her to know.

"Oh," she said. "Did it hurt?"

"A lot," I said, feeling a lump come into my throat. My friend pulled herself up to sit on top of the jungle gym. And life went on.

My stitches came out. The cut transformed into a thin scar, a sleek white line on my upper cheek that was smooth to the touch. Leigh sold her US house and moved permanently to the one in England. She was broken by the sight of me, of my mother, of my father. She didn't want to lose contact with us, but she couldn't bear to be around us. I was the reminder of what she considered her failure in raising Cadence to be a decent human being.

She remained a faithful best friend, even from a distance. She called my mother on the phone at least twice a week, and emailed her every day. After a while, my mother asked her if it would be all right to send pictures of me dressed as a stereotypical Native American girl for my school's Thanksgiving play. Leigh agreed. She sent a picture of her own, one of Cadence sitting on a swing in the England house's backyard. We were twelve by then. He was going to a private school at that point, and seeing a therapist on the weekends. I didn't mind seeing pictures of him. He still shone brightly, despite what he'd done to me. By then he had become something of a legend to me, this boy whom I had at one time called my best friend, this boy who had used me and left his mark on me forever. There was a period of time when I used to look in the mirror and trace my scar with my fingertip, wondering if the golden-haired boy in the pictures that Leigh sent to us had really done it. The good-looking boy who seemed so normal, painting at the easel he'd wanted so much, wearing the stiff uniform of the private school he went to. Was he real? Was Leigh even real, my mother's elegant best friend who had messed up her son, messed up the plan? I hadn't seen them since I was ten. It all seemed more like a scene out of a movie than like something that had actually happened.

And even though time often seems to stop after traumatic incidents, it was still unfolding, and I was growing. I became a teenager. I had my first crush. I went to the bathroom one day and found a red stain almost in the shape of a heart in my underpants. And the boy in the photos that came to us like clockwork grew too, tall and slender and perfect as always.

When I was thirteen, at Christmastime, Leigh and my mother exchanged photos of us as usual. A picture of me flew out over the ocean toward England, and in an envelope with a holly stamp came a picture of him wearing a red button-down shirt and skinny jeans, his feet bare, the blurred greenness of a Christmas tree splotched with smears of colored light behind him. For a long moment after my mother had pulled the photo out of the envelope, I was frozen, staring at it. The soft waves of blond hair framing his face were blurred slightly, illuminated from behind like a halo. And his head was held high, his thin eyebrows arched, his face dominated by those cold blue eyes.

His eyes were one of the only things I could always remember clearly, those icy eyes that were filled with fire at the same time. Still, Leigh said that she had framed my picture, and so we framed Cadence's. When my friends came over for a Christmas party, they asked me who he was.

"He's cuuuute," my then–best friend Kaitlyn trilled, picking up the picture for a closer look.

"He's my mom's best friend's son," I said awkwardly.

"What's his name?" she asked, still holding the picture.

"Cadence," I told her.

"Caaadence," she drawled. "What a cool name! He's really cute, Sphinx. Do you ever hang out with him?"

"No, he lives in England," I said. "He did this to me," I added, pointing to my scar. "He's in therapy."

She put the picture down like it had burned her. And I wanted to cover my mouth and take back my words.

It was the first time that I'd ever told a friend what had happened to me. The girls whom I hung out with had seen my scar, obviously, but no one ever asked about it. They probably all just assumed I'd been in an accident of some kind as a little kid and could do without having to explain it to people. And I was thankful for that. Aside from the fact that what had happened was a deeply personal thing, I also viewed it as too shocking for anyone to understand properly. I thought people would view it like something out of a crime drama, something fake. And I didn't want anyone interpreting it that way, didn't want anyone seeing Cadence as a one-dimensional shock story. That wasn't what he was to me, and I couldn't make anyone understand that. No one would ever be able to grasp it, no one would ever see the way that he'd looked at me when he'd cut me.

Kaitlyn's eyes were impossibly wide. "Are you serious?" she said, in a half-whisper. "He . . . he really *cut* you?"

I nodded. She pulled me into a hug that I didn't want, and blurted that I could always talk to her about it if I needed to, then changed the subject awkwardly fast, obviously eager to think about something else. And I wanted to take a step back in time, to untell her. I suddenly felt an overwhelming need to go to Cadence, to apologize for what I'd said.

I felt guilty for telling her that he was in therapy, as though I'd betrayed his confidence, as though information about him were a secret that he'd bestowed on me, meant for my ears only. I knew that I didn't have to feel that way — he couldn't hear me anyway —

but I felt disloyal. I couldn't blame Kaitlyn for noticing his picture, because he was beautiful.

I often thought about what had happened to me when I was younger. I knew the line of my scar as well as the story of my mother's and Leigh's plan. But it didn't matter. I was fine. And in all likelihood, I was never going to see Cadence again.

5

It was the year that we turned sixteen, in the fall.

I was still plain and a little heavy, brown-eyed, with brown hair pulled back from my face into a ponytail. I didn't like how I looked, and now I covered my scar up with concealer, smeared it over every morning and pretended that it didn't exist, that it had vanished over time and I didn't have to think anymore about the way it made me feel. My circle of friends was small, but better than nothing, and I thought a certain boy had feelings for me, and I had made it onto my school's soccer team. I wasn't really ecstatic about my life — for one thing, it seemed that everyone but me had, or had had, a boyfriend — but I was content enough.

I came home from the team's first practice feeling accomplished but frumpy. My ponytail was limp with sweat, and the studs of my cleats were caked with dried-on muck, on account of it raining the day before. I pulled them off and discarded them at the doorway.

My mother was on the phone when I went into the kitchen. She lifted her head when I came in, smiling, but her eyebrows were stiff; from the look on her face, I could tell that whoever was on the other line was upsetting her.

I watched her worriedly for a moment before opening the fridge and selecting a bottle of water. Then I walked over to the kitchen table and sat down, wrenching the cap off my bottle. There was crisp fall sun streaming in through the kitchen window, dancing over the tiled floor. I looked at my fingernails: short and bitten. Whenever I tried to grow them, they always broke, and whenever I bought those stick-on fake ones, they fell off. I took a drink of my water and watched my mother walk back and forth in front of the sink, pausing every now and again to tap her nails on the kitchen counter.

"All right. Call anytime. I love you." She stopped, her fingers curling around the counter's edge, squeezing ever so slightly. "Okay. Talk to you soon." She hung up the phone and shook her head once. Then she turned to face me, and the sun coming in from the window spread over her face. Her brow was furrowed now, and there was no trace of the smile that she'd put on for me when I'd first walked into the kitchen. There was definitely something wrong.

"How was soccer, Sphinxie?" she asked me, still missing her smile. "Did you have fun? What did you do?"

"It was okay," I said, shrugging. "We just did drills today, really. It'll be more fun when we actually play a game. Anyway, what's wrong? Was that Leigh on the phone?"

"Yes," she said, her voice measured.

"Oh, really? How's she doing?" I took another drink of water. I could see my shadow moving on the kitchen floor.

"She's having a bit of a rough time, actually."

"Oh," I said. I relaxed a bit. That was typical for Leigh; she was either being upset by Cadence's bad behavior at school or worrying about his health. For a long time, Cadence's rebellious behavior was all we heard about, although Leigh usually explained that away by saying he was just too smart to follow rules like other kids — and I was inclined to agree with her. But after a while, Leigh had finally opened up to my mother about Cadence's health problems, and they had taken center stage from then on.

Originally, she hadn't wanted to bring them up; she already felt as though she was burdening my mother by unloading the endless tales of her son's misfortune. And at first, she said, she hadn't thought anything of them. They were just bruises. Sometimes people got bruises and they just didn't remember bumping themselves. But then doctor's appointments and blood tests started to crowd up Cadence's schedule, and she'd told my mother what was going on. She was getting scared.

"How's Cadence?" I asked when my mother didn't elaborate.

"The same," my mother said. Her eyes fell to the floor, and we both looked at our shadows. "They gave Leigh a diagnosis for him, Sphinx." I looked up.

"It's acute lymphoblastic leukemia," my mother said. The first two words meant nothing to me, but of course, I knew what leukemia was. A girl in my school had had it, and she'd lost all of her hair during treatment. I knew it had been horrible for her, and it had been hard to see her looking sicker and sicker until finally she had to stop coming to school for a while. But she was all right now. She'd come back to school wearing a wig, and she was going to be fine.

"When are they starting chemotherapy?" I asked, without looking at her. I didn't want to think about the stuff Cadence would have to go through. I pinned my soccer team's game schedule to the fridge with a Mickey Mouse magnet.

"Leigh says his case is very aggressive. Odds are it won't respond well to chemotherapy," said my mother softly from behind me. I turned around.

"Well, they're still going to try it, right?" For some reason, I felt littler all of a sudden.

"No, Sphinxie," said my mother. "They're not."

"Why?" I demanded, shocked. "What's the harm in trying?"

"Cadence doesn't want it."

I felt like the air had been sucked out of my chest. How could he not want to try to survive?

"Why not?" I asked shakily, feeling stunned.

"I don't think it would do any good, Sphinx."

"How long did they give him?"

My mother covered her mouth with her hand, and her eyes glistened.

"Less than a year," she whispered.

I cried for him then, for the first time. I'd never done that before; I'd spent hours of my childhood crying *because* of him, never for him. But this situation was different. Cadence was special; he couldn't die. My mother hugged me as if I were little again, and I looked over her shoulder, sniffling.

"Leigh should make him try," I said insistently. "She should make him try."

"Sphinx, this way he'll be able to feel normal for as long as possible. He'll get a chance to enjoy the time he has left without drugs making him throw up all the time," said my mother, her voice cracking slightly. "I think Leigh . . . I almost think she feels it's better this way." As I stood there frozen, staring over her shoulder, feeling my hot tears coursing down my cheeks, the first thought that came into my head was a memory of staring over my mother's shoulder so many years ago, as blood dripped down my face from what was now a clean scar. An odd, unwelcome sense of relief flashed through me: The person who did that to me would be gone, truly gone. But the brilliant boy who had been my best friend and shone his burning light in my eyes — he would be gone too, and I realized that I wanted to see that boy before he died, that I wanted to talk to him one last time despite what he had done to me. But the person who had cut me and the brilliant boy were the same person, a paradox, just like the feelings that were filling up my chest and my throat. The next thing I thought of was the plan, the life plan that had been made and then undone, and the lump in my throat swelled even more.

"Mom," I said thickly, "what was the plan? You never told me what was supposed to happen."

"Oh, Sphinxie," she said.

"Please," I said, whining without meaning to. "Come on, what were we supposed to do, huh?"

"You were supposed to get married," she said hoarsely.

A tremendous chill surged through my body and suddenly I was the one holding her, thinking of an alternate universe where I had not been cut, where Cadence had not gotten sick, where the eggs that were inside me right now, dormant and sleeping as their grandmother cried into my shoulder, became children. His children. Instead, their grandmother was crying for the other half of the plan, the first best friend, the almost-father. But what was supposed to happen to me? Me, with Cadence's mark on my face, but no Cadence to grow up for, no one who would understand the plan, no one who would be able to comprehend what had happened to me. I wished that I could take my question back; I didn't want to know this part.

Soon, I thought, *soon he'll be gone.* I pushed the plan to the back of my head, and forced myself to swallow the lump. And suddenly I was thankful for the picture of him with the Christmas tree, the old magazines in the boxes in our attic, the videotapes of us as toddlers, even the scar on my face. They were all markers, pages in a life scrapbook that would remain, reminding everyone, reminding me.

Once, there was a person I called my best friend, my worst enemy, the shining one. He left these behind. He did this to me.

He was here.

6

Our phone wouldn't stop ringing. Leigh didn't have a husband or even a boyfriend to lean on; all she had was her faithful Sarah, her promised ally for life. She called at all times of day and night, and my mother always answered, never hanging up until Leigh had talked herself hoarse. I had to admire my mother for being so firmly grounded, so reliably there, ready to pounce on that receiver and offer sympathy, empathy, grief, anger, anything that Leigh needed.

Each day, my mother would get off the phone and relay Leigh's updates to me. She had pulled Cadence out of his private school. She'd asked him what he wanted to do. Did he want to see anything, travel anyplace, do anything in particular? Whatever it was, they'd do it. He mentioned Paris, the Louvre — he'd already been there, but Leigh took him again. She emailed us pictures of him standing in front of the *Mona Lisa* with his back to the camera, his beautiful long fingers clasped behind his back, his hair an organized wreck of golden-blond waves. And I found myself wishing that he'd turned around for the photo.

Leigh wanted to take him everywhere. She couldn't cure him, but she was compelled to do *something*, and day in and day out she begged him to tell her what he wanted. If he so much as brought up something in passing that he didn't own, she bought it for him.

But after a while, he didn't want anything any longer. My mother told me that at this point, it seemed Cadence just wanted to be left alone. I could understand why: Surely, he was struggling with the thought of dying and wanted to escape from the constant reminders that came with Leigh's hovering over him. He just wanted to *paint* . . . get him some canvases and leave him alone, he said.

And so he painted: little canvases, huge canvases. They filled the loft space of Leigh's England house, which had always been Cadence's art room. Leigh said he was a genius when he painted. Some of the paintings were of people, beautiful but twisted up and broken, and some of them were of birds: in trees, on lines stretched between telephone poles, airborne with their wings spread wide. Most of them were of water. The ocean, rivers, ponds, puddles, fishbowls with fat goldfish. My mother said Leigh seized upon the common theme and asked him if he wanted to go out on any kind of boat. Did he want to see any certain river, any particular stretch of blue? No, he didn't. Leave him alone, he said, he was *painting*. Leigh said he told her she was stupid to think that simply because he painted water meant he wanted anything to do with boats. I could understand that too, why Cadence was lashing out at her. People who are dying get angry at the world. It wasn't surprising.

Still, she kept on: Did he want to see anyone, anyone from school, anyone from when they lived back in the States? Did he want to see his father again? Leigh said that when she asked that, he painted a streak of dark, dark midnight blue across a blank canvas and told her bluntly, without looking at her, that he didn't. But then he turned around, she said, and his eyes were burning.

Sphinxie was what he said. Sphinxie. He wanted me.

"I'll understand," Leigh had said to my mother on the phone, in a pale voice, "if you don't want her to see him . . . but if it's all right with you, I'll pay for the plane tickets. I'll fly both of you out here, Sarah, so she can see him. Just a week. Just a little visit." Her voice broke.

When my mother told me the next day as we were driving home from one of my soccer games, I expected her to end the story by saying that she wouldn't allow it. That I had only to look in the mirror to see the reason why visiting Cadence — an older, smarter, more powerful Cadence, despite his illness — was not a good idea. I looked her directly in the eyes and waited for this verdict. I felt the line of the scar on my face, remembering how his cut had burned after the painless moment had slipped away, then stopped myself. He was dying, and he needed help, and I felt like I needed to go to him. Besides, he wasn't a stupid kid anymore, and neither was I. My breath was caught in my throat.

"I want you to decide," said my mother. "You're a big girl, you decide. Think about it."

I was stunned that the choice had been placed in my hands. People wait and wait until they're old enough to make decisions for themselves, and then things like this are thrust on them. In the case of my mother, it was especially shocking: She'd planned out my whole life and now she was dumping the responsibility on my shoulders all of a sudden? I wasn't sure I was ready. My mind was already too full.

When we got home, I climbed the stairs to my room and sat on my bed. A thousand different thoughts went through my head: I would miss soccer practice, I didn't want Leigh to pay for plane tickets. My kid self, shaking, with fresh blood on her cheek, was still alive inside me, heart still pounding. I didn't want any more pieces of myself to be held captive by his eyes and his smooth voice, only to be sliced away. And so for a moment, I was about to go downstairs and tell my mother that I had made my decision, and it was no.

But I didn't. Instead, I stayed there on my bed, and I thought about how shocking and beautiful it was that Cadence and I were alive at all — that the plan of two little girls, hatched under a bedsheet fort, had come to be. And the memory of the knife in his room wasn't the only one I had. I had all the shining days too, all the summers and the playdates and the birthday party and all the times he had ever made me laugh when we were little.

He was still shining, oh God, he was still shining in my mind. We were both human, and we were made of the same bones and blood and flesh, even though he shone and dimmed me, even though I was living and he was dying. We, the two eggs, the two chances in billions.

The plan that my mother had made and sown into me was never going to happen. It was time for me to take out her stitches and make my own. And I had cried for Cadence, I had known immediately that I wanted to see him. This was a journey I had to take, my new destiny unfolding before me. I had to go.

I went downstairs again, into the kitchen. "I want to see him," I told my mother. "Call Leigh and tell her I'm coming."

"Are you sure?" my mother asked me. She was standing at the sink, washing the dishes, but now she turned off the water and looked me in the eye. "Sphinxie, I have a feeling this is going to be very rough on you, you need to know that."

I gritted my teeth. I knew she was trying to be gentle with me, but she was stating the obvious, and it felt patronizing.

"Mom," I said after taking a deep breath, "he's dying."

She called Leigh. She fetched pencil and paper and wrote down dates and information, spoke about flights and fares. She bit her lip and held back her own tears, letting Leigh do the crying. And then she held the receiver out to me, looking uncertain.

"Say hello?" she asked, phrasing it as a question.

I hesitated slightly, but I reached out and took it. The entire situation seemed unreal; I hadn't heard his voice since the day he'd cut me. The plastic was warm where my mother had clutched it. Slowly, I brought the phone to my ear. My mouth was dry. I felt like I was auditioning for a play, as though if he didn't like the sound of my voice, the plane tickets would be withheld from me.

"Hi?" I said, questioning, just like my mother.

"Hello, Sphinx," said a cool, crisp voice. He'd picked up a British accent, and his voice had deepened, but only slightly: It remained high for a guy.

"Hi," I said, more firmly this time. If I was going to do this, I wanted to be kind and loving, but not naïve like I'd been as a kid. There had to be a balance.

"You already said that," he pointed out, which struck me as a very typical thing for him to say.

"Yeah, I know," I told him.

"Are you coming to see me?" he asked, and his voice went a little higher.

"Yep," I said, taking a shaky breath and trying to steady my voice. I felt tears prickling suddenly at my eyes. "I'm coming."

The line was silent for a minute.

"Thank you, Sphinx." There was a long silence, and I waited, clutching the phone. "I am going to die," he stated finally, and his voice shook slightly, like mine had when I'd last spoken. The line went silent again. It was as if he was waiting for my reaction to his statement. Perhaps he wanted to hear me cry for him.

"I'm really sorry," I said sincerely.

Silence. I wondered where he was in his house, if he was standing or sitting, if he was looking out a window. And if he was, was he looking down . . . or up, at the sky? The line was still silent.

Then he laughed and said, "You're a *good* girl, Sphinxie." And he hung up on me, leaving me standing openmouthed with the receiver in my hand, thinking, *What was that all about?*

Perhaps he was embarrassed. Perhaps he was just as nervous as I was and didn't know what else to do.

Leigh called back in a flash, apologizing. Apparently he tended to do that, hang up on people. She apologized again and again, thanked my mother and me so much for agreeing to come. It meant so much to her, she said, and it meant a lot to Cadence, too.

My father didn't want me to go. He looked at me and I knew he saw the scar, remembered the trip to the hospital, the paleness of my little face as the blood flowed down and down, staining my shirt collar on that side. He locked eyes with me, and I noticed the lines spreading out from the corners of his eyes, the furrows in his brow.

"I don't think you should go," he told me, and he wasn't shy about it. I could hear the anger that remained still in his voice, held there for always. I don't think he had ever forgiven himself. It was stupid, really; he hadn't been at Leigh's house that day, he had never been, and would never be, able to see into the future and give my mother and me precise warnings about the dangers of the world. Still, he was angry. He looked at my scar and he was furious. He didn't storm out like he had all those years ago, but I could sense that he wanted to.

"Dad, this is *my* thing," I said. "It's my choice. Cadence is dying, and I want to see him one last time." *Strong.* I had to keep repeating that word. I had to be strong with everyone, not just Cadence.

"Write him a letter if it means so much to you," said my father.

"You know that's not the same."

"I wish your mother had involved me more in this," he said, putting a hand to his forehead.

"Well, she didn't," I said curtly. "It's settled, Dad. Leigh bought the plane tickets. And it's okay, really. I'm going to be fine. Nothing's going to happen." I didn't usually speak to my father so brusquely, but I was afraid that if I listened to him long enough, I would start to second-guess my decision to go. And I couldn't have that.

"Sphinx, that kid is dangerous —" he began.

"He's dying," I said. "He's a human being who's dying. I'm going to see him. Besides, haven't you seen the pictures of him? He looks like he couldn't crush a grape, let alone me. I won't take any crap from him." I felt the need to shrink Cadence's tall, lithe form in my father's mind and make myself seem stronger in comparison. Still, there was a tiny twinge of fear inside my chest, pulling and poking. I stuck my chin out, and raised my head, determined. "I could take him down if I had to."

My father laughed then, weakly. He looked at me again, closely, carefully, but his eyes passed over the scar. I knew he was thinking that I'd gotten older, so much older, and so fast. I was making decisions about people who were dying. I was going to make decisions about what to pack in my suitcase, what magazines to read on the plane. And soon, I would leave the house and leave him behind, this man who still hadn't forgiven himself for something that wasn't his fault.

"I love you, Daddy," I said, tears stinging my eyes.

"I love you, too, Sphinxie," he replied, and pulled me into a hug.

Our flight was scheduled for a week from then, and we were staying in Leigh's house. I informed my soccer coach that I was going away. My mother got me off school, took time off work. I told all of my friends. They squealed over me — *England, England, it was so exciting, everyone loved England* — until I explained why I was going. Then their voices died down, their faces closed, and their eyes turned downward. They hugged me and told me to call them if I needed to. I promised them that I would, and promised myself that I wouldn't. That was the thing about my friends: I could tell them about secret crushes and rumors at school and new music to listen to, but I couldn't tell them about Cadence. They hadn't seen him shine as a child, they hadn't been cut, they hadn't been marked for life. My scar was like a wall between them and me.

I packed. Clothes, my iPod, books to read on the plane, shoes, my favorite hairbrush. I packed it all into my suitcase by myself, although my mother wanted to help me, to make sure that I'd hadn't forgotten anything. Did I have enough underwear? Yes, of course I did. Did I have my cell phone charger, my iPod charger? Yes, they were in my purse.

I laid out my clothes the night before our flight: a brown polo shirt, my good jeans, and magenta ballet flats, dug out of the back of my closet. I'm not one of those girls with impeccable fashion sense and a closet full of trendy clothes, but I wanted to look nice. I wanted Cadence and Leigh to see that I had grown up, that I wasn't always the tomboy kicking a soccer ball. I wasn't sure if an appearance in magenta ballet flats was enough to cancel out all the soccer photos, but it was worth a shot.

In the morning, I blow-dried my hair after my shower and left it down instead of pulling it back into a ponytail as usual. I dug a tube of mascara out of my purse and applied it. Then I stepped back from the mirror and looked at myself. I was all right, I supposed. I felt just the tiniest bit more confident than usual, and I thought it had something to do with the fact that soon I would be on a plane. There was nothing like the idea of getting flown to another country to make a person feel worth something.

I lugged my suitcase downstairs and ate a hurried breakfast with my mother. She had all the flight information printed out, and she spilled coffee on the papers. She had forgotten to plug in her cell phone to charge, but we had to leave in order to make the flight, and we ran out to the car.

"I'll charge it when I get there," she told my father. "Call Sphinx's phone."

"Okay," he said, starting the car. "Remind her to charge it, Sphinx, will you?"

"I will," I said. I was looking out the window as we pulled away from our house. Watching trees, sky, birds, neighbors, other cars. They rushed past my window in a blur, and the little fluorescent green numbers of our car's dashboard clock changed. Life was going past, and nobody realized it. I didn't usually realize it myself, but now it was different, because across the ocean, where I was going, Leigh was willing the clock to stop. Did Cadence watch it too, with those perfect burning eyes of his? Was he afraid of the passing of time, of how quickly a year went by? I felt an overwhelming sense of urgency. I had to get to him as quickly as possible. I needed to see what I could do to help before time ran out.

At the airport, my mother and I hugged my father good-bye. He kissed us both and told us to be safe, be safe, be safe. Call him, call him. Say hi to Leigh and Cadence for him. Charge my mother's phone, remember to charge it. He loved us, he loved us, and we loved him too. He stood there and watched us as we walked away from him and joined the line to go through airport security. When I looked back over my shoulder at him and waved one last time, he was smiling, but his eyes were worried.

My mother and I checked our bags, passed our purses through the X-ray machine, watched the employees go through our belongings with gloved hands, checking this and that. They took a spray bottle of perfume that I had in my purse; I'd forgotten to put it in my checked baggage. And, feeling like a stupid little girl, I started crying. I didn't want to lose that perfume. Deep down, I knew that I was really crying over everything else, over the fact that I was going, over the fact that my knees felt weak at the prospect of seeing Cadence again. The airport employee who had my perfume in her gloved hand gave me a sympathetic look, as though she could tell that there must be something else going on in my life to make me cry like that. She was a big black woman, and her fingernails were painted the same color magenta as my ballet flats.

"We match," she said, pointing to my shoes and displaying her nails for me. She smiled, and her teeth were perfect, a straight wall of white. "I'm sorry I have to take this from you. Have a good flight, honey."

"Thank you," I said, and wiped my eyes. I still felt so terribly stupid.

My mother and I hurried to our gate. The flight was waiting, and I was reliving it all, everything that had happened to me, over and over, inside my head. Every moment that had brought me onto that plane was playing in my mind like a movie on an old projector, images flashing in bright color. I took a deep breath in through my nose.

The clock in the terminal said eight thirty. We boarded the plane, found our seats, tucked our purses underneath. The pilot's voice came over the speakers, and we fastened the belts across our laps. The plane hummed and inched forward over the runway, and then up, and up, and up. My ears popped, frustrated with the change of pressure, and somewhere down on the ground, my father was walking back to our car, preparing to drive away from the airport, the distance between him and us growing with every moment. I had the window seat, and the passenger before me had pulled the shade down; I pushed it up and let in the blue of the sky.

A pregnant woman was sitting across from me in the other aisle, and as we ascended, she put her hand on her stomach and smiled.

7

It was raining when our flight arrived, and the clocks said 7:30 p.m.; we had lost the entire day somewhere over the ocean. We collected our luggage at the baggage claim and looked around for Leigh, who was supposed to be picking us up. She wasn't anywhere that we could see, so we went into the ladies' room. There was a mother in there with a little toddler boy at the sink, holding him up so that he could wash his hands.

"Rub your hands together first," she told him, moving his wrists back and forth. "Make some bubbles before you rinse the soap off." I loved the sound of her voice; she had such a perfect British accent. It seemed a waste for her to live in England; she should have moved to the United States where everyone would really appreciate it.

I still couldn't believe that I was actually there, that within the next few hours I would be seeing Cadence. Thinking about it made my chest tighten. There was this weird mix of Christmas-Eve excitement mixed with death-row apprehension running in circles around my heart.

I chose a bathroom stall and slipped in, sliding the little lock into place. My mother was in the stall next to me. I heard the door of the restroom open: The mother and her toddler went out and someone new clicked in on high heels. When my mother and I came out, the woman with high heels had already disappeared into another stall. My mother pressed the soap dispenser over her sink with the palm of her hand, but nothing came out.

"There's no soap in mine," she said, pressing again, to no effect. "Is there soap in yours, Sphinxie?"

"Yeah," I said, shifting over so that she could get some.

In the mirror over the sinks, I saw one of the stall doors behind me open. The woman with high heels came out, clicking over the bathroom tile floor. Her hair was shoulder length, hanging in a mass of bouncy blonde waves, a pair of sunglasses with shiny lenses perched on the top of her head. She wore a brown coat over a white blouse and well-fitted jeans, and there was an elegant string of chocolate pearls around her neck.

"Sphinxie," she said. "Sarah!"

Her wide blue eyes were beautiful, enhanced with a tasteful amount of eye shadow, but with noticeable dark circles underneath them. It was Leigh, I realized suddenly. It was Leigh. I'd almost forgotten what she looked like. Seeing her in front of me was almost like seeing a fictional character suddenly sprung to life and standing before me in the flesh. Ever since she'd been gone, she'd just been part of my mother's story, a past-tense presence. Now here she was in front of me, staring at me as though she felt exactly the same way I did.

My mother whipped around from her sink, her hands still soapy and dripping wet, and pulled her best friend into a hug. Leigh bit her lip as they hugged; her eyes looked glossy with tears under the fluorescent overhead light in the bathroom. She smiled at me, but her eyes were dancing over my upper cheek, looking for the scar. I'd covered it up with concealer as always, and when she couldn't find it, her smile spread wider. She and my mother broke apart, and she came for me, wrapping me into a tight hug. Her perfume filled up my nose, a light, rosy scent; her nails were long, and they were digging into the skin of my back through my shirt. I hugged her back as best I could without feeling awkward. I knew before setting out that it was going to be strange to see her again, but I'd underestimated just how strange. This woman had been like a second mother to me, yet I felt wooden in her arms, strained between buried childhood memories that made me want to pull away from her and hug her tighter at the same time.

"Did you have a good flight?" she asked breathlessly when she had released me.

"Yes, it was fine, really easy," my mother said, looking a little teary-eyed herself. "No turbulence, right, Sphinx?"

"No turbulence," I confirmed, pulling a wad of paper towels out of the dispenser on the wall and drying my hands.

"Isn't this weird . . . we find each other in the bathroom, of all places!" said Leigh, moving to the sink to wash her own hands.

"We were looking for you out there, but we figured we'd make a quick stop in here when we didn't see you," my mother said, laughing.

"Same," said Leigh, flipping her hair over her shoulder. "Can I have a few of those paper towels, Sphinx?" I still had extra clutched in my hand, and I gave them all to her. "I guess you already picked up your bags," she said to my mother.

"Yep, got everything." My mother turned to me. "Sphinxie, why don't you call your daddy? Let him know we got here safe and sound." I obeyed, pulling my cell phone out of my purse and dialing my father. I talked to him as we walked out of the bathroom, relayed the story of finding Leigh, marveled over the change of time zones, and promised at least three more times to be safe and remember to have my mother charge her phone at Leigh's house. He wanted to talk to my mother then, and Leigh, looking slightly shy, asked if she could say hello too.

"Tell him to get off the phone," my mother said teasingly after a few minutes, linking arms with Leigh. "We have some driving to do." My cell phone was finally snapped shut and handed back to me.

We found Leigh's car in the airport parking lot, a sleek black Lexus. Leigh opened the trunk and helped us put our suitcases inside, the bags falling to the trunk floor with dull thuds. I blinked and stared at them lying there in Leigh's car; this was really happening.

"Who calls shotgun?" Leigh asked as she climbed into the driver's seat and took out her keys.

"You can have it," I told my mother, and got into the backseat while she climbed into the front. There was a pair of brown lace-up guys' shoes on the floor, thrown in a haphazard jumble with a deep purple scarf and a little paperback book, pages splayed open and bent. "There's stuff on the floor," I said, holding my feet up so I wouldn't step on it.

"It's Cadence's," Leigh said. "You can move it to the side, Sphinx."

I buckled my seat belt and reached down to pick it all up. I hadn't even seen Cadence yet, but I felt like his things were paving the way for his re-entrance into my life, giving off a presence that was distinctly *him*. And those shoes weren't little-boy shoes; they were big, they belonged to a young man who was obviously taller than I was. I hesitated for a moment before my fingers brushed against the shoes: I knew the old Cadence would absolutely hate it if he knew I was touching his things. I shouldn't be thinking like that, though, I reminded myself: Cadence had grown up, just like I had. He was different now. I couldn't think about him the way I had when we were little.

I grabbed the scarf and pulled it out from under the shoes, sending them toppling over, the book splaying out farther in protest. I winced involuntarily, hoping that I hadn't permanently creased the pages. Carefully, I put the scarf on the seat next to me in a neat little pile of purple, letting my hands linger momentarily on the soft material. Then I tucked in the shoes' laces and moved them out of my way, but not without inspecting them and making sure I hadn't somehow scuffed them when I'd knocked them over by pulling on the scarf. Thankfully, I hadn't. I picked up the book last, smoothing the pages down as best I could until they lay flat again. Then I turned it over to read the cover: *The Metamorphosis*, by Franz Kafka. I'd read that book for school, not all that long ago.

I put the book down next to the scarf and turned toward the window, feeling a little better now that Cadence and I had something more recent than childhood memories in common. We were already a little way from the airport, and I pressed my nose against the glass, taking in all the sights, fear and excitement mingling in my belly. We'd flown straight into London, but Leigh's house was a fair way from the airport, and we had at least an hour's drive ahead of us. I took my iPod out of my purse and put in the earbuds. My mother and Leigh were talking, catching up, and I turned the music up, not wanting to listen in. Later, I took out my cell phone and took a few blurry pictures of the view outside the car window with the phone camera, feeling guiltily like a tourist.

We left the highway, entered a more suburban area, then a more rural one. I leaned my head against the window and watched the raindrops course down, racing each other, touching each other and merging. Soon we would be there, at Leigh's almost-legendary England house. And *he* would be there, waiting. I traced the raindrops with my fingertips and turned off my iPod. The car radio was on, and all the radio hosts had such perfect voices.

✳

Leigh's house surprised me; it rose up out of nowhere and pulled us up the driveway. It was a beautiful house, huge and relatively new-looking, but modeled after those old Victorian mansions that you see every now and again, looking like pages out of dusty old books. The lights were on in the windows, looking warm and inviting. Leigh pressed the button on her garage remote and the door slid open mechanically, flooding the driveway with light. I unbuckled my seat belt and opened the car door, feeling faintly giddy as I got out. My knees were a little weak, but I stood up as straight as I could and mentally promised myself that I wouldn't let the butterflies in my stomach show. I couldn't.

"Do you want me to bring Cadence's stuff inside?" I asked before I shut the door.

"Oh, you don't have to do that," Leigh said as she helped my mother get our suitcases out of the trunk.

"It's no problem," I said, and slung my purse over my shoulder so that I could gather up the shoes, book, and scarf in my arms. The scarf smelled like autumn leaves and guys' cologne, and I found myself breathing more deeply than usual, wanting to be able to remember the scent clearly. When we got inside, we were in a little mudroom. I saw a low shelf on which a bunch of shoes was lined up, so I put the shoes down there. Above the shelf was a row of hooks for coats, and I hung the scarf over one of the hooks. Then all I had left was the book. I was clutching it far tighter than I intended to, making the cover buckle slightly.

"Cadence!" Leigh called. "We're home!" My eyes darted from side to side. Where *was* he, and why wasn't he answering Leigh? I wanted to know exactly when I was going to see him. I licked my lips, trying to bring a little moisture back into my mouth.

Leigh led us through the house, showing us the kitchen, the entryway where you came in if you went through the front door, the living room, the dining room. Everything was artsy and stylish and matching, with eccentric accents here and there. The living room had more window than wall to its name, and I could imagine that in the morning, when light was streaming in, it would be particularly beautiful. But where was he? My stomach was doing a complicated little dance, and I was still squeezing the book hard enough to turn my knuckles white.

"Leigh, it's gorgeous," my mother said, smiling at her.

"Yeah, it's really nice," I managed to say, even though my mouth was a desert.

"Thanks, guys," she said, looking almost embarrassed. She had kicked her high heels off in the mudroom and discarded her coat somewhere along the way. She went over to her fridge and opened it, sticking her head inside. "You didn't eat dinner yet, did you?" she asked.

"Nope," my mother said.

"I didn't think so . . . you're probably all confused because of the time . . ." She emerged from the fridge. "Do you want dinner?" We didn't, but thanked her anyway. She put water on for tea instead, and said, "Let's go upstairs and find Cadence. He's probably in the attic, working on one of his paintings."

I swallowed and tucked a loose strand of hair behind my ear. So this was it.

We followed her up the wide staircase. She pointed out her room and Cadence's room on the second floor, showed us where we would be, showed us where the bathrooms were. Standard, typical, easy hostess, as though this were a simple visit, no big reason, just friends visiting. Then up another, smaller staircase we went, up toward the attic, where he was. I squared my shoulders and held my head a little higher. Here I went, up a flight of stairs and off a cliff.

It was a wide, open attic, nothing but white walls and canvases. On the far side there were shelves for paints and brushes, and a sink to wash everything off in. And up against one wall was a giant canvas, taller than me and far, far wider. He was standing in front of it with his back to us, painting.

The three of us stood at the top of the staircase and looked at him: me feeling apprehensive and eager and frightened and strange, my mother's feelings unreadable. And Leigh, yearning, yearning. Her mother's heart seemed to be bursting into shreds in her chest, underneath those chocolate pearls that looked so nice on her. A giant, painful buildup of tension was rising in my chest, growing and growing. He didn't even turn his blond curly head.

"Cadence," Leigh said, her voice strained all of a sudden, "Sphinx and Sarah are here."

He turned suddenly then, and made me suck in my breath. He was wearing blue jeans that were torn at the knees and a white button-down shirt smeared with color. And although he was thinner and paler than he'd been in the last picture Leigh had sent us, he was still captivating, his eyes still that brilliant shade of icy blue. I couldn't look away.

He held a thick brush dabbed with midnight-blue paint in one hand, and the thumb of his other hand was hooked through the hole of an old-fashioned wooden artist's palette. He cocked his head to one side, and a bit of the old glare flashed through his eyes as he took in my mother and me. The eyes darted over my face, looking, just as Leigh's had, for the scar. And I remembered the playdates, the games, the lies, the switchblade. The mass of tension in my chest swelled suddenly and pushed my heart into my throat, choking me. *Click.*

Then he looked right at me, and he smiled, his grin wide and inviting. "Hello!" he said brightly. "I'm so glad you're here!" He tossed a stray blond wave out of his eyes and went on, "I'd hug you both, but I'm absolutely covered in paint." And then he turned on his heel and faced the canvas again. His feet were bare, his long toes spread out on the attic floor.

"How are you doing?" my mother asked. "You still love to paint, I see."

"I'm fine," he said, without looking at her. He didn't have a smile for her like he'd had for me. Instead, he reached out with the brush and painted a streak across an upper corner of the canvas. "And yes. I love to paint."

"I put water on for tea," said Leigh. "Do you want some tea, Cadence?"

"Yeahhh," he drawled softly, mixing two blues together on the palette.

"Okay." Leigh turned to go downstairs. My mother went to follow her, but looked at me, putting a hand on my shoulder. Her eyes asked me if it was all right for her to leave me, if I wanted to talk to him alone. I nodded my head, and she left. Slowly, I walked into the attic, closer, closer, until I stood next to him in front of the canvas. I felt like I was creeping up to stand next to a wild animal. No sudden movements.

One side of the canvas was filling up slowly with many different shades of blue, swirled expertly together, melting into one another and bursting out again anew.

"What's it going to be?" I asked him.

"Don't you know me well enough to guess, Sphinx?" he said, and I looked up at him. He was a head taller than me.

"No," I said firmly, fighting the urge to apologize. There was no reason for me to apologize. It was just a big smear of blues so far; there was no way for anyone to tell what it was.

"Then maybe you aren't worthy of knowing." He painted a blue circle, separate from the flowing mass, and stepped back from the canvas. "Or maybe if you look long enough, you'll start to understand." Briskly, he walked over to the sink on the far side of the room and turned on the water. He began running his brush under the flow from the faucet, rolling the bristles between his thumb and forefinger in order to preserve their shape. "Are you just going to stand there?" he asked, glancing at me from under his ringlet fringe. He turned and began scrubbing the palette with a little sponge.

"I'm just —" I began, but he cut me off.

"If you're just going to stand there, then you might as well do something." He dropped the sponge and the palette into the sink and dried his hands on a towel hanging over the faucet. "Here. Wash this." He left the water running and came across the room again, passing me, passing the canvas. "I'm going to go and change. It looks like a rainbow threw up on me."

"Wait a second," I said. I still had his book in my hand. "I have your *Metamorphosis*."

He came back to take it from me, and as he did so, his fingers brushed against mine, trailing over them like a soft breeze. His skin was still damp. He lingered there for a moment, and I felt my own hands freeze under his touch, unsure and wondering. Then he pulled the book out of my hands, looked deep into my eyes, and smiled as he dropped it on the floor at my feet. It fell on its back, pages opening wide, words upturned toward the attic's overhead light.

And then he disappeared down the attic staircase, leaving me alone, heart racing, with the paints and the canvases and the running water. I wanted to tell him to clean his own palette, that I wasn't the Sphinx he bossed around when he was younger, but then I remembered that he was sick, that he was dying, that in less than a year he'd be gone. That someday in the near future I would see that Christmas picture of him at home and think of this, being in his attic before he died, and him leaving me with his painting things. The water in the sink, splashing over the palette, gurgling down the drain. I would think of this. And I had done it, I had faced him again, I was here and I was being strong. I could strike a balance and be helpful without losing the real me. I could figure this out.

I went over to the sink and picked up the sponge. I started to scrub, methodically, making sure that I did a good job of it. I wrung out the sponge and dried the palette with the towel. All of Cadence's blues swirled down, down, down into watery tendrils before vanishing from sight.

8

After I'd washed Cadence's palette, and picked up his book yet again, we had tea downstairs. Cadence had discarded his paint-covered shirt and donned a plain, loose blue T-shirt. We sat in Leigh's living room and drank our tea, my mother and I on one sofa, Leigh and Cadence on the opposite one. All of the tea mugs were art-themed; I had a Georgia O'Keeffe flower, my mother had a Mary Cassatt mother and child, Leigh had a broken-up Picasso, and Cadence had Van Gogh's *Starry Night*.

My mother was updating Leigh on our lives, and vice versa, and their words were adult, but their voices sounded like young girls'. They were best friends, brought back together again by unexpected circumstances. And I felt small again, returned to those days of playdates every week after school, of Cadence and the butterfly. I didn't like it. I didn't know how I had expected my mother to behave around Leigh, but the sight of her talking with her best friend as though nothing had changed put a bitter taste in my mouth. I didn't expect my mother to give Leigh the cold shoulder, of course not. But to giggle casually with her the way she was doing? I couldn't quite stomach that, either.

Cadence put his mug down on the coffee table. He picked up one of those little puzzles made out of swirling metal shapes and started playing with it, clever fingers darting all over it with elegant precision. I had a similar puzzle at home, but I could never figure out how to solve it. In a few moments, though, this one was apart in Cadence's hand, the two shapes separated like hands letting go of one another.

"Those things drive me crazy," I said as he set it down next to his mug on the coffee table. "I can never get them apart."

"Perhaps you don't try hard enough," he suggested.

"Maybe," I said. I took a sip of my tea, feeling slightly glamorous: Having tea in England seemed classy. Then I said, "I put your book on a bookshelf I passed on my way downstairs, the one in the hall on the second floor."

"All right, thank you," he said.

"Do you like that book?" I asked. "I read it for school once. It was really weird."

"I love Kafka," he said sternly. "He's one of my favorite authors."

"That's cool," I responded awkwardly, feeling stupid again. I should have known he'd have liked that book. He'd surely have understood it far better than I ever could.

After that, we were mostly silent, just listening to our mothers, answering the occasional questions. Cadence went to bed first, and then I stayed downstairs for more than another hour, waiting for my mother to finish speaking with Leigh. She didn't seem to want to finish, so I went upstairs to the guest room Leigh had assigned to me, changed into my pajamas, and called my father on the phone. His voice sounded happy, but a layer of tension and worry was hovering just beneath the surface of his questions about how I was holding up so far. He kept stumbling over his words, repeating himself.

"I'm fine, Dad, really," I said after he'd asked me for the third time if I really wanted to be there and reminded me that I could come home whenever I wanted to. "I can do this. It's only a week."

"I know, Sphinxie," he said, releasing a strained sigh. "I know." He paused. "How's your mother? Can I talk to her?"

"She's still downstairs with Leigh," I said slowly, feeling a sudden sourness in my chest. "I'm sure she'll call you later, though." After a moment of uncomfortable silence, I added, "You know, Dad, I'm really tired. It's late here. I think I'm going to go to bed now."

"Okay, Sphinxie," he said, sounding disappointed that I was getting off the phone so quickly. "I love you. Get some rest, I know you need it."

"I love you too, Dad," I said, and hung up. Yawning, I put my phone on the bedside table and turned out the light. Despite my exhaustion, I resisted immediately giving in to the wave of sleepiness that hit me as soon as my head touched the pillow; I wanted to see if my mother was going to come quietly into my room to see how I was holding up on our first day there. But she didn't, and eventually I rolled over onto my side, digging my fingernails into the unfamiliar pillowcase, and closed my eyes.

I woke up late the next morning, my body confused by the time. The sun was coming in through the windows of the room I was staying in, and I could hear people moving around downstairs. I rubbed the sleep from my eyes and sat up in bed. Was Cadence awake too, or was he the kind of person who liked to sleep in? The image of his bedroom in my head was a leftover imprint from years ago — I still imagined the painted trees on the walls, the sky on the ceiling. I wondered what his room looked like now.

The polished hardwood floor was cold against the bottoms of my feet when I got out of bed. The guest room that Leigh had given me was beautiful, decorated like a teacup from one of those china sets with the blue pictures on them. It had its own little matching bathroom off to one side, and a little walk-in closet. My suitcase was sitting on the floor of the closet; I hadn't brought anything that required hanging up, which made me feel slightly dull. It was a really pretty room, and it made me feel as though I were in a hotel, but it also made me feel intimidated. It was an awful lot nicer than my little, messy room back at home, with my unorganized homework and clothes and shoes and various electronics strewn all over the place.

I rummaged in my suitcase for a pair of socks before leaving my room and padding down the stairs. My mother and Leigh were at the stove, both still wearing their pajamas, a drippy bowl of pancake batter on the counter beside them. Leigh was smiling and seemed happy enough, but then I noticed that her eyes were red and the area around them was puffy. It looked as though she'd had a rough night.

"Good morning!" she and my mother chorused together.

"Good morning," I said, stretching. "Where's Cadence?"

"Out in the backyard," Leigh told me as my mother began flipping pancakes. "Why don't you go find him? You can tell him breakfast is almost ready — finally. We all got a late start this morning, didn't we?"

I went back upstairs to my room to get a sweatshirt and my tan Uggs. I had stuffed them in the bottom of my suitcase, and they were all crumpled up, the tops folded over and out at an angle. I pulled them on, hoping that the wrinkles weren't permanent.

The backyard was an expanse of green field with a forest at the far end, and it looked like a postcard image in the morning rays of sun. The air was crisp enough to make me cross my arms over my chest, pulling the sleeves of my sweatshirt over my fingers for warmth. Not far from the back of the house stood a wooden play set, complete with a green plastic slide and two swings. He had had a set just like it back at his house in the States when we were little. I remembered it perfectly: how the swing on the right side was always his, how we hid in the little fort area at the top of the slide, how we much preferred to run up the slide than to sit on it and go down, like you were supposed to. And of course, I couldn't help thinking of our birthday party, of that moment when he'd flown from the swing and taken my hand, magical and smiling.

He was sitting on the right-hand swing now, his feet firmly on the ground, sunlight catching his hair and making it look even lighter than it was. As I approached, he ran a hand through it, smoothing back the blond curls.

"Hey," I said, sitting down on the left swing. "Pancakes·are almost ready." We were too big for the swings now, our legs grown like long vines.

"Oh," he said disinterestedly. I didn't blame him. After all, what did pancakes really matter when you were dying?

"It's really pretty here," I told him, taking a deep breath. The morning air smelled good, damp earth and the grass of the field mingling together. "I wish my backyard looked like this."

He rocked back and forth slightly on the swing. He was already dressed for the day, wearing jeans and a red sweater, the shoes I'd brought in from Leigh's car laced up on his feet. His head was bowed slightly, his gaze inclined toward the ground.

"Does this swing set remind you of when we were little?" he asked me, lifting his head and looking at me. He pushed off from the ground and held his feet up so that the swing could move back and forth unhindered. I couldn't stop thinking about little Cadence at the party, swinging back and forth, higher and higher. I could feel the heat of long-gone summer days on my skin, see little him silhouetted against a blue sky, his hair flying back from his face. When he'd jumped off, little me was sure that he'd hovered in the air for a moment, beamed up by the sun, light taking back light, like an alien ship coming to Earth to retrieve something it had left behind.

"Yeah, it does," I said as he went back and forth beside me. "It makes me think of our party."

"My mother invited all those other kids to that party, you know," he said. "They weren't my choice. None of them were like you, Sphinx. Never like you." He put his feet down suddenly, halting the swing, and looked at me. His hair was falling into his eyes, softening them.

"Oh, yeah?" I said. There was a time when I would have loved to hear him say things like this, back when my idolization of him won out every time over his mistreatment of me. Once, I would have been elated to know that my perfect friend Cadence didn't like playing with anyone else. Now I didn't know what to do with myself. I didn't know how it was making me feel. I wanted to be more grown up, more sensible, stronger. Unaffected. But he was smiling at me, and my breath caught in my throat. I couldn't help smiling back.

"Well, of course," he said, still smiling. "You were my best friend."

"That's what I used to say about you," I said, looking away from him.

"That's what I'll *always* say about you, Sphinx. Always. Until the day I die."

I looked back at him. My heart felt like it had run into a brick wall. Until the day he died. In front of me, he let out a laugh and tossed his hair out of his eyes. I bit my lip and asked him a thousand questions inside my head. *Are you at peace with dying? Do you want to die? Are you happy to die? Are you really dying? Is this real?*

Still smiling, he looked out over the backyard and repeated, "Until the day I die." Like an oath, like a mantra, like a vow.

And I thought, *It doesn't seem like you're dying. Can you hear me? Your eyes are very, very bright and you know it. Once, I had a friend named Kaitlyn, and she thought you were good-looking. I told her you were crazy. But she was right. And now you're smiling at me.*

"Sphinxie," Cadence said. "Do you want to hear my secret?"

"Sure," I said, feeling suddenly apprehensive. The smile had vanished without a trace, making me stiffen. It was like he had set off an enormous flashbulb and then turned out the lights, leaving me reeling in the dark, a ghost of the brightness that had been still floating in front of my eyes.

"Come here," he said, edging his swing closer to mine and reaching out a hand, gesturing for me to move closer. When I did, he put his hand on the back of my neck, fingers intertwining with my hair, holding me where I was. His lips were right next to my ear, his breath warm on my skin, and his closeness was tantalizing, exciting. A chill ran up my spine, a terrific tingling chill that electrified me. Then I felt myself freeze up, as though my brain was putting my body on lockdown, safeguarding me just in case I decided to lean in to his touch.

"What are you afraid of?" he whispered. "I'm just telling you my secret, Sphinx." He took a breath, and went on, in the softest whisper yet, "Did you know that my doctors said there was something wrong with my mind? You didn't, did you?"

His hand moved slightly; now the bottom half of his palm was over my lower cheek. The tip of his nose was touching me just

above my ear. "Well, they were wrong. When a doctor doesn't understand something, they have to say it's wrong, to make themselves feel safe . . . but that doesn't mean it's true. There's nothing wrong with me, Sphinx, nothing at all . . ."

I was frozen. His hand was warm on my face, the movement of the words falling from his lips sending fresh chills through me with every moment. My first thought was that I was scared, terribly scared. I didn't know what he was talking about, and I didn't like the sound of it at all. But then I recalled how many times I had imagined myself in a situation like this: sitting somewhere with a boy like Cadence, his hand in my hair, and his lips so close. A good-looking boy, with blue eyes locked onto mine and blond hair falling over his forehead. Suddenly, a voice in my head reminded me, *We were supposed to get married.* An involuntary shudder went through my body; I should not have thought of that. *He cut you,* I said to myself, and shuddered again. *He is not an ordinary boy. He cut you.*

It didn't matter that he could make his voice soft and layer it over my skin like a blanket; it didn't matter that he had the ability to veil his eyes with temporary warmth, like an Indian summer floating in after the frost had already killed everything. And it was completely inconsequential that he could give out these moments of gentleness, cracks of light pushing their way through the dark. Yes, his hand was warm, a sign of life, but I knew about the ice in his eyes.

"What are you afraid of?" he repeated, in a murmur, and pulled away from me. The hand came away from my face, and I

was left chilled and burned at once, my mind reeling in confusion. The swing set creaked as he let his swing take him back to its original position. His head cocked to the side as he looked at me, as those piercing eyes focused on my face. On my upper cheek. On the scar that was no longer covered in concealer. I had washed my face the night before, and hadn't applied makeup since.

"You hid it yesterday," he said, his eyes flashing. "Don't you dare hide it again!"

"Cadence, it's *my* face," I said, my voice trembling. "I'll cover it up if I want."

"No!" he snapped, sounding like an irritable toddler. "Don't you dare!" He got up from the swing, growing taller in a second, and I stood just as quickly, trying to catch up to him. We stared at each other, his eyes blazing, mine wider than usual, but defiant. "Sphinx," he burst out, his entire frame tensed and shaking, "don't you dare!"

"Why not?" I asked, raising my head higher. My eyes met his, soft brown against the hard wall of icy blue. And his eyes darted back and forth in their sockets, and I had this sudden urge to clear my mind. This terrible, irrational fear that he would reach in and read my thoughts, see that I had been thinking of the plan, of the marriage that would never be.

His eyes narrowed, and then softened. And I wondered so many things. Why did he act like this, how could he go from gentle to vicious in the blink of an eye, was it only because he was dying? And what if he had indeed seen into my head, what

if this shining and wild boy was picturing me in a white dress that would never exist? My hands clenched at my sides. *No, that's impossible.*

"Sphinxie," he said, his voice calm again. "Why would you want to hide it?" He reached out and put his forefinger at one end of the scar, traced it to the other end as I stood strong, determined not to let him scare me. "I don't understand. Don't you know that you have been touched by an angel? I thought you knew that." He looked at me for a minute, and his eyes were perfect smooth walls in his head.

Then, as though nothing had happened, he turned on his heel and strode toward the house.

"Let's go have some pancakes," he said casually. I stood motionless, stunned yet again by the sudden change in his demeanor.

Did you know that my doctors said there was something wrong with my mind? His words flooded back into the forefront of my thoughts. And yet I could feel his hand still on my cheek, his lips by my ear, his finger on my scar. *Don't you know that you have been touched by an angel?* My mind seized the newer question, turned it over and over, looked at it from all angles, held it up to the light, racing to provide an answer to the question.

And for a moment, there in the green of the backyard, next to the swing set that was just like the one we'd always played on, watching him walk toward the back door of the England house, I considered it. Was that why all those twisted feelings had blossomed in my chest when he'd first cut me? For a moment, I thought

I had the answer. Didn't I know that I had been touched by an angel? Yes, I thought I had . . . for one minuscule, burning, shivering, shining moment in time, in the green, green backyard, with the long yellow rays of the sun touching down around me.

Just for a moment.

9

My mother and Leigh had given the pancakes smiley faces: lopsided globs for eyes, long snakelike curves for grins. They used syrup to make hair and beards and mustaches that flowed out and dripped all over the plates, turning amber in the sunlight from the kitchen windows as it spread out into sticky pools.

"Leigh and I used to do them like this when we had sleepovers in grade school," my mother explained. I stared at her as the realization washed over me that she had no idea what had happened to me out on the swings. If she'd only stepped away from the pancakes to look out the window, she would have seen everything, but she hadn't. And evidently, the look on my face now was escaping her notice too. Couldn't she see how wide my eyes were?

"We used to try to make them look like our teachers," Leigh said, stacking two on her plate.

I took a shaky breath and looked down at my plate. The pancake's wiggly smile looked back up at me, and I felt a weight settle on my shoulders. Leigh was trying so hard. She just wanted us to be happy on this visit, just as happy as if we hadn't come for any reason but to have a good time with old friends — to remember grade-school sleepovers, old teachers who had been made fun of, good times.

Across from me at the table, Cadence sat ramrod straight in his chair and cut his pancake face in half, then in quarters.

"Aren't you hungry, Cay?" Leigh asked, watching him with those fierce mother's eyes, that sad intensity, the longing for time to freeze in place.

"Not particularly." He skewered one of the pieces on a single prong of his fork, biting off one of the corners before returning the piece to his plate.

"So," my mother said, pouring herself a glass of orange juice, "do you two have any plans for today?" She looked expectantly at Cadence and me.

"Just tell me what you guys want to do, and we'll do it," Leigh said.

"Ask Cadence," I said, feeling like he should decide.

Cadence merely shot me a glance out of the corner of his eye, gave me a little smile, and shrugged his thin shoulders before returning his attention to his breakfast. His calmness startled me. How could someone who had less than a year to live and breathe and see, to move and do things, to learn and listen and soak up everything the world had to offer, just shrug casually when asked what he wanted to do? If I had been in his place, knowing that every second brought me that much closer to dying, I would have had so many things on my list. So many little, beautiful, last-minute, hurried things. *And I would eat that pancake,* I thought disconcertedly. *I would eat five of them.*

In the back and sides of my mind, crowded around my present thoughts, was the fresh memory of what had happened out on the swings — of Cadence's hand on my face. It was shaking me up. My last memory of him had been Cadence at his most intense, eyes burning as the knife dragged across my skin. I'd forgotten how soft his voice could get. My pancake turned to rock in my throat and I had to take a huge gulp of water to get it to go down, like it was a tremendous pill.

"Come on, what do you want to do?" I said, sensing an unintentional urgency behind my voice. "We have to do something. We're not just going to sit around all day, are we?" I wanted us to be busy, to be doing something. If we were busy with some kind of activity, he wouldn't have the chance to whisper anything else into my ear — and I wouldn't have time to listen. Enough was enough for one day.

He pushed his plate away with the tip of his finger and rose from his seat.

"I'm going to play the piano," he said, with a tone of finality. He was going to play that piano all day long. That was all.

"Well, I'm going to take a shower," I told him. "I'll come find you when I'm done. But we should do something later, okay?"

He left abruptly, without answering me. Leigh stood up.

"I'll get you some towels, Sphinx," she said, and came upstairs with me. She handed me a little stack of fresh, crisply folded beige towels, a little washcloth on top, and showed me how to turn on the shower. "All set?" she asked me.

"Yeah," I said, unzipping my sweatshirt. "Thanks."

The shampoo in Leigh's shower was in a purple container that claimed it was scented *Moroccan Violet*. It smelled heavy and persuading, like some kind of exotic honey. I wasn't sure if I liked it or not, but I hadn't brought shampoo from home, so I had no choice but to use it. When I got out of the shower, I wrapped my hair in one of the towels and went back into my room to get my little blow-dryer out of my suitcase, but found that I had forgotten it, so I had to use Leigh's. When I was finished, I got out my makeup bag and dug around inside it for my concealer. I only hesitated for a moment before carefully covering up my scar — just a moment, and then it was hidden, like a secret. The place where I had been touched by an angel. I couldn't stop thinking of those words. Was that how Cadence had really viewed cutting me all of these years? Had he really always thought of what he'd done to me as something beautiful? The idea was shocking, and thinking about it made my hands shake as I added the final touches to the concealer over my scar.

Stop thinking about it, I thought firmly, giving myself a mental kick and forcing myself not to dwell on the next thought that immediately popped into my head: *It isn't that simple.*

When I went back downstairs, there was another woman in the kitchen along with my mother and Leigh. Her dark hair was pulled back into a bouncy ponytail, and she stood in front of the sink, washing the breakfast dishes and talking to Leigh over her shoulder. She turned around, her hands soapy, and smiled at me when I came in the room.

"Hi," she said, pushing a loose strand of hair out of her eyes with her wrist. "You must be Sphinx. Such an unusual name. I love it." Her voice was just as bouncy as her hair.

"This is Vivienne, Sphinx," Leigh said. "This is the woman who organizes my life and keeps it from steering off the road!" She and Vivienne both laughed.

"I do what I can," said Vivienne, going back to the dishes. It took me a few moments to realize that she was some kind of house-keeper. "It's nice to meet you, Sphinx," she said, turning back to me. "Everyone's been really looking forward to your visiting here."

"I'm happy to be here," I said. Her brightness was contagious, and I wished that my mother had someone like her around our house, to organize our lives.

"Good," she said. "That's good." There were soapsuds piled up high in the sink, smelling lemon fresh. I could hear the sounds of a piano drifting into the kitchen from somewhere else in the house.

There was another living room off the dining room: It was more formal and fancier, and it didn't have a television in it. Instead it had Victorian furniture, a chandelier, posh art prints on the walls, and the piano. It stood big and black on the shiny hardwood floor, underneath a wide window. Its back was propped open, sheets of music spread out on the music stand over the keyboard. Cadence was sitting on the bench in front of it, his feet bare on the pedals, his hands flitting over the keys. He was playing something high and beautiful, vaguely sorrowful, something that reminded me of light on flowing water, slipping easily over gray stones.

I had known for a while that he played the piano: Leigh had sent pictures of him playing several times over the years. But this was the first time that I was witnessing it in person, and I was transfixed. He had as much of a gift for music as he did for painting, and yet it was all impermanent. Within months, he'd be gone, leaving the piano and canvases behind, silent and blank.

I sat down in one of the armchairs and hugged my knees to my chest. There was a little end table next to the chair, with a vase of fresh white lilies on it. Next to the vase, in a little black case, was a silver digital camera. I picked it up, slid it out of the case, and pressed the button on the top. It turned on with a quiet beep, the screen lighting up. I pressed the button for storage, wanting to see what was on the memory card. It was empty; no pictures, no movies. Nothing.

I changed it from the picture-taking mode to the movie mode and focused it on Cadence and the piano, framing it to include as much of the wide, beautiful window as I could. Then I pressed the start button. A little green circle appeared in the upper corner of the camera screen, letting me know that I was filming successfully.

"Cadence, what's the name of the song you're playing?" I asked.

" 'Sacred Ground,' " he said, still playing. "By Jon Schmidt."

I zoomed in on his hands. They were so graceful, gliding across the keys like ballet dancers, never missing a note. He played excellently . . . he did everything excellently.

I leaned forward slightly, taking a close-up shot of his profile. He was concentrating intensely, his lips pressed together. His head was dipping ever so slightly back and forth, matching the inclinations of the music. I raised the camera so that the shot was filled with the light coming in from the window. And then I zoomed back out again, showing the whole scene once more before pressing the button to stop it. And I put the camera back into the case, and placed it back on the end table, exactly where I had found it. I felt accomplished. He hadn't noticed me filming him, and now I had his playing recorded, forever.

"You're really good," I told Cadence.

"Yes," he said bluntly.

"I can play a tiny, tiny bit," I said. "Only with one hand, though. Not like you."

He finished playing and folded his hands in his lap, and I waited for him to say something. He ran a forefinger along one of the piano's black keys and examined it, as though checking for dust. Then he smoothed his hair back from his forehead and turned to look at me. The light from the window accentuated his angular face, outlining him in a soft golden glow. His ice-blue eyes were focused intently on me. I was glad I had put the camera down.

"Come here," he said.

"What?" I stiffened. What had happened out on the swings was still brutally fresh in my mind, and that had begun with this same phrase, this casual *come here*. I didn't want to "come here." I didn't want to be close to him. The chair that I'd settled in was a safe distance away, and I intended to stay there.

He put a long-fingered hand down on the piano bench next to him, indicating where he wanted me, and said, "You heard me. Come here."

I could hardly breathe.

Our moms are in the kitchen, I reminded myself. *Vivienne is in the kitchen.* I could call my mother into the room at any time; I could make her watch us if I wanted to. I rose slowly from the chair and he turned back to the piano.

It was as if I couldn't help myself. In the next moment, I was sliding carefully down next to him on the bench, trying to make sure that there was a gap of empty space between our bodies. It was a futile attempt: He scooted over and suddenly my right leg was pressed against his, our elbows brushing. I felt my jaw clench.

"You can't play anything with both hands?" he said.

"No." I didn't know what he was leading into, but I assumed it was going to be a stinging jibe about my lack of musical talent.

Instead, he laid his hands on the keys and said, "Put your hands on top of mine."

"Why?"

"You'll see. We're going to play a song. I'll help you, Sphinxie."

Slowly, I lifted my hands and obeyed. It took me a moment to arrange myself: I had to weave one arm underneath one of his, and the fact that I was determinedly trying not to touch any other part of him besides his hands didn't make it any easier. My elbow brushed against his chest and I winced, but he acted as though he hadn't noticed, smiling softly as I lined my fingers up with his. They were longer than mine, but far more slender, the skin paler.

And he was cold to the touch. The skin around his fingernails had a vaguely disturbing bluish tone, as though his blood wasn't circulating correctly. The sight of it sent a little chill down my spine. My fingers might have looked stubby and awkward compared to his, but at least my hands looked *alive*.

Then there we were, next to each other at the piano, hand to hand. He began playing, slowly, his fingers dipping down over the keys, and I let my own follow. The song he was playing was unrecognizable to me, slow and measured. I looked at his face and then down at our hands, biting my lip. His skin might have been cold, but it was soft. I could feel the bones of his hands moving underneath my fingers, like a machine sprung to life. These hands had scarred me. These hands were terrible, beautiful, and running out of time.

And I was touching them. Next to me, he was smiling vaguely, his eyes half closed.

"How do you feel, Sphinxie?" he asked, his voice soft. "How does it feel to be here at last?"

"What do you mean?" I said, looking away from our hands for a moment to try and gauge his intentions. He inclined his head slightly toward me, still smiling.

"You're here with me. Finally. After all those years, you're back to where you're meant to be." I stared at him, my mouth open, trying to form words. "You do know that, don't you, Sphinx?" he said when I couldn't answer him. "You know that you're meant to be here with me."

I swallowed, thinking of the way I had felt at home when I'd heard that he was sick, how I'd known that I had to come to see him. His hands were still moving gracefully underneath mine, the notes of the piano echoing softly in midair. I looked away from him, and finally found my voice.

"Yes," I said slowly, so quietly that I almost couldn't hear myself. "I know."

"Good," he said, in an even quieter voice, as though he were a figment of my imagination.

Then he stopped playing and slid his hands out from underneath mine, like a ghost receding into invisibility. I hovered over the piano for a split second before lacing my fingers together in my lap, shivering.

"What was that?" I said, my voice trembling.

"What was what? The song? I composed it. It's my own song."

"Really? That's amazing." He was silent for a few minutes while I looked at him, waiting for him to respond. "Are you going to play anything else?" I asked when he still didn't say anything.

"Is there something you want to hear?" he asked, sounding suddenly impatient.

I tried desperately to think of some piano piece to request, but the only songs that came to my mind were pop and rock. I felt incredibly uncultured. And he waited, his shoulders slumped idly.

"Play whatever you want," I said finally.

He played something faster and louder, with lower notes that bounced around in a furor.

"What was that?" I asked curiously.

" 'LoveGame,' " he said. "By Lady Gaga."

I was fairly stunned by the idea that any song like that could be translated into piano, but there it was, right in front of me. Notes drumming out like footsteps marching.

"Do you have sheet music for that?" I asked interestedly.

"No," he said, sighing. "I just listened to the song and figured out the notes. It's not as hard as people think it is." Cadence reached out and slid the cover down over the keys with a gentle thump. He turned his head and looked out the window, and his hair became golden in the sunlight. His head was leaning back slightly, as though he was looking upward.

"Are you looking for God?" I blurted, startling myself. I hadn't even known that I was going to say anything. All I knew was that if I were dying, sitting on a piano bench in front of a wide, wide window, with that sun coming in and the last notes I had played echoing into nothing, I would look for God in the view outside that window. I wasn't a particularly religious person; I knew all the Bible stories, but my mother never took me to church and I wasn't exactly sure if I believed in God or not. But I knew that if I were dying, I would look for Him. I would try to believe.

"There is no God, Sphinx," he said.

"Oh," I said quietly. "I just thought maybe —"

"You thought I'd want God," said Cadence coolly. "Because I'm dying."

"Well, yes," I admitted. "I mean, it'd be comforting to believe in something . . ."

"I believe in myself," he said, rising from the piano bench and folding his hands behind his back. "I am the only thing that I have. My art, my thoughts, my body, myself." He paused. "And anyone who believes otherwise is an idiot. All anyone has is their own self."

"But even if you don't believe in God, you have other people," I said insistently. "Your family and friends, and everyone around you. You have them."

He laughed, and it was a cold laugh. *"Other people,"* he spat, and laughed again. "I don't need other people, Sphinx. I have all I need right here in front of me, and everywhere I stand is sacred ground." Like the name of the song he had played on the piano. Sacred ground, a holy place. Beautiful, but vaguely sorrowful. A church, a temple, a mosque, a place of worship. And Cadence stood alone in the light under the window, alone in his holy place, praying to no one, covered by a wall of self-sufficiency and talent and young genius. Dying rapidly, on his sacred ground — but maybe I could join him there, just for a moment, before he slipped away . . .

A lump came into my throat. He turned to face me.

"Are you crying?" he asked me blithely.

"Not yet," I told him truthfully.

"You're a big girl, Sphinxie," he whispered, shaking his head. "And big girls don't cry."

He had moved on already. He was no longer thinking of his life, of his philosophy. His mind had already found a new focus. How silly of me to cry over nothing, over another person.

And the sun was gleaming on the shiny black of the piano; and in the digital camera on the end table, the video of Cadence playing was held in an invisible limbo, a few moments in time. *I'm going to cry when he's gone,* I thought suddenly, feeling very small. *I'm going to see things that remind me of him, and I'm going to think of this.*

He was preserved in the camera, in my memory, in the molecules of my skin where his fingers had brushed against my cheek. Traces of him were everywhere. No, it didn't matter that Cadence was wrong — he was still beautiful, he was still going to affect me, he still mattered. In front of me, he stood with his head tilted, watching me so closely. Impulsively, I smiled at him.

A veil came over his eyes, smooth and perfect. He smiled back vaguely, the edges of his lips pulling up ever so slightly at the sides, and left the room. And the sun streamed in through the window, and danced lightly over the piano, as though it were just another endless, timeless day on planet Earth.

10

I took the digital camera with me when I left the room with the piano. Cadence flitted away up to the attic to paint, and I felt that he didn't want me to shadow him all day, so I went into the living room with the television and sat on the sofa next to my mother. She and Leigh were talking, drinking tea out of the art mugs. Leigh's eyes were bloodshot, but she wasn't crying.

"Whose camera is this?" I asked her, holding it up by the wrist strap of the case. She took it from me and opened it, sliding the silver device out and peering at it.

"I think this is Cadence's old camera," she said, handing it back to me. "He got a new one last Christmas. He hasn't used this one in a while. Why?"

"I didn't bring mine," I told her, which was actually true; I hadn't thought to bring my camera. "I was just wondering if maybe I could use this one while I'm here."

"Sure, Sphinxie," she said. "You can use it. Do you need a new memory card for it?"

"No, there's one in there," I said. "And it's empty."

"Then you're good," she said. "Fill it up." She smiled, a trembling, weak smile.

And my mind was made up. Every chance I got, I would film Cadence, capture him, save a few more moments of him each day — leaving something for me to hold on to, for Leigh to hold on to. I would have to do it without his knowledge, though; I was fairly sure he would object to being filmed if I asked him outright about it. I slipped my hand through the wrist strap and tightened it, binding myself to my new mission.

"Okay, thanks, Leigh," I said.

"You're very welcome," she said, and did that smile again.

We had arrived at Leigh's house on a Monday. The rest of Tuesday passed without event. On Wednesday, we managed to get Cadence out of the house and went to the movies, then out to dinner afterward. We sat in silence around the table in the restaurant as Cadence first flirted with and then abused the waitress, telling her that she was too slow and that he'd never been in a worse restaurant in all his life. I stared down at my lap, trying not to notice as Cadence raised his voice and people sitting near us turned to look at our table. When I looked up, my mother's eyes were wide with shock at his behavior, and Leigh's cheeks were burning pink with embarrassment.

"I'm so sorry," she whispered feebly, tears welling in her eyes.

"That's all right," said my mother, shaken.

I couldn't say anything. When we were finished, Cadence swept out ahead of us all, and the waitress began to clear away our dishes, scowling.

Leigh shakily opened her wallet and handed her a fifty-pound note. The scowl disappeared from the waitress's face as she carefully tucked the money into the pocket of her jeans.

"Thank you," she told Leigh, suddenly glowing with surprise.

"No, thank *you*," said Leigh. "You were very patient with my son." As the waitress walked away, Leigh glanced toward my mother and me, and said in a low voice, "I know that doesn't really make up for it, I know I should have said something to him, but he's —" She hesitated, her eyes tearing up again. "He doesn't have a lot of time left and he's scared and I don't think he can help acting up."

"Of course," said my mother, her voice still wobbly as she tried to compose herself. "Of course. It's fine. Don't worry about it. Sphinxie and I know that."

All I could think was that the waitress did *not* know Cadence was dying, and she did not know what I was doing there with him. She only knew that she had just spent an hour waiting on the most awful teenage boy she had ever met in her life, one who sat surrounded by silent women who didn't even try to tell him off. She didn't know that he was sick, that he was part of his mother's precious life's plan. She had gotten money for not blowing up at us, and she liked that. Money was good. I saw her speaking to another waitress as we walked out, showing her the money. It was the best tip she had ever had, she said.

Later that night, I overheard Leigh and my mother talking while I got ready for bed. They were sitting on Leigh's bed, cross-legged, with the door of Leigh's room cracked halfway open and the television on to drown out the sound of their voices. It was a failed strategy; I could hear them anyway.

"He used to have more control," Leigh said. "He used to be able to charm anyone. Girls fell all over him at his school." She took a shaky breath. "It's like he's breaking down, or something . . . losing his touch. Giving in to the side of him that just wants to bite, you know?" There was a pause. "Sometimes I think I shouldn't have stopped the therapy," Leigh muttered. "But he hated it . . . he really hated it, and it didn't seem like it was going to fix anything."

I felt an uncomfortable prickle at the back of my neck, like there was an insect crawling on me, and I stepped back from Leigh's door. What was I doing standing there anyway? I'd learned my lesson about eavesdropping on my mother and Leigh a long time ago. It seldom led to hearing anything that I wanted to have weighing down on my mind.

I went to my room and closed the door behind me. Would Cadence dissolve completely by the end? He was losing his touch, Leigh had said. Would the side of him that terrified me get more stage time eventually than the side that captivated me?

The digital camera was on my bedside table, and I reached for it, turned it on, and played back the clip of him on the piano.

✳

On Thursday, there was an explosion. He disappeared up into the attic, or so I thought, and this time I followed him, ascending the stairs and stepping out into the spacious room filled with paintings of blue, blue, blue. He wasn't there. He must have gone into his bedroom instead. I went over and stood in front of the tall canvas, wanting to see if he'd filled it out more.

He had. More blues; what seemed like hundreds of different shades of blue stretched out over the canvas in spirals. Weaving through each other and coming out again, like fluid, melting serpents, their bodies made of water. I stepped forward for a closer look.

"Sphinx!" came his sharp voice from behind me. I whipped around and he flew into the room, up the stairs and straight toward me; I looked and his eyes were on fire, flames rising higher behind a thin layer of ice. "What do you think you're doing?" he demanded, rounding on me. He'd crossed the room in an instant to where I stood in front of the blue canvas, a too-bright light turned on before my eyes had time to adjust. He was already looming over me, his entire body tensed with anger, seeming taller than he ever had. His hands were clenched, shaking, at his sides. I shrank backward.

"I thought you were up here," I said, fighting to keep my voice steady. I reminded myself that Leigh and my mother were just downstairs. One scream, and they would come running. All I had to do was scream. "I'm sorry, I won't come up here again . . ."

"What were you thinking? No one is allowed up here without me. You can't just come up here," he said, his voice louder and higher, as piercing as his eyes.

"Cadence," I said, taking another step backward from him.

I wanted to escape. I wished the floor would open up and swallow me right out of the situation. Instead, I was trapped, standing underneath the skyscraper as it rose, tremendous and earthshaking, out of an icy wasteland — just like when I was little. I was still little. I was on the ground, head back, as the skyscraper became taller, and I was inside it on the top floor with the door locked, all at the same time.

Did you know that my doctors said there was something wrong with my mind? You didn't, did you? The words that he'd whispered to me on the swings echoed suddenly in my mind, and mentally I was kicking myself for letting his touch, his piano-playing, his everything distract me. I hadn't thought anything through. I hadn't bothered to dwell on it, to wonder what he meant. What was wrong with him? What was I thinking?

"You're just as stupid as you were all those years ago," Cadence hissed. "You're just as stupid. You didn't even know enough to run away from someone with a knife." His breathing was hard and raspy. "It's just like all those years ago," he said again. His mouth was pulled taut in a line, but there was an air of excitement about him, an eagerness, like a dog bouncing in front of someone holding a tennis ball. In my mind I saw the reflection on the surface of the switchblade. *Click, click, click.* I screamed, and downstairs the footsteps started pounding, reminding me further of that day he had cut me.

He jerked his head around, hearing our mothers coming, and when he turned back, his entire face was narrowed, his teeth bared, like a snarling animal. His arms jerked forward in a flash and he shoved me; I fell over backward and landed on my butt, my heart beating out of my chest, feeling panicked. Our mothers were on the attic stairs now, and he knew it. *He won't do anything, he won't do anything,* I told myself. I wanted to get up and run, but I was frozen to the floor, my hair falling into my eyes. He stared down at me for a split second, and his face was unreadable; I was terrified of what I didn't know, of what was going on inside his head. And he was just staring and staring, his eyes turning brighter and brighter, perfect jaw taut, looking as though he was teetering on the edge of charging at me again.

What is wrong with him? And why, why, why does he want me here?

I found my ability to move again and began scooting backward across the floor. I didn't want to stand up just in case I ended up being weak at the knees; I wasn't sure I could trust my legs to support me yet. He let out a shriek of frustration and stamped his foot against the floor like a two-year-old having a temper tantrum, and then I saw Leigh in the doorway, white-faced and frantic, my mother right behind her.

"Cadence!" she yelled, her voice shaking. "Cadence, don't you touch Sphinxie!"

He whirled to face her and burst into tears: loud, childish, rasping sobs that shook his entire body. My mother disappeared from the doorway and reappeared at my side, her hands gripping my shoulders. And relief, warm and firm, enfolded my chest and began thawing out the buildup of ice.

"Are you okay?" my mother gasped, out of breath.

"I'm fine," I said, stumbling to my feet. I was shaky, but not as much as I had expected to be. I did a ridiculous and involuntary little jog in place, like an athlete trying to shake off an injury. "I'm totally fine."

When I looked over, Cadence had slumped to the floor; Leigh came up and hugged him, letting him cry passionately into her shoulder. He was sobbing and clinging to Leigh like a very small child. It didn't look right; it was like a bad acting job, an over-the-top B movie.

"I'm sorry!" he wailed, and she stroked the back of his head; I felt an exquisite kind of pity for her as she sat there trying so hard to be a mother, a good mother, comforting this child who was too old to be crying like this. Why was he doing this, forcing tears from his eyes as though he was trying to prove something? Was it all just because he was dying, all just misplaced emotions that he couldn't hold back? I looked over to my mother and saw her brow furrowing in mixed confusion and discomfort. Just like me, she couldn't make sense of his actions.

"It's all right," Leigh said, and she went on stroking his hair, smoothing down those blond waves that were so like her own.

"I'm dying," Cadence whimpered into her shoulder. "I'm going to die."

"I know, Cay. I'm so sorry," she said, kissing the top of his head. He sniffled and turned in her arms to look at me. His face was streaked with tears, his hair sticking to the damp skin of his hollow cheeks.

"Sphinxie," he said, holding out his hand to me. "Please forgive me."

Only a moment ago he had been tall and frightening, furious and delighted all at once. He had shoved me, and I had sat on the floor of the attic with his artwork all around me, remembering the feeling of the cold blade slicing into my cheek. He had looked eager and hungry, and I had thought he was going to hurt me again. But now he was the one on the floor, quivering and pitiful. He had shrunk himself, becoming suddenly fragile, a rabid dog that had lain down suddenly, tail tucked between its legs. I took a deep breath and knelt next to him and Leigh on the floor.

I let him wrap his arms around me, let him beg me to forgive him, let him attempt to be remorseful. I was years older than him inside my head, whole and complete, and he was so young and terrible and raw. His hair was brushing against my face, tickling my skin. That made it worse somehow; he had gotten up that morning and showered and dressed, and walked downstairs and eaten breakfast, done everything perfectly, but then he had fallen apart. He was talented and bright and shining, but he had failed before he had even started.

"Don't be mad at me, Sphinxie," he said into my ear, his voice still trembling, his arms holding me tightly. "Please. I *need* you here."

"It's okay," I heard myself telling him, my heartbeat pounding in my ears. "I'm not mad."

11

I really decided it then, on the floor of the attic, when I told him that I wasn't angry. But it was later that day, when we were all in the living room downstairs, that I realized it. My mother and Leigh were watching a sitcom on television, filling up their eyes with the antics of people who didn't exist, and Cadence and I were reading: I had a novel with a picture of pink high heels on the front, while Cadence was flipping through *The Picture of Dorian Gray*. I had my iPod out, the earbuds stuck firmly in my ears, shuffling slowly through my songs.

And then the nurse comes round, and everyone lifts their heads, sang a soft male voice, mingling with piano that sounded like water overflowing past the edge of a sink. "What Sarah Said," by Death Cab for Cutie. They weren't my favorite band, but they were soft and good to listen to while reading. *But I'm thinking of what Sarah said . . . that love is watching someone die.* I looked up. Cadence turned a page in his book. Outside the wide living-room window, a flock of little birds descended on Leigh's lawn and pecked the ground.

So who's gonna watch you die? asked the singer's voice, and I lowered my book. The digital camera was sitting on the coffee table. I picked it up, slowly slid it out of its case. Cadence's eyes moved back and forth, following the words on the page, and I turned on the camera.

So who's gonna watch you die? I focused the camera on the cover of his book, then moved up to his face, filming those striking eyes as they went back and forth, back and forth. He looked intent, firmly interested in the words on the pages before him, his lips parted slightly, peaceful — or as close to peaceful as he could come.

So who's gonna watch you die? I kept the camera on him for a moment longer, then stopped before he could look up and notice me. He turned another page. And I thought of the way he had broken down in the attic, the torrent of emotion that he had released. And there was less than a year left, and even now the hands of the clock on the kitchen wall were moving, and the stove clock was changing, new numbers popping up. Time was flowing, rapidly, like the running notes of the piano . . . flowing, flowing, overflowing. The huge canvas in the attic filling up every day with more blue. Cadence, thinner, paler, losing his grip further every second. He had less than a year, and that meant I had less than a year to understand him, to know him, to do whatever I could for him. And love, the song had said, was watching someone die.

So who's gonna watch you die? There — that was when I knew. I was not going to leave at the end of the week. My mother would have to get on the plane and go back home without me, because I was staying. I was not going to leave until Cadence was gone.

But why? My mind was swirling even as I felt invisible threads tie me down to Leigh's house, securing my position. I was perfectly capable of leaving at the end of the week, of getting on that plane and leaving Cadence behind forever. I would never see him again, never need to fear him again, never need to let myself think about what could have been. I could do what everyone would say I should do: Move on. I had school. I had friends. I was normal, wasn't I? And I had done my part, I had done my good deed and visited him at his request. It was as simple as that.

And yet I was beginning to realize that I was not as simple a person as I'd always believed I was. My entire life I had been clinging to my belief in my ordinary existence, covering up fears and past memories and emotions as I smeared concealer over my scar morning after morning. I was my mother's good girl, my school's nobody, another pair of feet on the soccer team. And I'd been born right and raised right and I shared my toys and I didn't sneak out at night and my eyes weren't full of ice. Ordinary. And yet there was nothing ordinary about my mother's plan, nothing ordinary about the situation it had put me in, nothing ordinary about Cadence and me.

I was older now. I was sixteen. *Sixteen.* I knew things. My feelings were changing, dotted with question marks. I could form my own opinions. I wanted to make my own way, my own ending.

There was this thing called love that I was beginning to understand was more complicated than a boy and girl making out after school, than a mother kissing her daughter on the forehead at bedtime. Love could be painful, frightening.

I could go home. I could keep on covering my scar. I could listen to my mother forever. It was an option . . . a safe and warm and comfortable option.

Or I could take a risk, I could enter the danger zone on purpose, I could make a sacrifice, I could do what I knew I was meant to do. *Love is watching someone die.*

Outside, the flock of birds raised their wings and flew off into the open air.

12

My mother came into my room that night to talk to me, to ask me what had happened up in the attic. Her eyes were filled with concern and worry as she looked at me. A lump started forming in my throat the moment she sat down on the bed next to me, but I felt an urgent need to prove to her that I was all right.

"It was nothing, Mom," I told her, brushing off the incident like an annoying fly. "He threw a fit because I went up there alone — apparently nobody's allowed in the attic unless he's there too." I rolled my eyes, to show that it had been silly, nothing big, just something stupid. She still looked anxious, her brow furrowed.

"I just want you to be careful, Sphinxie," she said. Sighing, she put a hand to her forehead and smoothed her hair back from her face. "Well, we'll be leaving in about three days." She said that last part more to herself than to me; it was a reassurance that there was

only a small amount of time left in our visit, that nothing too horrifying could possibly happen to me in only three days.

"About that," I said slowly. My tongue was sticking to the roof
of my mouth. I knew what she was going to say when I declared
my intentions. She was going to be a mother and insist that I come
home. But I had to try. I had to try.

"What?" my mother said, and I took a deep breath.

"I'm not leaving," I stated, supposing that I might as well put
it right out in the open.

My mother opened her mouth and froze that way for a
moment, shocked, before she recovered enough to speak. "What
are you talking about, Sphinx? Of course you're leaving." Her
voice was firm, but I sensed a quiver of emotion underneath the
outer shell of stern parental insistence. "We have things to do at
home, and —"

I started talking again, interrupting her before she could say
anything more. "I have to stay, Mom. I just really have to. I have
to stay until he's gone, Mom, I *gotta* stay with him." I was talking
faster than I meant to. "He's so empty, Mom, he doesn't think he
has anyone but himself. He's always alone, even when there's people all around him. And I don't think he's ever been happy, not
really, he's —"

"Sphinxie," my mother said, her voice cracking, "I know you
want to help him, but you can't make him better. You can't make
him happy."

"But I can try!" I said, my voice rising, louder, louder. "He's
got less than a year! I think he should get a chance to be happy,

don't you think? And maybe I'm that chance. He asked for me, he wanted me to come here!" It seemed so clear to me, it made perfect sense. And didn't mothers always teach you to be unselfish, to put others before yourself?

"Sphinx —" My mother tried to speak, but I cut her off abruptly.

"And think of Leigh, Mom! Don't you think it would mean something to her if one person other than herself stuck around to watch her son dying young and broken? If one person other than herself cared enough? I'm staying, Mom. I have to do this. I really have to."

My mother's mouth quivered.

"Sphinxie, he might hurt you again," she said, taking my hand. "I can't let that happen."

But you already did, said a quiet little voice in the back of my head. *And your plan for me broke and now I have to make the choices. And you were the one who told me, Do unto others as you would have them do unto you.*

I lifted my head and met her eyes. I squeezed her hand and attempted to smile, if only to keep myself from crying. "He's just a kid, Mom. And he's dying." I squeezed her hand again, and her fingernails dug into the skin of my palm. "What if it were me, Mom?" I asked. "Wouldn't you hope that someone would do for me what I want to do for Cadence? Wouldn't you want someone to stay with me?"

She bowed her head and didn't say anything. Maybe she was realizing her part in it all. I hoped she was.

"You would," I said assertively. "I know you would. Anyone would."

When I went to sleep that night, I dreamt that I went up to the attic by myself and found a blue heron lying on the floor in front of the huge canvas, its wings twisted and broken.

I woke up to rain pattering against the windows and roof, a clap of thunder echoing in my ears.

"Not a very nice day, is it?" Leigh said during breakfast. "I thought we could go out and do something today, but I don't know if I want to go out in this weather."

"I certainly don't," said Cadence at once. He inclined his head toward me, his eyes softening. "What do you think, Sphinx? Wouldn't you rather we just stay inside today?"

"It's pretty nasty out," I admitted, looking over at my mother. She dropped her eyes to her plate, as though she hadn't been looking at me just a moment before. We hadn't reached a resolution, nor any kind of decision, the previous night: We had just talked until two in the morning and cried, and neither of us could fully understand where the other was coming from. I bit my lip. It was Friday now, leaving only two more days before it was Monday and we left on another flight in the afternoon, flew out over the wide ocean, and crossed over into another time. It'd be morning when we got home, if we left in the afternoon. It would be like starting the day over again.

"I always hated thunder when I was a little girl," my mother said thoughtfully. "It scared me out of my wits."

"But I loved it," Leigh said, grinning. "I used to try to convince Sarah here that it was the most beautiful sound in the world."

"And she never succeeded," my mother told us, laughing. "I thought she was crazy."

"Thanks a lot," Leigh said teasingly. "I still love it, you know. I just hoped that we could get out again today. It was fun when we went to the movies, wasn't it?" She left out the part where we went to the restaurant, I noticed. I wondered what the waitress had done with the money. She hadn't really known what it was for; she had just thought that Leigh was some rich pushover with a spoiled, rude son. I wished I had stopped to tell her. I suddenly wanted her to know Cadence's name.

"Well," said Cadence, shaking his blond curls out of his eyes and pushing his chair back from the table, "I'm going to paint." He stood up, leaving his plate on the table, and loped off in the general direction of the attic, his arms crossed over his chest.

"Why don't we *all* paint today?" Leigh suggested, looking timidly toward Cadence for approval. "Would that be all right, Cay, if Sarah and Sphinxie and I came up and painted with you? We'll just use regular paper instead of a canvas."

Cadence stopped with his back to us, and his arms unfolded themselves; his head tilted to one side, and I knew that he was thinking: Did he really want us painting in his inner sanctum? But then he turned around. "Yes, that's fine," he said curtly, then strode briskly off toward the stairs. By the time we got up to the attic, he was already at work, standing before that gargantuan canvas, filling it up with more blue.

Leigh had a stack of computer paper and three paper plates for us to put our paint on. We went over to the shelves where the tubes were lined up, neatly organized according to color. I ran my hands over them, and they were cool to the touch.

"Is there any paint we shouldn't use?" my mother asked Cadence before we made our selections.

"Don't touch the blues," he said, never once taking his eyes off his work.

"Okay," I said, and reached out.

I took a light purple, a pale brown, a buttercup yellow. My hand hovered over a robin's-egg blue before I quickly remembered. Carefully, I squeezed my chosen colors out onto one of the paper plates. As I did so, my eyes darted over to my mother, who was busy collecting her own colors. I felt like we were tiptoeing around each other, like I'd opened up some kind of a rift by telling her about my decision to stay. But wasn't that how people grew up — opening rifts, cutting boats loose from their docks, until it was easy to step away and live your own life? And people were supposed to grow up faster when they had to deal with tragedy. I guessed it was normal, but it still made me feel vaguely sick.

Cadence was suddenly beside me, the tube of robin's-egg blue in his hand. Slowly, he unscrewed the cap and then made the tube hover over an empty space on my paper plate, in between blobs of brown and purple. For a moment, I thought he was taunting me; I almost expected him to yank the paint away. But then his fingers clenched around the tube and a circle of robin's-egg blue appeared on my plate, bright and beautiful. Out of the corner of my eye, I saw my mother and Leigh watching, and an involuntary feeling of pride that Cadence had chosen to offer one of his blues to me, and me alone, swelled in my chest.

Once he'd finished pouring out the blue for me, I knelt in a little semicircle on the attic floor with my mother and Leigh. My mother had picked out pinks and greens, and Leigh had reds and purples. Leigh had taken a glass mason jar filled with brushes from one of the shelves, and put it out on the shelf within easy reach of all of us. I noticed an empty jar on the shelf, and filled it with water from the sink so that we could wash our brushes. And then we began, there in the attic.

I painted a table with my brown, and above it a long, wide rectangle of yellow. I put lines across the yellow with the brown, making window slats. The window panes themselves were the blue, the sacred blue that had been forbidden to everyone but me. Around it all, I spread the purple for a background, and then with the brown I made lines to show that there were walls and a floor, instead of just a lavender mass. I made the yellow come in through the window in rays and land on the surface of the table. It was a lopsided table, with stick legs that could have been painted by a five-year-old. Typical for me. I've never had any talent for art.

Beside me, my mother was painting a flowering vine. Long green tendrils swirled over her paper and burst into pink flowers. She borrowed some of my yellow to add detail to her petals, and then took some of my brown to make a background: the crisscrossing lines of a lattice. Next to her, Leigh's reds swirled over her paper in a way that reminded me of Cadence's work. The strands of crimson formed the shape of a bright red woman holding a little, deep purple child in her arms. The woman's hair rose up from her head in jagged streaks like lightning and turned purple at the ends, shooting up into the top of Leigh's paper and becoming billowing clouds.

"You're really good," I told Leigh, turning my head sideways to see her picture better.

"Oh, thank you, Sphinxie," she said, but she kept her head bowed over her paper, her blonde hair falling forward and hiding her face from view. After a moment, she looked up. "Can I see yours?"

I dutifully held up my painting, feeling slightly ashamed of how childish I thought it looked.

"I like your style," Leigh said. "It reminds me of some famous artist's style — I can't remember whom I'm thinking of . . ."

I looked down at my work. "I don't think it's very good," I confessed. "The table looks silly."

"No, it doesn't," Leigh told me. "It's simple, but it has elegance."

"Thanks," I said, feeling pleasantly surprised by her comments.

"What do you two think of mine?" my mother asked, pulling her brush away from her paper with an air of decided finality. "I went a little crazy with the swirls." Her vines had grown out of control on her paper, looping around each other and clinging to her brown lattice, leaves and flowers shooting out this way and that.

"Now that reminds me of a Georgia O'Keeffe," Leigh said. "The flowers definitely do."

"I like the swirls," I said. I wished that I were more art savvy, that I had something to compare my mother's work to — and I wished that I didn't sound so stiff, that I wasn't still on edge from our talk. I swallowed, picked up the water jar, and stirred the brushes around like spoons in a pot of soup, trying to get them clean. The water had turned a grayish shade of brown. "Isn't it weird that when you mix all those great colors together, you just get this?" I asked, holding the jar up.

"You would think it'd look prettier, wouldn't you?" my mother said, looking thoughtful.

I took the jar over to the sink and dumped it out. The brown water swirled away down the drain and disappeared as I turned on the faucet and began to wash the brushes. I rolled the tips between my fingers as I had seen Cadence do the night I had arrived in England.

"What do you think, Cay?" I heard Leigh ask from behind me.

"You used an awful lot of red," he said. "And Sphinxie's table is lopsided. Your flowers, though, Sarah, remind me of a Georgia O'Keeffe."

"How did you know whose was whose?" I asked, looking curiously over my shoulder. He had had his back to us the entire time, and now even our brushes and paints were cleared away, leaving only the paintings.

"It's easy," he said, without actually explaining why or how.

"What about your painting?" my mother asked. "Are you just going to fill it with blues?"

"Perhaps," he said simply. "I like blue."

I looked at my mother's painting, at those delicate flowers blooming and seeming to move as they filled the paper, leaving no space unfilled; at my own, my spindly little table weak at the knees and imperfect, but with light shining on it from that rectangle of yellow; and at Leigh's, at her raw red mother's love, bleeding furiously all over her paper and exploding into those angry purple clouds.

And then at Cadence's: his wide, swirling ocean of blue, blue, blue. It was artistic and free-flowing, steady and firm; beautiful, painted with a delicate hand, different shades and nuances, rising up and down . . . but really nothing at all, when you looked. When you remembered that there was a whole world of other things to paint, a world of flowers and mothers, children, the sun, the earth, people everywhere, it was nothing.

It was nothing but blue.

13

Leigh pinned our paintings to the door of her refrigerator with magnets. Before that, the door had been bare. I supposed that there used to be artwork there, when Cadence was little and didn't work on canvases, but now there was nothing — until our paintings came along. Leigh smiled and stepped back.

"I like seeing art on my fridge," she said, resting her hands on her hips.

"We used to have tons of Sphinxie's pictures up on our fridge at home," my mother said. "She liked to draw the Disney princesses, and horses."

I felt a rush of hot embarrassment flood into my face. My childhood attempts at art were so clichéd, and when compared to Cadence's work, they became downright pathetic. I used to like drawing as a really little kid, when I was still locked blissfully in the stage of believing that every scribble that came out of my pencil was a masterpiece and looked exactly like whatever I was trying to draw. Later, I got frustrated with my lack of talent, and gave up drawing. Then I tried poetry for a while. It was always in a stiff rhyming format, concerning a typical subject: rainbows, for example, or flowers in a garden. I'd given poetry up too. Now the only things on our fridge that had anything to do with me were my soccer practice and game schedules. At least I was good at soccer.

"I don't really draw anymore," I explained to Leigh, hoping that I wasn't visibly blushing. "Sports are more my thing."

"Your mom tells me you're a great athlete," Leigh said. "We have pictures of you in your soccer uniform somewhere around here. You look like a pro." I doubted that I really looked like a professional player, but it still made me feel proud. "Do you want to play for a living someday?"

"Not really," I said. "I'm actually not sure what I want to do."

"Don't worry, you'll figure it out eventually," she said, and looked at the fridge again. "I really do like your painting, Sphinxie."

"Thanks," I said, for the second time. I wondered if Leigh looked at my painting, with its wobbly, poorly executed table, and wished that she had had an ordinary child. It must be so difficult to be a mother to Cadence.

I supposed at one time she had yelled at him in frustration, tried time and time again to get him to conform, stop breaking rules, stop stabbing people in the back. But somewhere along the line, as he got older and older, she must have gotten weary. Exhausted. Thoroughly tired from trying to bring up this child who shone so brightly into her eyes that it hurt. And then his sickness had come, and although her motherly side still screamed to correct him when he did wrong, she didn't. He was dying and she'd just had to give up. It was like me and my poetry, amplified a million painful times.

It was just Leigh and my mother and me down in the kitchen; Cadence had stayed upstairs, locked in place in front of that canvas, his fingernails caked with blue. Vivienne wasn't in that day. Most days, she would have been moving things around in the kitchen, or organizing something in another room. The house was still without her around; she added a liveliness to the place that Leigh sadly seemed to have lost. There had been a time, I was certain, when Leigh would have been the one who was moving around, smiling, talking animatedly to everyone. She seemed older than my mother now, even though they were the same age. She was leaning on her kitchen counter as we stood there, her palms braced against its edge.

"Are you okay, Leigh?" my mother asked gently.

"I can't say yes," Leigh answered. "But I can't say no, either."

My mother stepped forward and hugged her tightly, and the two of them rocked slowly back and forth like a toy horse. I stood nearby, feeling as though I was intruding on something terribly private, and averted my eyes, staring at the floor.

"Sphinxie," Leigh said, and when I looked up, she was staring over my mother's shoulder at me, her blue eyes glittering with tears under her kitchen lights.

"Yeah?" I asked. My mouth was dry, and I licked my lips.

"You're a really good kid," she said, and the tears fell from her eyes, running down her face and dotting the back of my mother's shirt. "You have a lot of compassion for my son, I can see it . . ." Her breath rattled in her throat. "You're just a really good kid."

I didn't know what to say. I didn't want to say thank you, it somehow felt wrong, but at the same time I didn't want to stand there, stony, and not say anything. I opened my mouth, but nothing came out, so I closed it again. Tomorrow was Saturday, and after that there would be only a day of our visit left.

"Don't worry, Leigh," I blurted, without meaning to. "I'm staying."

"What?" she said, breaking away from my mother.

"Sphinx," my mother said, her voice lowered in warning. I hesitated, looking at her, but only for a moment. She had brought me here, I reminded myself. She raised me to this position. And now I was older and I was paving my own way and I knew where I wanted to go. I took a deep breath, willing strength into my chest, and thought firmly, *Don't back down.*

"Mom, I told you, I have to do this," I said, my voice trembling. Then I looked at Leigh, making perfect eye contact with her, and stated, "I want to stay with Cadence until . . . until he passes away."

Leigh's hands sought the kitchen counter again and gripped it once more.

"Honey," my mother said, "we talked about this. You can't —"

"Why not? Because I have school?" I laughed, that short, barking kind of laughter that's more of a derisive breath out than an actual laugh. "Mom, this is more important than anything I have to do at home. I want to stay with Cadence."

"Oh, Sphinxie," Leigh said, her voice breathy.

"Honey," my mother said again.

I could barely hear either of them. Even though my feet were firmly planted on the floor, I felt the kind of reeling, anti-gravitational panic that comes with slipping and falling backward off a staircase. I had to get a foothold.

"Let me stay!" I said, feeling like a toddler spiraling into a temper tantrum. "I just have to stay." My cheeks began to burn; I was embarrassed about what I was doing, I felt like I was making a scene, stirring up trouble . . . but at the same time, I desperately needed to speak. I had to convince them. I was staying. I needed to stay. I was *supposed* to stay, it was part of some plan, I was convinced of that.

"I want to be here for him," I said, and my voice sounded pitiful in my ears. "And don't you say that he won't care whether I'm here or not, because you don't know that. I'm not taking any chances. If there's the slightest chance that my being here could make him happy, then I want to take that chance."

Leigh was looking at me with her mouth open, the tears rolling in waves down her face. I couldn't tell if she was pleased with me or horrified, if they were happy tears or not. I shut my mouth, sealing my lips tightly. I didn't want to offend her. That was the last thing I wanted to do. I clasped my hands together behind my back, feeling supremely nervous all of a sudden. Had I just upset her, or had I affected her in a way that was deep and good? What was I doing? The kitchen was silent.

"I'm . . . I'm really sorry," I stammered out. "I shouldn't have said anything."

"No, no," Leigh said. "You're okay, Sphinxie, you're okay."

My mother closed her eyes briefly, and put her arm around me, but said nothing. My face was still burning. The more childish part of me wanted to leave so that I wouldn't have to look at Leigh and wonder if I had hurt her, if she was just saying that it was okay. The rest of me, though, was almost proud of myself. I had spoken out. I didn't often speak out for myself like that: It was a rare occurrence. It was a step forward. I thought I felt some of the hot embarrassment begin to drain out of my face. I wasn't *almost* proud of myself — I *was* proud of myself.

No one seemed to know what to say. My mother's arm felt like a line of bricks on my shoulders, and Leigh's eyes were filling up her face. She reached over onto the counter and took a napkin out of the holder and wiped her face. She crumpled the napkin into a ball in her hand and pressed her lips together, trying to get a hold of herself. And I looked at the fridge, at our paintings, and thought of the mass of empty blue upstairs. It was like the wide blue of the ocean, deep and cold and dangerous. Beautiful, but so dangerous. And here I was, and I had spoken up, and suddenly I was feeling like I could swim no matter how deep the water was.

And then the ocean came into the kitchen. Cadence stepped out from around the corner, his head held high, his hands folded behind his back, reminding me somehow of Napoleon. He came forward and stood in front of us, his eyes alight with something that was, as usual, unreadable.

"She's a good girl, isn't she?" he said, nodding his head in my direction.

"You're good, too, Cay," Leigh said weakly.

"Don't say that," he said, scornful. "No one is *good*." He turned to me and asked fiercely, "Why do you want to stay? So you can have a nice vacation in England, is that it?"

"No," I said softly, shaking my head. "I just want to be here for you."

His eyes flashed, and it was almost as though I had said something completely foreign to him.

"I just want to be here for you," I repeated, and my eyes were pulled into a lock with his. They were such strange eyes. It was as if they were made of three layers: the first, a layer of ice; the second, the normal blue that was so like Leigh's; and then the third, a flickering flame, dancing out of reach inside his head. And I wanted to reach that flame, to understand it.

He was looking at me like a person looks at a famous painting in a museum. He was studying me, all of the lines that made up my being, fascinated. I just wanted to be there for him. Perhaps, for a genius like Cadence, seeing that in me was like going up to a wide, detailed canvas and realizing suddenly that the whole thing was a mass of multicolored dots, far more complicated than one would originally assume. It seemed like Cadence was leaning into me, peering closer and closer, although I wasn't sure if that was real or just my imagination. Had I really been a painting, one of the museum guards would have stuck out their hand and told Cadence to take a step back. I saw the beginnings of a smile tugging at the edges of his mouth, drawing them upward. His eyes were alight. And I still couldn't look away.

Then he seemed to draw back into himself. His eyes closed up again, the ice thickening over the dancing flame, and he pulled himself up to his full height, ramrod straight.

"Sphinx," he said gravely. "There is no reason for you to want to stay with me." He stated it like a scientific fact, like something undeniable. As though once he said it, I would immediately realize the error of my ways.

"But that's the whole point," I told him, feeling a terrible lump rise in my throat. "That's why it matters so much, that's why I want to be here so badly."

He looked at me, his expression detached, like a cat staring at a mouse underneath its paw. Then he turned slowly to face Leigh, and smiled. Such a dazzling, breathtaking smile.

My eyes had been released at last from his gaze when he turned to Leigh, but I wanted him to look back again. Had I pleased him? Had I actually made him happy?

"She's a good girl," he said again, and the smile pulled wider. We were frozen again in the kitchen. Leigh was leaning forward slightly, looking as though she might simply pitch forward to the floor at any moment. It was like a scene from a movie; the soundtrack would have been high and soft, suspenseful in the background. It seemed unreal. My newfound pride was still with me, but it was taking a backseat now: I felt like it was my fault for beginning it, for starting this strange heaviness on the air when I had started talking about wanting to stay. It was just like the tenseness after my talks with my mother, except now that it involved more people, it had bigger consequences.

"I would love if —" Leigh began after a moment, and then halted, taking a shaky breath. She swallowed. "I would love if you would stay, Sphinxie." Then she looked toward my mother, and I watched their eyes meet. "But of course, that's really up to you, Sarah," said Leigh, in a lower voice.

Leigh looked like a frightened child asking for permission, her eyes moist. My mother opened her mouth and closed it again.

Cadence looked at the clock over the stove. "It's close to dinnertime," he said, suddenly conversational. "What are we having?"

"I thought we could order in," Leigh said, her voice wispy and thin. Everyone was shaken but Cadence, who breezed away from the group, floating over to the table and slouching in one of the chairs like a prince waiting to be served. People always said they wished they could get over things, not be so affected, so hurt. Cadence was a master at that. He wouldn't remember the awkward sadness and stiffness in his own kitchen, the words he had overheard, the way Leigh had called me a good kid. He moved on so easily. And here I was with pain in my throat, sourness in my chest. Inside me there were colors, swirling about and bruising and growing and changing every moment.

Not a single one of them was blue.

14

My mother let me stay.

She protested until the very end of the designated week, even though I gathered up my courage and went into her room every night and talked to her about it, trying to drill it into her head that I was not going to give up. I wanted to stay. I *had* to stay. I had to open up the rift and unclench her fingers from around me and let her know that this was okay, that this was the plan now. That I needed Cadence just as much as she needed Leigh, that I knew she'd want to do the same thing for Leigh if she were dying, even though Leigh wasn't nearly as extraordinary as Cadence. There was something important that needed to be done here, and it was my job to do it.

On Saturday night, she shook her head and closed her eyes. But on Sunday night, she gave in — at least partially.

"I don't want you to stay here for long," she said, "but I've talked to Leigh, and we decided to let you extend your visit another week." She ruffled my hair as though I were littler than I was. "I have to go back to work, there's a meeting I can't afford to miss," she said. "Are you sure you'll be okay without me? And are you okay with flying home alone?"

"Yeah, I'll be okay," I said, and hugged her, really hugged her, for the first time since we'd been having our nightly talks. "Thank you so much." I looked over her shoulder. There was a mirror hanging on the wall above the dresser in her room. I saw my own reflection in that mirror, and although I was smiling, thankful for the one more week, my eyes were hardened. Another week was too little; I needed to stay until the very end. But I bit my tongue to avoid saying anything. Once my mother was gone, I supposed it would be easy to keep pushing the end of my visit further and further back. Without her there, the only one who could get me to the airport was Leigh, and I knew she wanted me to stay.

And if Leigh wanted me to stay, then so did my mother, even if she wasn't fully aware of it. For my mother, when it came to helping Leigh, the answer was always yes; it always had been.

"Call me every day," my mother said. "More than once a day, if you can."

"Don't freak out if I miss a day," I told her wryly.

"I'll try not to," she said, and touched my hair again. "I love you, Sphinxie."

"I love you too," I whispered. She kissed me on the top of my head, and then I walked through the dark hall of Leigh's second floor, heading for my room. It was dark in Leigh's bedroom, but when I looked in the direction of Cadence's, a thin strip of light was glowing, pushing out from the cracks around his slightly open door.

I tiptoed over and stood in front of the door, my hand raised to knock, wondering if I wanted to talk to him or not. I just felt like telling him that I was going to stay, and making sure that it was okay with him. There was a little voice in my head telling me that maybe I was being selfish by pushing to stay; maybe it would make Cadence happier if I left. After all, I hadn't stopped to consider that, had I? I knocked softly on the door, three hesitant, shy taps.

"Yes?" he said.

"Um, it's me," I said, in a low voice. "Can I come in?"

"No" was the curt answer.

"Oh, okay," I said, feeling slightly dejected. Perhaps he wasn't decent? I stayed outside the door. "Well, I just wanted to tell you that I'm staying another week."

"That's nice," he said, his voice suddenly softening. "I hoped you would." From inside the room, the faint sounds of a pencil scratching against paper reached my ears. I wondered what he was writing. Perhaps it was a list of things that he wanted to do in his remaining weeks . . . or maybe he was writing a story. Did he like to write fiction? He certainly read a lot.

"Are you going to go to bed anytime soon, Sphinx?" he asked after a few minutes, making me wonder how he knew that I was still there. I could have tiptoed away in that moment of silence. For a brief moment, I was suddenly convinced that he could see through the door, that he had been staring at me the whole time, and I simply hadn't known.

"Yeah," I said softly. "I just wanted to tell you that I was stay-ing," I repeated after a pause.

"Thank you" was the smooth, murmured response. There was a soft *clack*; he had put the pencil down onto a hard surface — a desk, probably. Was it the same desk with the drawer that he had taken the switchblade out of all those years ago?

"Good night, Sphinx," he said. I imagined that he was smiling when he said it. He sounded like he might have been.

"Good night, Cadence," I said, stepping back from the door.

I was glad that he sounded pleased with me staying, but a heavy feeling of disappointment dripped into my chest and lin-gered there. I had envisioned him letting me into his room, had seen us having another talk like the one we had had out on the swings or in the piano room — but it was not to be. The light went out in his room, plunging the hallway into even deeper darkness. I suddenly felt much smaller than I had just a moment before. Things were not always the way that one envisioned them; that was always the problem.

Instead of going to my room, I went back into my mother's. Like all mothers, she woke up as soon as I neared her bed. "Are you okay, honey?" she asked, her voice thick with sleep. "What's the matter?"

"Can I sleep with you tonight?" I asked. All those years ago, when I had been cut, my mother had offered to sleep with me, to stay with me. And I had been trying to grow up all week, trying to pick apart the threads that bound me to my mother, but now I wanted to cash in on her offer from years ago. Now I didn't feel like I'd done any growing up at all. I felt like I was ten again, a little girl who was scared of the dark.

"Sure," she said groggily, and so I climbed up onto the bed next to her as she shifted over to make room. I curled my knees up to my chest, and she pulled the comforter up over both of us. It covered half of my face, and underneath it the air was warm and smelled like my mother's lavender bodywash. The rift closed up; I needed her, and she was there.

The next morning, I sat on the bed next to my mother's suitcase as she made sure that she had all of her things packed. Her clothes were neatly folded within, a stark contrast to the mass of wrinkles and crumpled fabric that my suitcase had become over the past week. I smoothed a line out of one of her shirts.

"Don't worry too much if you forget something," I said. "I'll still be here."

"I keep forgetting," she said ruefully. "I wish you were coming home with me."

"I know," I told her. "But —"

"But I know this is important," she said, smiling and closing her suitcase. "Don't worry, Sphinxie, I'll be fine on that big plane all by myself!" She laughed and zipped up the outer pockets. "And I know you'll be fine too." She lugged her suitcase off the bed and put it down on the floor with a gentle thump.

"Do me a favor," she said, her smile suddenly growing more serious. "Be there for Leigh, too. She needs someone here for her even more than Cadence does." She was right, I realized. Leigh was the mother who would be left behind, a piece of her eternally broken off and lost.

"Do you think she'll be okay?" I asked my mother. "When Cadence is gone, I mean."

"I think she'll make it," my mother answered, squeezing my shoulders. "It'll be so hard, of course, but people are resilient. She won't forget, but she'll be able to go on, I think. She's strong, she always has been."

"That's good," I said quietly. "I feel so bad for her, Mom. She's going to feel it, forever."

After breakfast, we all got in Leigh's car to drive my mother to the airport. Cadence sat next to me in the backseat, wearing a floppy red jacket and clutching a travel mug of tea so fiercely that his knuckles had turned white. His hair was falling into his eyes, a mass of golden tangles. His iPod earbuds were in his ears, and he wasn't responding to anything that any of us were saying. I leaned over slightly so that I could see what he was listening to: Beethoven's Fifth Symphony.

Outside the car, the sky was gray but clear. As we drove away from Leigh's house, I noticed a man jogging with his dog on the side of the road. It was a shaggy golden retriever, pink tongue lolling, tail wagging happily as it followed its owner.

"Look at the dog," my mother said from the front passenger seat. "That's a really pretty dog. I always wanted a golden retriever when I was a little girl."

"I remember that!" Leigh said. "I was going to help you sell lemonade on your street so that you could get enough money to buy a puppy!" They laughed together, enjoying the memory.

"Did you ever get the dog?" I asked my mother curiously.

"No," she said. "Grandma is allergic to them, remember?"

"Plus your lemonade was too watery," Leigh remarked. "We had one customer, this little girl from the block over, and she took one sip and spat it out. Then she told all the other kids not to buy Sarah's disgusting lemonade. I thought she was the rudest child in all the world."

"I never liked that kid," my mother said. "She was in my class at school that year. She used to make fun of the bad haircut I had."

"What was her name again?" Leigh asked.

"Polly? Lucy? I don't know," my mother said, and giggled for no apparent reason. That was when I realized how nervous she was about leaving me behind.

We were nearing the outskirts of Leigh's rural town, coming closer every moment to the tall city of London and its airport. Soon my mother would be on a plane, rising higher and higher, while my feet remained firmly on the ground. Just as I had wanted. Still, a pang of nervousness suddenly stung the inside of my stomach, making me shudder. I was the one Cadence had hurt the most; I knew his dark side better than anyone. And I was still determined to stay. But no matter how old you get, there's always a part of you that wishes your mom could always be there to protect you, even if you are trying to be an adult, even if it was all your idea to make her go home without you in the first place. My stomach was in knots, conflicted. In that moment, I hated that I had the capacity to hold such a twisted assembly of emotion inside me.

When we arrived, I carried my mother's suitcase for her into the building and stood with her as she checked it in, wrapping the tag that the man behind the counter gave her around her suitcase handle. As we walked through the airport toward the line for the baggage check, Cadence aligned himself so that he was walking next to me, close enough for his hand to accidentally brush against mine every now and again. I looked up at him and he gave me a smooth smile, his eyes sparkling. I felt a chill run through my body.

"Sphinx," he said casually, in a low voice. "Look at this."

When I turned to see what he was talking about, he put his hand in his pocket and pulled out a Swiss Army knife. When I saw it, I felt a terrible chill run through my entire body, as though someone had dumped a bucket of ice water over my head. And I remembered, with a sick feeling in my stomach, that he'd introduced me to the blade that he used on my face with almost identical words. *Look at this.*

"What are you doing with that?" I whispered, trying not to look at the little blade. "Cadence, we're at an airport, you can't have that out! They take things like that very seriously!"

"So sorry," Cadence said, in a smooth voice, as he slipped it back into his pocket. "I forgot I had it. I was just showing you, Sphinx." That was a lie. He'd brought it along in his pocket on purpose, I knew that. But what had he meant to do with it? Was it a threat? For a moment, I wondered frantically if it was too late to change my mind and fly home with my mother. Maybe I was crazy to be letting her leave me alone in a foreign country with a boy who'd used a knife on me before. But there was nothing I could do now. The knife was out of sight. No one had seen it but me. And Cadence was probably just trying to see if he could get a reaction from me, if he could cause trouble in the airport. Just a little fun, a little game. He was always playing some kind of game.

We waited with my mother as she procrastinated going through security, as she hesitated over and over again and filled the air with empty conversation in order to avoid the inevitable. When we finally hugged and said *good-bye* and *I love you* a thousand times, she paused yet again before walking off to remind me of all the things I was supposed to do, to call her and be careful and be a good houseguest. And I promised that I would. Then she disappeared through baggage check and was gone, leaving an imprint of herself on the air behind her, still trying to watch over me.

"Well, Sphinxie, it's just you and us now," said Cadence casually.

"Yep," I said, taking a deep breath and trying not to think about the knife.

"Do you want to eat lunch out on our way home?" Leigh asked.

"Sure, if that's okay with you and Cadence," I said.

Leigh smiled and put an arm around my shoulders, giving me a quick squeeze. Behind us, Cadence had wandered over to a magazine stand and was peering at the headlines: gossip and scandals and who cheated on whom.

"Of course it's okay," said Leigh, still smiling. "You know, I can't tell you enough how much it means to us that you're staying, Sphinx."

"It means a lot to me, too," I said, still looking out the window at the sky, at the place where my mother had disappeared. There was no turning back now.

We went to a restaurant near Leigh's house, a casual little place. It didn't feel like we had really left my mother at the airport, and I kept having to remind myself that she was in the air, flying home. The waitress was grandmotherly, with gray hair pulled back from her face and wrinkles around her mouth from a lifetime of smiling. When we gave her our orders, she didn't write anything down.

"I keep it all safe up here," she said, and tapped the side of her head when she saw us looking quizzically at her. She had little earrings shaped like carrots dangling from her earlobes. When she brought our orders out, everything was exactly correct; she really had kept it all safe in her head. I admired her for that, seeing as she was an older lady. You would think she'd have problems with her memory.

Leigh and I were sharing a large basket of fries, but Cadence had a bare salad in front of him. He was rearranging the leaves of lettuce, moving them around and around in circles, and staring through my head to the window behind it. It had begun to rain again. I wondered if he was feeling sad or just tracing the path of a certain raindrop, watching it to see if it would beat the other drops to the bottom of the window. I twisted around in my seat and picked out a drop. If he was upset, I wanted to distract him.

"Let's play raindrop racers," I said, pointing. "This one's definitely going to win."

He only stared at me, seeming unimpressed. I knew he probably thought I was behaving like a little kid. I waited for him to roll his eyes and return his attention to his salad. Instead, he watched me for a moment, his head inclined slightly to one side, and then pointed at the window too. I felt myself let out an involuntary breath of relief.

"I think *that* one is going to win," he said, showing me his choice.

And for a minute, we stared intensely at those drops, cheering our chosen racers on.

They both reached the bottom at the same time. I looked back at Cadence, and he turned to look at me almost at the same time. His eyes were cold as they quickly swiveled around to meet mine. For a moment, I wondered if he was angry that he hadn't "won," even though a raindrop hitting the bottom of a window was a random event and not a skill to be mastered. I felt one corner of my mouth quirking into a quivering involuntary smile, like a frightened dog pulling back its lips.

And then he smiled too, the corners of his own mouth stretching almost in sync with mine.

"Did you see that, Sphinxie?" he said.

"See what?" For a split second, I thought he was referring to his own smile. I'd made that happen. I'd pointed out the raindrops for us. And managing to do these little things for him meant that my choice to stay was not going to waste. I had my purpose here.

"The raindrops, Sphinx. They ended the race together."

"Yeah," I said, feeling suddenly uncertain. His tone sounded as though he was trying to make a point, but I didn't know what it was.

He nodded and looked back to the window, still holding my smile on his face. I wondered what he was trying to tell me. And then Leigh said something in her forced cheery voice that I was only half listening to, and the pattering of the rain on the roof slowly came to a halt.

15

Now that I was its sole guest, Leigh's house seemed larger and more imposing. I walked through her front door and into her entrance hall feeling as though I had never really noticed how big the place was. In a daze, I left my shoes on the communal pile in the mudroom and followed Leigh into the kitchen while Cadence disappeared out onto the back patio, letting the door slam behind him.

Vivienne was at the stove, a large pot simmering gently in front of her. She had a wooden spoon tucked behind her ear like a pencil, and the silver bangles around her wrists jingled happily when she moved. Her shirt had a humongous purple peace sign spreading across the front of it. She turned and smiled at me when I came into the kitchen.

"I heard you'll be with us a little longer, huh?" she said, taking the spoon from behind her ear and sticking it into the pot. "I'm glad you like it here so much." She stirred the soup, back and forth. "It's so nice that you want to be here for Cadence."

I bristled without meaning to. This particular thing had been quietly grating on me ever since it first came up: the way that it was "so nice," "so good" of me, to stay with Cadence. Some girls I knew from school at home might have thought of me as a goody two-shoes; I didn't sneak out at night or party, nor had I ever experimented with drinking or drugs. Even so, I was not a saint. And I thought there was something sad about it, that everyone thought of me as so good when I wasn't, and of Cadence as so terribly bad. Nothing was ever said aloud, but it was still sad. We were both just teenagers; I was just as prone to getting in trouble for a stupid mistake as he was. And it was very possible that my continued presence in the house was a stupid mistake in itself.

"You could move into the room your mom was using, if you want to," Leigh said, tearing me away from my thoughts. "It's bigger, and it has its own little bathroom attached too."

"Oh, thanks," I said, still feeling slightly uncomfortable. The fact that my mother was no longer there was making me feel insecure; I didn't want to take her room and be constantly reminded that I was really on my own now. Not to mention being constantly reminded of *her*, and our discussions, and the plan, and the rift. It was a paradox. I wanted her back and I didn't. "Maybe I will, but I don't know. I really like the room I'm in now, it's so pretty."

"Oh, good, I'm happy you like it," Leigh said. "I wasn't so sure about it when I decorated it."

"I think it's great," I told her. Not only did her house seem to have grown, but her conversations with me had grown suddenly awkward. "Do you know where Cadence went?"

"Probably up to the attic," she said, moving to the stove to help Vivienne add ingredients to her soup. "You can go up if you want, Sphinxie." She said it sheepishly, recalling — just as I did — the incident when he had shoved me for accidentally going up there alone.

"I'll go up," I declared, trying to exude confidence. I left the kitchen and slowly traveled up the stairs. When I reached the second floor, I turned toward the direction of the attic stairs, but the sound of movement from inside Cadence's bedroom caught my attention. He wasn't in the attic after all. Just as it had been the night before my mother left, the door to his bedroom was not closed all the way, but hung open a crack. And just like I had that night, I went over to the door and knocked quietly.

"Yes?" he said.

"Can I come in this time?" I asked bravely.

There was a pause.

"Yes," he said finally, and his voice was higher and softer, enticing. I was pleased he wanted me with him, but his tone put me on my guard. I didn't know what to expect, but I swung the door firmly open anyway.

He was sitting in a chair in front of a writing desk, shirtless. His stained painting shirt was laid out on his bed, making me think that he had simply been changing his shirt when I knocked on the door, and then decided to invite me in just to shock me.

And it worked. I had never been alone with a half-naked boy before.

His shoulders were fairly broad and his waist narrow, but his collarbone jutted sharply out from his chest, as did his ribs, and across his chest there was a gigantic bruise, deep purple and blue and black, yellowed around the edges. It covered almost the entire left side of his chest. I recoiled; it looked horribly painful. And this wasn't just any bruise on just any body. This was Cadence. Beautiful Cadence, fading away before my eyes, disintegrating into a painful and stark frailty.

"There's more," he said softly, noticing me staring. "I've got bruises everywhere. Do you want to see, Sphinxie?" He got up and moved to stand close to me. Too close.

"No," I said shakily. "That's, um . . . that's okay."

He smiled down at me, then quickly stepped away, his eyes flashing brightly. He grabbed the painting shirt off the bed and pulled it on, buttoning it up. I swallowed, unable to erase the image of his pale body from my head. Did it terrify him when he looked in the mirror? If I could see the fact that I was dying written all over my body, I would be scared. So very scared.

He was sitting on the bed now, leaning back slightly, with his arms out behind him, his fingers splayed out across his bedspread. It was white, everything on the bed was white, and everything in the room was either white or made out of dark, shiny wood. Except for the walls — he had painted on the walls in every hue imaginable, and he had painted everything he could think of. Animals, flowers, water, mountains, trees, cars, clouds, houses. Planets, stars, swirling galaxies. He must have started when he was little; some of the paintings were done more crudely, and were situated at a height much nearer to the floor than the rest. My eyes darted over the walls, searching for something. I didn't realize what it was until I figured it out: There were no people. He had painted everything except for people.

"I like your walls," I said, trying to distract myself from thinking about his body. I looked up. Even the ceiling was covered with paintings: fish and sea creatures, mostly. "Why did you put fish on the ceiling?" I asked.

"Why do you think?" he said.

"I don't know," I told him. "You tell me."

He sighed. "Lie down."

"Lie down?"

"Yes!" He seized my shoulders and forced me down onto the bed, then lay down next to me. "There!" he said firmly, as though that explained everything. I stared up at the ceiling, unsure of what to say, and then suddenly I understood.

"Oh, I get it!" I exclaimed. "You put fish on the ceiling so that when you lie in bed and look up, it's like you're underwater, watching them swim around above you."

"Exactly," Cadence said. I stared at the ceiling for a moment in silence, realizing that he hadn't admonished me for not knowing why the fish were on the ceiling. He'd simply shown me the answer. I turned to look at him, feeling a small smile making its way across my face, but that didn't last long. Turning to face him made me realize that he was too close to me again. I shifted backward slightly, needing to put some distance between us.

The top few buttons of his shirt were undone, and I found myself staring at the harsh line of his collarbone, jutting out from his body like a mountain ridge. After a moment, I tore my eyes away. One corner of his mouth quirked into an almost imperceptible smirk.

"Sphinxie," he said, breaking the silence with his softer voice. "When you first came, I told you my secret. I told you that my doctors said there's something wrong with my mind." He paused, looking thoughtful. "But I never told you what it was."

"Oh," I said uncomfortably. The back of my neck was suddenly alive with chills, and I wished that I could rewind time and leave the room before he started talking about his secret again. I had shoved what had happened between us on the swings that day to the back of my mind, refusing to allow it to take over my thoughts. "What is it?" I managed to say when he didn't continue. He was looking away from me, his head tilting back to gaze up at the ceiling fish.

Then he turned back to face me, and his eyes were shining.

"They think I'm a sociopath," he said, in a voice so soft that I could feel it on the air.

Sociopath? I stared at him. The word made me think of crime shows, serial killers, grainy photos of Ted Bundy, stringy men luring children into their basements. Instantly, my mind placed Cadence in a line next to the television killers and the rapists on the news, and he looked so out of place, with his smooth blond hair and striking eyes, and his voice the way it sounded right now — a gentle breeze against my skin. I shook my head.

"They didn't say that," I said. Denying it was instinctive. I thought he was trying to scare me, to impress me in some twisted way.

"They did," he said calmly. "It's my diagnosis. They told my mother. And she didn't tell yours, Sphinx, because she was afraid you wouldn't be allowed to come if your mother knew."

I opened my mouth, but nothing came out. Had Leigh really kept what was wrong with Cadence secret from us, and had me walk unaware into her house? Was that true? I shook my head again, still firmly denying it, but inside, I already knew it had to be true. There had always been something wrong with Cadence. My father had known it when the butterfly died. We'd all known it when my cheek was split open. And here it was, named at last.

"Are you scared, Sphinxie?" he was whispering, his eyes still fixed on me. "Are you scared of me?" He laughed, so softly, so lightly. "Remember what I told you. When doctors don't understand something, they have to label it just to make themselves feel safe."

I couldn't speak. I couldn't move. I was shrinking into myself next to him, thinking about the knife, thinking about all the times that I had wondered just why he'd done that to me. My fingers grazed the comforter on his bed and gripped it. Next to me, Cadence ran a hand back through his hair.

"Sphinx," he said, almost casually, as though there was nothing wrong. "Don't just lie there. I've told you my secret now. It's your turn. You have to tell me yours."

My head was spinning, and my mind gladly seized the distraction of having to think of a secret for him. I swallowed and tried to clear my thoughts. Then I quickly scanned through the collection of embarrassing moments and hidden crushes on boys in my head, trying to find something that sounded vaguely secretive but wasn't too revealing. My mind rebelled against my intentions, giving me the exact opposite of not too revealing: I thought about the way my scar was a wall between my friends and me, about how Cadence was a secret of my own, about how my old best friend Kaitlyn had picked up his photograph and thought he was cute, about how she ended up being the first person I ever explained my scar to. After a few minutes of fervently pushing unwanted thoughts to the back of my brain, I settled on telling Cadence that I had never had a boyfriend. That wasn't really a secret per se, but it sounded like one, in my opinion.

"I've never had a boyfriend," I said, in a tone of confession.

Immediately, I regretted my choice of secret. I shouldn't be talking about boyfriends with him, I shouldn't. It was a risky subject; there was a possibility of the conversation veering off in a dangerous direction. And he'd just told me that there was something terribly wrong with him. I considered getting up and leaving the room. But how could I? I was supposed to be there for him.

Cadence seemed entirely unmoved.

"I knew that, Sphinx," he said seriously.

"How?" I asked him, thinking that he had probably over-heard my mother talking to Leigh about the subject before she left for home.

"Because of us," he said, as though it made perfect sense.

"What do you mean?"

"We were made for each other, Sphinx. It's only natural that you'd be waiting for me."

I recoiled. "What?"

"Waiting for me. Hoping you'd someday find a way to be good enough to fulfill the plan."

When I only stared at him, wide-eyed and silent, he added, "You know. Our mothers' plan." He raised his eyebrows briefly and then shrugged, shifting into a more comfortable position. "Our children," he said, in a softer tone.

"Our children?" I said, louder than I intended to.

"Calm down. We were supposed to have children. You knew that, Sphinx." He was quiet for a moment, then he rolled onto his side and faced me, resting his head on his hand. "Imagine that, hmm?" His lips parted and drew back into a smile. "They'd prob-ably look just like their mother. They'd have hair like yours."

He reached out toward me and I jumped. "God, Sphinx," he said, in a mild tone. "You're so jumpy." He extended his hand again and I stayed still, hearing my own heartbeat pound in my head as he tucked a loose strand of my hair back behind my ear.

"There. That's all," he said lightly.

That's all? When he'd fixed my hair, he'd been so gentle that he might have been a breeze passing over my skin — I almost hadn't even felt it. I swallowed and reminded myself that he could be dangerous. The fact that he was being so gentle didn't mean anything — you didn't feel anything when you watched the swirl of a hurricane push its way across a weather map on the television. Just because it felt like nothing didn't mean that it was nothing. But I was questioning myself. Was this really somehow the reason that I'd never had a boyfriend? Did I have some kind of an air about me, was I taken on the inside without knowing it? Was I waiting for children with a terrible, shining father? And did he really think about those children, did he really picture them in my image? . . . No. That was idiotic. That was terrible. He was sick, he was all wrong, he'd said the doctors had diagnosed him. And this was exactly why I shouldn't have brought up boyfriends.

I took a deep breath and managed to roll my eyes dismissively, like I just thought he was ridiculous and I was over it. Now he was staring at me, looking at me like a cat watching a piece of string being dragged across the floor. And I found myself torn between the lingering echo of Cadence's hand tucking my hair behind my ear and the instinctive feeling in my stomach that told me to be wary. Danger was all around.

"Okay, then, what about you?" I asked, forcing the words out of my dry mouth. To have him staring without saying anything was too unnerving. "Have you ever had a girlfriend?"

"Of course," he said dismissively. "But none of them were right for me."

"Oh," I said. I couldn't think of anything else to say. It sounded to me as though he'd always ended the relationships, after the girls undoubtedly failed to live up to his expectations. I was wondering what those girls had been like. I was wondering if he'd ever compared them to me before deciding to throw them away.

"Well," said Cadence after a few moments of silence, "this is getting a bit boring."

"What do you want to do, then?"

He rolled over onto his stomach and hung one of his arms down over the side of the bed, reaching under it. He dragged a box out from under the bed and up onto it, sitting up as he did so. It was a chess set.

"Let's play chess," he said, and took the board out of the box, unfolding it.

"I'm terrible at chess," I said. When I sat up to make room for the board, I realized that I was shaking slightly. I wrapped my arms around myself to try and stop it.

"I don't care," he told me. "Chess is one of my favorite games. It always has been." He stood the white queen and king up in their places on the checkered surface of the board. "Start setting up the pieces, will you? I'll be white." Obediently, I collected the black pieces and stood them all up in their proper locations. "White moves first," he reminded me.

"I know that," I said as his elegant hand hovered over the board, making its decision. He moved one of his pawns forward. Then it was my turn, my little soldiers facing off against his. I moved a pawn, too. And so on it went, until he beat me in seven moves. The fact that we had started with essentially the same move didn't seem to matter. He had thoroughly trounced me.

"Good game," I said politely. "You're a really good player." Chess, it seemed, was another one of those things he could do seemingly effortlessly.

I reset my black pieces and took back the one bishop that he had captured, but then Cadence swept the pieces back into the box, put the lid on it, and lowered it down to the floor, shoving it back under the bed with a flick of his wrist. There, done. The game was over. For a moment, his eyes had lit up, the corners of his mouth curving in a self-satisfied grin. All of that was gone now, receded back into the smooth wall. He looked toward his desk, at a little digital clock placed in the center.

"It's almost time for dinner," he said. "I'm going downstairs."

He swept out and left me in the white, white of his room, surrounded by the colors and the swatches of paint and the fish swimming in streaks above my head, and not a single person to be found. I slid off his bed, my neck prickling with chills again, my feet padding softly across his sterile white carpet. And then I closed the door behind me, sealing the crack, leaving behind the world where there were no others.

16

That night, before I went to bed, I asked Leigh if I could use her computer. She was sitting on the sofa in the living room, but I didn't approach her, choosing to voice my question from a safe distance. I didn't know what to think of her anymore. There she was, putting down her magazine, smiling, saying yes, getting up from the sofa and fetching her laptop for me from another room. And there I was, my brow furrowing, wondering how she could keep what was wrong with Cadence a secret. Was it really true that she would keep something like that from me, from my mother?

Leigh held the laptop out to me and I took it slowly. "Thanks," I mumbled, avoiding looking directly at her.

"No problem, Sphinxie," she said, and then noticed the look on my face. "Are you okay? Is something wrong?"

"No," I said, shaking my head. "I'm okay." I turned and walked toward the stairs, holding the laptop tightly against my chest.

When I got to my room, I put the laptop down on the bed. I knew exactly what I was going to do with it, but I had a terrible sinking feeling that this was going to be similar to when I was little and had listened to my mother's phone conversation. I was going to learn things that I did not want to learn. Instead of opening the laptop, I procrastinated by going through my suitcase, pulling out all of my clothes in a giant heap, and throwing them into the laundry hamper in Leigh's room. I had run out of clothes by then, since I'd brought only enough for a week. The shirt I was wearing at the moment was wrinkled, the edges of the sleeves turning up in a funny way, the result of stuffing the shirt into the bottom of my suitcase at the beginning of my visit. *I should have kept my clothes neater,* I thought ruefully. *I don't want to look like a mess.* I shut the hamper and changed into my pajamas, feeling a lump of apprehension and discomfort forming in my stomach.

Then I finally sat down on my bed and turned on the laptop, because I couldn't put it off forever. It was the first time I'd been on a computer since I'd been there. It hummed to life, loading up much faster than my old desktop at home. The home screen came into view and I saw that Leigh had a picture of Cadence at the piano as her wallpaper. Quickly, I opened an Internet window. *Sociopath,* I typed into the search engine, and clicked on the first result. The glow from the computer screen made my hand on the touch pad look alien as I scrolled down the page, feeling my breath catch in my throat.

One in every twenty-five people is a sociopath, the first line of the website declared. *Sociopaths are born, not made.*

So it wasn't Leigh's fault that he'd turned out the way he did. My mother had been right all those years ago on the phone; some things couldn't be helped. It was a mere accident, a mistake of genes and chromosomes and sperm and egg, the one egg that had happened to be at the front of the line, at the right time. No one's fault.

Characteristics of a sociopath include pathological lying, superficial charm, a lack of remorse or guilt, a grandiose sense of self-worth, a complete lack of empathy, and behavioral problems from an early age.

I shivered. This was everything that Cadence was, in one sentence. The doctors had said this was what was wrong with him. And after reading that sentence, I knew they had to be right.

Many people who have had encounters with sociopaths will mention their piercing eyes. Sociopaths often stare because they are trying to discern and understand the emotions of people around them.

I understood, at last, the significance of him crying after he had watched me closely, the day he crushed the butterfly. He had had to take the cue from me first.

Sociopaths do not have true emotions; they only imitate them. They can never be truly happy. What little pleasure they can gain is derived from harming others around them. A sociopath can never truly experience love.

After this, there were pictures, two scans of human brains, the active parts alight with red and orange, the resting parts soft with mingled blues and yellows. I exited the Internet window and closed the laptop, my hands trembling.

What did it feel like, I wondered, to have no true emotions, to go about imitating them forever? I couldn't imagine it. If I had faked everything, from the first day of my existence, slunk through life with a fake smile, fake tears. Never felt my heart leap with absolute joy, never felt it sink with grief — just felt it remain still and cold and unmoved by anything. Would I try to jar it, perhaps, by stirring the emotions of others? By arranging them like game pieces, making them laugh and then tearing them to shreds, hoping that when they cried, so would I? Would I even feel hope at all? It was impossible to imagine: I'm one of those people who gets laughed at because she cries too much at sappy movies. I couldn't picture myself going through each step of my life in such a level of constant detachment.

And to never experience love. Never look up one day and see my perfect match looking back at me, feel the warmth fly between us and rise in my head, dizzy and bright? Instead, I would stand there, my eyes piercing, staring, staring into the depths of everyone's souls, not knowing why they smiled and clung to one another. Who doesn't want to find their soul mate? Who would want a fairy-tale wedding if they weren't going to feel it in their chests? It made goose bumps break out over my skin to think about it.

And there was no cure. Cadence would stay this way for the rest of what little time he had left. Trapped, no way forward, no way out. Staring and staring, imitating everything so perfectly, shining and shining but so, so dead. He would never really smile. He would never really cry. He would never really fall in love, no matter how softly he could speak or how gentle his hands could be.

And he would never understand what he was missing. I felt a lump rising in my throat and I thought, *This is it, this is it right here. I'm feeling sorry for him.* It was reassuring. Even if the scar never faded from my cheek as I got older, even if I was shy and a nobody at school and the boys never noticed me — I was still normal, I was all right, I could feel it all. The realization jolted me. And at that moment, a few rooms over, he was alive, breathing just as I was, and he was cold, just as cold as his eyes, and empty like a dusty ceramic vase.

Suddenly I understood why he was so terribly good at everything. It was because there was nothing else for him to do. He couldn't work on building relationships with people. So what was left? For most people, it was people who came first, and hobbies and learning came second. For Cadence, there was no people element. There had never been. He had literally nothing to do but throw himself into other things — working, pushing, succeeding at all of them — shining, as I used to see him. But people were still missing from his life, just as they were missing from the paintings on the walls of his bedroom.

The digital camera was lying out of its case on my bedside table. I had filmed Cadence secretly for the third time that day, not too long after he'd told me his terrible secret. We'd just finished dinner and he had sat down on the couch and swung his feet up onto the coffee table and fallen asleep. His head was lolling back against the top of the couch, his blond hair spreading over the dark leather of the furniture. Asleep, his face lost that wall-like quality he sometimes had and opened up slightly, becoming more childlike, more human. And more sickly. His eyelids looked thin and translucent, his cheekbones pressed out, creating shadows below themselves, and in the light from the living-room lamp, I could see a thin web of blue veins spreading out from his temple and over his forehead.

Vivienne had left for the day, and Leigh was still in the kitchen, talking to someone on the phone, her back to the living room. I was trying to ignore her. I didn't want to think about her yet, about what she'd done. Determinedly, I'd focused the camera on Cadence's still face and filmed, just a minute of him in sleep. Then suddenly my hand shook. What if he wasn't sleeping? What if I was filming him dead? I'd turned off the camera and put it down on the coffee table, and then reached forward to touch him, shake him. I hesitated, afraid that he would wake up angry with me for touching him . . . but what if he didn't wake at all?

I settled on raising my foot and using it to nudge his ankle. He shifted, and his head turned to the side. I let out a breath of relief. My heart was beating at a faster pace than usual. I had been so scared when I thought he was gone, when I thought he had died in front of me, when I thought that the person I had loved and feared in equal measures had left my life.

As I watched the minute-long clip over again before I went to bed, that same feeling rose in my chest, making me feel very small. It was dawning on me that someday not very far in the future, I would see Cadence after he had died — if I managed to stay until then, as I intended. The shining one would go to sleep and never wake up, and I would see his body when the life had left it. I'd see those terrible, beautiful eyes without any light in them. All of a sudden, I wasn't sure if I could handle that.

And now, alone in my room, the laptop put away, I wasn't sure if I could handle what came before that, either. If Cadence was a sociopath — if he was dangerous, if he was that ill — then what would he do in the days before his death? What would he do to *me*?

I took a shaky breath. In that moment, I wanted to call my mother and say that I wanted to go home. If I told her the secret, I knew she would immediately buy me a plane ticket and rush me out of there. And I'd be safe. All it would take was one phone call, and I could get on the phone right now.

But you have to be here for him no matter what, said a small voice in my head. *You have to make the most of the small amount of time he has left. You're meant to be here, you're meant to do this. You know that. Even Cadence knows that. He said we were made for one another.*

I reached over and switched off the lamp on my bedside table. In the dark, I pulled the covers up to my chin and curled into a ball. I suddenly wished that my mother were still in the other guest room, just in case I needed to be little again and run into her room during the night.

17

The next day, we all went out after breakfast. Leigh drove us into a little village near to her house, mainly made up of small, family-owned shops and restaurants. It was the perfect picture of what everyone thought of as a little British village. Quaint. Cute little houses and buildings, all in a row, all looking like a kindly grandmother's abode. Flower boxes in all the windows. Chickens pecking around some of the yards. I thought it was absolutely adorable. It reminded me of a kids' picture book.

"I love this place," Leigh said. "It's so picturesque, and the shops have some really cute stuff in them."

Cadence seemed either unimpressed or depressed, if he was capable of feeling that way. He pulled his jacket more tightly around him and lagged behind us, his eyes hidden behind a pair of thin sunglasses.

In one of the shopwindows, a cage filled with young budgies sat in a sunny spot. The birds darted all over the place, chattering to one another and flapping their clipped wings. Leigh stopped in front of the window and tapped her finger against the glass, making the birds swivel their heads to look at her.

"I had a budgie when I was a teenager," she said, smiling. "His name was Orville."

"That's cute," I told her, standing next to her in front of the birds. Cadence came up next to me, and I asked him, "Do you like birds?"

"Yes," he said after a moment of contemplative silence. He took off his sunglasses and peered at them, his eyes darting around to follow a particular one: blue and white, with a dash of yellow at its throat.

"Do you want one?" Leigh asked eagerly, almost leaping forward. The fact that Cadence had shown a relatively cheerful interest in something had sprung her into action, as though she was hoping she could freeze time and keep him that way. "Do you want that one you're watching, with the yellow on it?"

"All right," said Cadence, surprising me. He didn't strike me as the type that would enjoy caring for a pet, and I wondered why a common budgie had caught his interest. We went inside the pet shop, a little bell ringing over our heads as we did so. We watched as the man came out from behind the counter and opened the budgies' cage, as Cadence pointed out the bird he wanted, as the man captured it in his fist, as easy as could be. He put the bird in a little cardboard box with air holes on the top and set it down on the counter to wait while we browsed through cages and bird toys, seeds and dried-fruit treats.

"I want to get one of those cages that hangs down from a little pole," Leigh said. "That's the kind I had for my bird. It was really convenient, you could just move it around. I used to put it out on the porch so he could get some fresh air." The man showed us where that type of cage was located in the shop, but Cadence didn't seem interested in picking one out, so Leigh chose instead: a circular cage with a domed top, metal swirls painted a robin's-egg blue.

We paid for everything and left, not wanting to leave the bird in the box while we browsed around the village. In the car on the way back to Leigh's house, Cadence held the box on his lap, and the bird chirped softly from within. Occasionally, it tried to flap its wings, making little thumps against the cardboard.

"Poor little guy wants to get out," Leigh said sympathetically. "What do you want to name him, Cadence?"

"I'm sure I don't know," Cadence said dryly, his slim fingers tapping lightly against the side of the box. "What was yours named, again?"

"Orville," Leigh said brightly. "For one of the Wright brothers. The guys who designed the first airplane."

"This one could be Wilbur," I offered. "For the other brother."

"Fine. Wilbur it is," said Cadence, smiling at me. Inside the box, the newly christened Wilbur made little scratching noises with his feet against the cardboard bottom. And I smiled too, feeling pleased that Cadence had allowed me to name him.

"I hope he's all right in there," Leigh said. "He doesn't sound happy."

When we got back to Leigh's house, we set up the cage in a relatively empty corner of the living room before opening the box. The budgie stared up at us from within for a split second before flapping his clipped wings and fluttering a few feet out, making us all jump. He landed on the floor not more than a few paces away. Leigh reached forward and caught him neatly in her hands.

"Got you!" she said triumphantly. "Sphinxie, open the cage door for me, please." I unlatched the little hook and held it open for her so that she could deposit Wilbur inside. He fluttered to one of the perches, looking about with bewildered eyes that were like black beads in his head.

"He looks totally confused," I said, chuckling. "He's not used to being in a little cage without other birds to hang out with." His little head was swiveling around, looking at each of us in turn. Cadence stepped up and leaned in closer to the cage, making the bird focus on him. The little yellow beak opened slightly, as though preparing to bite if necessary.

"Silly bird," said Cadence softly, sticking a finger through the bars of the cage and flicking one of the mirrors that Leigh had hung up. "Silly, silly bird."

"He's not all that silly. Birds are actually quite intelligent," Leigh pointed out. She set out the little plastic food dishes that had come with the cage and tore open one of the packages of birdseed. Carefully, she poured out enough seed to fill one dish, and then sent me to the kitchen sink to fill the other with water. "We have to make sure that he always has food," she informed us. "Birds need to eat all day." She set the seed dish down on its little ledge in the cage, and the budgie slid down the bars to reach it, pecking eagerly.

I thought there was something very desperate and sorrowful about the way that Leigh had carefully poured out the birdseed and reminded us that we must always make sure the dish was full. She was jumping around, like a child excited by her new pet, but there was something very heavy about her excitement. It was as though she was overcompensating with her happiness lest she show any sadness. Cadence had wanted that bird so badly in her head, and she had bought it for him . . . but he had not responded with normal joy, as usual. I thought she was trying to feel the childish excitement and happiness for him, and it was saddening. I was starting to understand. She was so desperate. *Feel this, feel this, feel it.*

It was like that for Leigh every day, in everything she did. And it must have been that way ever since Cadence was born, and he grew up strange and detached, a wall behind the emotions that he had taught himself to fake.

When I realized that, I thought that at last I understood what he wanted me there for. I was the first person he'd really learned to take emotional cues from, the first person he'd studied. Once upon a time, playdate after playdate, he'd modeled his mask by looking at me, like the day that he killed the butterfly and I'd unknowingly taught him that he was supposed to cry. I was the model who stood at the front of the art class, my heart on my sleeve, laid bare for the student to try and capture my likeness. And oh, how he'd tried.

He didn't really have any interest in the bird at all. Leigh and I dutifully cared for Wilbur the budgie, taking turns at cleaning out the newspapers from the bottom, seeing to it that there was enough seed, filling up the dish with fresh water every morning. He seemed happy enough for a caged bird. He fluttered from perch to perch, talked to his reflection in the mirror, and sang when we left his cage in front of the window, allowing him to see wild birds outside. Every now and then Cadence seemed to remember that he was there, and went over to the cage, sticking a finger through the bars and petting the little feathery head.

Leigh and I liked to let Wilbur out so that he could explore the living room; his flight feathers still hadn't grown back out since we had bought him from the pet shop, and so he would simply run around on the living-room floor, nibbling at the carpet. Cadence would retreat to another room when we did this. I supposed he preferred the bird through the blue lines of the cage bars, but I enjoyed watching Wilbur run around. It was a little release from the serious feeling in Leigh's house, just following this winged creature, watching his bewildered curiosity at everything in Leigh's living room.

When I was little, we had a cat, an old cat that really just belonged to my mother. I would try to pick the poor cat up like a baby, and always got scratched for my overenthusiastic displays of affection. Seeing the budgie dart around made me want to get one of my own, from the same little pet shop, and take it home with me as a reminder.

Later, during that same week, we were watching television in the living room. Leigh had Wilbur out, sitting on her lap like some sort of a substitute for a lapdog. He'd become friendly and used to us quickly; he was perfectly content to hang out on your lap. Leigh was petting him rhythmically, running her forefinger down his back over and over again.

I thought Cadence was asleep, or at least dozing. His eyes were half closed, and they weren't focused on the television set whatsoever. He was starting to sleep an awful lot during the day, something that was hard to see. I knew it upset Leigh too. She didn't want to watch him getting slower and slower, more and more exhausted as his body gave in bit by bit. I stared at him for a moment, checking, as I always did when I noticed him sleeping, to see if he was still breathing. He was, very slowly. His chest was rising and falling, but almost imperceptibly. His head had fallen to the side and was resting on his shoulder. *He's going to wake up with a stiff neck,* I thought. Then, all of a sudden, he woke.

His eyes literally snapped open; they went from drooping peacefully to becoming wide holes of ice blue in his head, all in a matter of seconds. I jumped and looked away, thinking that it would be weird for me to get caught watching him sleep. Out of the corner of my eye, I saw him raise his head and look around the room almost wildly. Had he woken up from a nightmare? His eyes were darting all over the place, seeming never to settle on any particular object or person in the room.

"Cay?" Leigh asked nervously. "Are you all right?"

"Let me hold the bird," he said, and his eyes stopped finally, resting on the budgie. And for a moment, he stared, watching Leigh's finger caress the little feathered body, watching how she smiled and imitated the sound when Wilbur chirped contentedly.

"Sure," Leigh said, sounding slightly confused. She took Wilbur in her hand, rose from the sofa, and passed him to Cadence. He put the bird in his lap and watched for a moment as the tiny beak explored the wrinkles in the leg of his pants. His slender hand reached out and covered Wilbur's back, stroking him slightly, softly. But then his hand came down harder and harder. Wilbur squawked in protest, but couldn't get away; Cadence's hand was practically pinning him, flattening him, his wings and little pink feet splaying out in protest.

"Cadence!" Leigh said, her voice rising. "You're hurting him!"

Up and down went his hand, harder, harder. The bird screamed, high-pitched and raspy. Cadence's face was blank and stony. Harder and harder and harder. His eyes burned, brighter, painfully.

"You're crushing him!" I said, and without thinking, I reached over and grabbed his thin, bony wrist. My fingers met my thumb and overlapped each other; Cadence's wrist felt fragile in my hand, but he was stronger than I'd imagined. After what seemed like forever, I pried his hand up, off the budgie. Wilbur was silent, but he wasn't dead: He fluttered haltingly off the sofa and dropped to the floor, where he shook himself and scuttled under the coffee table, trembling. I still had my hand around Cadence's wrist, gripping tighter than I meant to.

Suddenly angry, Cadence jerked his arm away from me, his eyes narrowing. Before I could think to back away, he had balled his other hand into a fist and tried to punch me in the face, but he missed, only grazing the side of my cheek. I leaped away from him and he came after me, grabbing my shoulders as he got up from the sofa; our feet twisted together, and we fell onto the coffee table in a tangle of limbs and a crash of breaking glass.

I was aware of nothing but Leigh screaming, the bird flapping wildly out from under the table, the table itself seeming to disappear underneath us. And Cadence yelling hoarsely, and breathing hard and fast and roughly, as though his breath were caught in his throat. I was on top of him, I realized.

I rolled off and something crunched painfully under my back. Cadence lifted his hand for no apparent reason and then let it fall back again; it landed on my shoulder, and when I raised my own hand to push him off, there was blood dripping down my palm, coursing down my wrist, and a shard of glass was glistening, stuck cleanly through the palm of my hand.

18

My voice was trapped in my throat, and I couldn't move. For a moment, all I could do was stare up at the ceiling overhead, my eyes locked there involuntarily. Leigh was screaming for Cadence and me to stay still, that she was going to call an ambulance. As soon as I heard the word, I started sobbing and yelled back at her, frantic.

"Don't call an ambulance!" I begged. "Please, Leigh, my mom will freak! Please don't call an ambulance!" Beside me, Cadence was panting, his hand pressed to the side of his chest. Vivienne came pounding down the stairs; she had been folding laundry on the second floor but dropped everything when she heard the commotion downstairs. She appeared next to Leigh, white-faced.

"Honey, I need to call!" Leigh said. She tried so desperately to be calm, but her voice was high and terrified. "We need to get you to a doctor!"

"I can't wait for an ambulance to get here!" Cadence gasped. "Just take me to the hospital!"

Leigh dithered on the spot, panic flashing in her eyes. "Okay, okay," she said, her words running together. "Vivienne, can you please pull my car around front and get the back doors open?"

Vivienne darted away, her dark ponytail flying out behind her. And Cadence and I lay in the pool of broken glass on the floor, listening to each other's breathing. His still sounded unnatural, too forced and rough.

"Why are you breathing like that? Are you okay?" I asked him, turning my head to the side to look at him. There was a thick fashion magazine under my head; it had been sitting on the coffee table. That was lucky, I realized. The magazine must have protected my face.

"I don't know," he snapped, still hoarse. "It hurts." He grimaced and added, "There's glass in the back of my head, I can feel it."

Leigh let out a moan, but then she said, "You guys are going to be just fine," in as a comforting a voice as she could muster. "I'm going to help you stand up one by one, and then Vivienne is going to help you out to the car." She got me up first, grabbing the hand that didn't have glass in it and heaving me to my feet, the only parts of me that weren't hurt. I swayed at first, and she steadied me with an arm around my waist. I could feel the pain of the glass in my skin now, little stabbing pains all through my body, especially in my back . . . but none in my face or my head, as far as I could tell. That magazine had saved me.

When Vivienne got me out to the car, I tried to sit down on the backseat and yelped in pain. "There's glass in my butt!" I said, and then laughed, a wild and frightened laugh that burst out of me without my consent.

"Are you okay with sitting here alone while I go and get Cadence?" Vivienne asked me, her brow furrowed with concern.

"Yeah, I'm fine, just go help him," I said, brushing her off. And then I was by myself in the car for the small amount of time that it took for Vivienne to rush back inside the house, to help Leigh get Cadence to his feet. I perched stiffly on the edge of the backseat, my hand throbbing with pain from the big shard of glass that stuck out from my palm like a little mountain. I stared at it; I couldn't stop looking, even though the sight of it was making me feel sick. Then I thought I should try to keep my hands over my lap, try so hard not to let blood drip onto poor Leigh's car, but three crimson drops fell and soaked in even so. And then four more, and then six more, and then more than that. I spat on my uninjured hand and tried to rub the blood away, but it was useless.

By the time Leigh and Vivienne came outside, supporting Cadence between them, I was crying. I did not want to cry, and I was not actively crying; that is, I wasn't sobbing or anything like that. I simply sat there shivering and dripping, while cold tears flowed silently down my face. Leigh was sitting in the front passenger seat while Vivienne drove, and she reached around, trying to hold my hand. I wouldn't let her.

"I got blood on your car seat, I got blood on it," I babbled. All I could think about clearly was the car.

"It's okay, we'll get it cleaned," she told me. Her hand fluttered around, looking for something to do, and started rubbing my knee.

"My mom's going to be really mad at me," I said, sniffling. My voice sounded wet.

"No, she's going to be mad at me," Leigh said. "I'm the grown-up, I'm responsible."

Yes, I thought distractedly, staring at her. *I probably wouldn't even be here at all if you'd told the truth.*

Vivienne turned the car abruptly around a corner, and I pitched to the side, bumping into Cadence, who gritted his teeth in pain. He glared at the back of the driver's seat, at Vivienne's now-messy ponytail swinging around behind it.

"Drive smoother, will you?" he snarled.

"Cadence!" Leigh said, his name wrenching itself from her throat in a raw half-scream. Her head whipped around as she twisted in her seat to look at him. Her face was pinched with worry and a sudden overflowing of held-back frustration. "That's enough, do you hear me? That's enough!"

He glared at her. His hand was still clamped over that one side of his chest, his breathing still off. "Are we almost there?" he asked after a moment of glowering silence. Behind his head, the car seat was smeared with blood. I squeezed my eyes shut and gripped the seat with my good hand.

"We're almost there, just hold on, you're fine," Leigh said. The terrible, pitchy voice that she had used to yell at Cadence moments ago had vanished just as quickly as it had come, dissolving back into a shaky mass of worry. Her head was practically on backward from twisting around to look at us. "Look, here we go, here it comes." I opened my eyes and saw a hospital building coming up on our left. There were two places to turn in, but we went into the first one, and then almost immediately realized that we'd gone in toward the visiting entrance. The other way had been where to go for the emergency room. Vivienne backed up awkwardly and was almost rear-ended by a passing car as she did so.

"Stop it!" Cadence snapped, his face twisted in pain. "Somebody else needs to drive!"

"Cadence! It's okay, we're fine!" Leigh yelled. The car wheeled precariously around and made it into the right entrance; Vivienne stepped on the gas and we jerked forward, finally skidding to a stop in front of the emergency room doors.

And then we were flying, out of the car, through the automatic doors that slid open to let us in. We tracked red through the waiting area, over the hospital's crisp white tiles. A nurse came out and put towels out on the chairs for us, and we sat on the edges, feeling stiff and sharp all over. We waited there for what seemed like forever, and I became so aware of the shard in my hand that I could feel the outlines of it under my skin. Leigh kept begging for them to let us in faster, to get us a room, a doctor. "They're bleeding," she kept saying, her voice high and frantic. "My kids are bleeding." She couldn't sit still; she paced around in front of us and kept going over to the place where you were supposed to sign in, pleading for the wait to be shorter.

When they finally took us back into the rooms, we were separated: Leigh went with Cadence, and Vivienne came with me. A young doctor with short brown hair came in and looked at me. He pulled the shard out of my hand with a pair of tweezers, and then looked through my hair, searching for any stray pieces. I had to take off my shirt and pants so that he could get the rest out of me, and it was freezing in that hospital room. I felt like I had stitches all over me, I couldn't keep track of how many I needed. My clothes were in a little pile on the floor by Vivienne's feet, smudged with red, turning brown in the dry air. Vivienne had a tank top under her shirt, and when the doctor was finished, she took it off and gave it to me so that I wouldn't have to put my bloody shirt back on.

Vivienne and I sat in the emergency room by ourselves for more than half an hour. I couldn't stop thinking about the strange way Cadence's breathing had sounded in the car. It scared me that they were taking so long. Finally, Cadence and Leigh emerged. Cadence looked terrifying, angry and bitter and vicious. The back of his head was a mess of tangled hair and blood.

"He wouldn't let them shave the back of his head," Leigh told Vivienne. "They stitched it up with all the hair in the way. It's a mess."

"I'd rather have it like this than not have it at all," Cadence spat.

"What's up with the breathing?" I asked, still worried.

"He's got a broken rib," Leigh said.

"What do they do for that?" Vivienne wanted to know.

"Nothing, apparently. They used to put bandages around the chest to hold everything in place, but now they don't do that anymore because it stops people breathing deeply enough."

I was frozen, feeling sick. Even though I knew that it had been beyond my control, that he had grabbed me and made me fall, that I couldn't have helped it, I had still fallen on him. I had broken his rib. It was me.

"I'm really sorry," I said, and my voice sounded whiny and annoying.

He wouldn't answer me. I hadn't expected him to.

When we got into the car, most of the blood had dried already. It was then that I remembered the budgie. I hoped Wilbur hadn't been grazed by a piece of flying glass, and that he was safe. No one had bothered to put him back in his cage, I realized as we neared Leigh's house again.

I looked at the palm of my hand, at the thin lines that were suddenly all there was to hold my skin together, and I felt fragile. Breakable. And mortal. When you're living day to day, just ducking and dodging what life throws at you as though you're playing in some cosmic game of extreme dodgeball, you don't realize that one day you could fall the wrong way and never get up again. I rested my hand on my knee, palm facing upward.

Cadence had his head turned away from me, looking out the window. The back of his head looked awful where they had stitched it up; his blond hair was matted and sticky, looking tight and unnatural plastered just above his neck. I wished I could have known what he was thinking. Was he somehow grateful, for being alive and fixed when just a short while ago he had been lying next to me in the glass, bleeding and bleeding? Or was he just angry, filled with spitfire that he wasn't sure where to direct? I had a twinkling of a desire to reach out and try to touch him. If he had been anyone else, I would have, knowing that he, as another person, would gain comfort from touching someone who had just been through the same thing, and who had come out all right . . . but he wasn't anyone else. He was Cadence, alone on his sacred ground even when he was hurt. I knew that. But my desire to try to reach him was only growing stronger.

How had he felt when he was frightened, when we had first fallen and he had begged Leigh to get him to the hospital? I had drawn comfort from seeing the faces of Vivienne and Leigh above us, from knowing that they were there and worried about me. But he, alone and with no one but himself — how had he felt? He was lying on the floor, breathing painfully with a cracked rib, and he had no one but himself there in his head. And that must have been terrifying. It must have.

"Hey," I said quietly as we came up on Leigh's driveway. "Hey, can you believe that happened to us?" I knew that it wouldn't mean anything to him, but I wanted to try even so. "And we're fine," I continued. "We're really fine."

I was trying to project what I felt outward. I wanted to feel thankful enough for both of us, lucky enough for both us, and to cover us both in those feelings. He was always searching; I wanted to put it right out there in front of him. I was still thinking about reaching out to him, touching him. Just once.

"We're so lucky," I said, and slowly, oh so slowly, I reached out and put my hand over his. It was the first time I had ever dared to do something like that, and my heartbeat sped up at once. My fingers were trembling, and I bit my lip, trying to make them stop. For a moment, I forgot the stinging pain that was still present all over my body, in all of my cuts.

Then he turned his head slowly, and my hand stiffened involuntarily over his, in fear of what his reaction might be. I watched his eyes adjust. He was examining me closely again, like the day that I'd stood in the kitchen and declared that I was staying. And I realized that all of those years when we were little — when I'd stared at him and wondered how he could read so well, draw so well, speak so clearly, think up such clever games to play — he'd been staring at me and I hadn't noticed that he was also wondering. How I felt so deeply. How I screamed so loudly. How even though he knew he could best me in all other areas of life, I still lived so much more intensely than he did.

He looked away from me, pulling his hand away from me and closing his eyes as he did so, as though he was turning away from a disconcerting sight. "It is not lucky," he said, his voice thin, a little snip of sound in what was suddenly a gigantic car. "I'm going to have so many scars."

And I felt sunken all of a sudden, as though I were watching the middle seat in between us slump into a great divide. The scars. That was the first place his mind had gone: the physical marks.

He was smarter than me, better than me, and more talented than me, but he was more lost than me, too, and we both knew it. And that was impressive, because I felt incredibly lost myself. I was sitting in the back of a car stained with my own blood, and I wanted my mother and didn't want her, and it was her fault but it wasn't, and I was trying so very hard to do something right, even though the plan was broken and ruined and stained with my blood just as much as the car was. I swallowed and it hurt, and I wondered if I'd gotten glass in my throat, in my chest, in my lungs.

The car trundled slowly along the road. I reached out to put my hand on Cadence's shoulder, but then all of a sudden we were in the driveway and life was continuing on, and I had kind of forgotten how lucky I was to breathe and feel and live.

19

We found the budgie sitting on the floor next to the shattered remains of the coffee table, pecking curiously at a piece of glass that was sparkling in the light from the windows. Leigh grabbed him and stuffed him unceremoniously into his cage, and then stood over the mess, surveying the damage. I stood awkwardly in the kitchen and watched her, dread rising in my chest. She was going to call my mother any minute, there was no doubt about that, and then she would make me go home. But now Cadence was hurt on top of everything else. How could I leave him now? I'd already decided that nothing could prevent me from being there — not his diagnosis, not his behavior, and certainly not a stupid accident with a coffee table.

"Nobody take off their shoes," Leigh said finally, turning away from the remnants of the table. "We don't need glass in anyone's feet." She sighed, pushing her hair out of her eyes, and continued,

"I'm not even going to try to clean this up, I'm going to call some-one to come in and do it safely. And I have to call Sarah."

I cringed, as did Leigh. She looked almost as pained by the idea of calling my mother as I felt, or maybe even more so. This was the second time I'd had to go to the hospital as a result of something that belonged to Leigh. Her kid, her coffee table. I couldn't decide whether I felt worse for her or for myself.

She called my mother first, and cried when she explained what had happened. They talked for a few moments, and then Leigh handed the phone to me. I took the receiver gingerly in the hand that didn't have stitches in the palm.

"Hi, Mom," I said, my voice quivering with apprehension.

"Sphinxie! Oh my God, are you okay?" Her voice was loud in my ear, high and strained. I tried to reassure her, to tell her that I was really fine, the doctor at the hospital had fixed me up just as good as new. And there had been a magazine on the table, it had protected my face. I was so lucky, I was so thankful. And the stitches hadn't really hurt, not really.

"Please don't make me come home," I added at the end of my speech. "I mean, I really wish you were here to hug me and stuff, but I can't come home. Not now."

"If I had my way, I'd have Leigh put you on a plane today," she said. Her voice was almost angry, but I knew she wasn't mad at me, just angry that she hadn't been there to hold my hand in the hos-pital, to tell me that it was going to be all right. Angry that anything had happened at all. "But I can't really do that, can I, not with you all cut up. You'll have to stay until you're somewhat healed."

I imagined how she would feel about the situation if she knew what Leigh was hiding from her. But then suddenly my heart leaped. Maybe it was a twisted blessing to have gotten hurt. I hadn't even stopped to think that if I was hurt, my mother would wait before making me take the long flight home.

"Okay," I said breathlessly.

"I love you, Sphinx," she told me. "You have no idea how much your father and I wish we were there to be with you."

"I know, Mom. I love you too," I said. "But I'm fine. Really. I got lucky."

"I'm happy you're feeling positive," she said, and let herself laugh briefly. "Here, talk to your father. He wants to hear your voice."

My father hardly let me speak when he got on the line. His voice was far louder and angrier than my mother's had been, and although I knew his anger wasn't really directed at me, I felt a sinking feeling in my chest. I held the phone to my ear with a shaking hand and listened in silence as his declarations that he'd known something like this would happen melded together with questions about how I was feeling.

"I love you, Dad," I said, in a small voice, when he finally trailed off into silence of his own.

I could hear him breathing, sounding slightly winded.

"I want you home as soon as possible," he said, his voice hardened. I felt tears stinging my eyes. I knew that meant he loved me too. He just couldn't say the words right then. He was still too angry. It was like all those years ago, when he'd stormed out after I'd gotten cut.

A half hour later, a man came to clean the glass and the blood from Leigh's living-room rug. Cadence and I sat in the kitchen and watched him do it, and took Tylenol with large glasses of water to stop the throbbing in our wounds. The cleaning man looked at us out of the corner of his eye as he worked. He was probably wondering what had happened, pondering what events could have led up to two sensible-looking teenagers catapulting through a glass coffee table. I almost wanted to ask him what scenario he had come up with in his head.

For a few days afterward, it felt like we were all walking on eggshells. Leigh was feeling guilty and traumatized, and the table itself was missing, a void in the living room. Cadence and I were still hurting, although I found an odd sense of comfort in knowing that we were hurting in the same ways, because we'd gone through the table together. Now Cadence had marks that connected him to me, just like I'd always had my scar to connect me to him.

Leigh ordered another table online, a wooden one this time. She was through with having glass tables in her house, and I couldn't blame her. While we waited for the new table to arrive, we sat in the living room holding our mugs of tea instead of setting them down, and watched movie after movie. We were trying to do nonactive things, because Cadence was supposed to move around as little as possible, but he ditched us and went up to the attic in spite of the doctor's orders, and painted more blue onto his canvas.

Leigh and I watched television alone then, chick flick after chick flick. Thankfully, she remained silent while we did so. When I found myself getting embarrassingly teary-eyed over the soppy parts, she didn't call attention to my quiet sniffles.

I tried to let myself get lost in the endless parades of superficial characters and humorous situations that wiggled their way across Leigh's television screen, but my mind refused to tune out. No matter how many movies we watched, my brain wouldn't stop thinking over everything, running through what-if scenarios in which Cadence and I had both been gravely injured by the glass, in which my mother had forced me to come home anyway, in which I didn't actually accomplish anything by staying here, in which something broke further inside Cadence's head and he did something horrible to me. And I was in pain. The cuts were prickling all over my body, the palm of my hand an almost constant throb.

Then slowly, as the days passed, I healed. The pain became less, I began using the hand that had been cut again, the stitches pulled out like loose threads, my skin having formed the necessary bonds again. Leigh's new table arrived, a shiny, dark mahogany, and she and Vivienne set it up in the living room, refilling the void. My mother called every day, asking me how I was doing, if I was feeling healed enough to make the flight home. And in my heart, I knew that I was healed enough, that enough days and weeks had passed for my cuts to be considered closed . . . but I didn't admit it. I dragged out the visit, dragged it out longer every time I got off the phone, dragged myself out of my chair to find the digital camera because I noticed another opportunity for filming Cadence. I refused to let the fall through the table take anything out of me; I was still on a mission, firm in my will to complete it. Nothing could make me leave Cadence.

He hadn't healed as nicely as I had. Some of his cuts reopened, looking angry and red. His body was focused on the mess that the leukemia had created, and didn't see fit to attend to the newer injuries. He was more tired than usual now, too; he slept even more than he had before, and sometimes when he woke up, he mentioned pain that had nothing to do with the cuts and the broken rib. New pain, new bruises spreading out, taking over. And I felt guilty, because it seemed as though he had taken a turn for the worse after I had fallen on him. It wasn't my fault, of course, I kept reminding myself. He had been too rough with Wilbur, he had lashed out — I wasn't responsible for any of that. And this was supposed to happen, this was expected, the way that he was getting more and more exhausted, closer and closer to giving out.

It seemed hard to believe that something as stupid as an illness could ever take him. Yes, he looked frail and delicate and drawn, all the color sucked away from his face and dark hollows under his eyes, but those eyes were still burning. And he was still reaching outward, doing this and that and shocking everyone he could, blazing like the fiery surface of the sun, trying to convince everyone that he was a god, that his sacred ground was real. When I thought of it that way, it seemed like idiocy to think that he was dying. How could he be dying? He was still burning so brightly.

I followed him outside and sat next to him on the swings before dinner one day. He had just woken up from a nap, and his hair was fluffed up at the back. The part where he had gotten stitches over his hair stuck out in odd little wisps and points. He held on to the ropes of the swing with a tight grip, making his knuckles pop out. It was cold outside, and I worried that maybe he shouldn't be out there, that maybe it was bad for him. Fog hung in gray waves over the expanse of Leigh's backyard and veiled the trees at the far end, making everything look ghostly and somehow older.

"It's getting colder," I remarked, and immediately felt that I should have said something more interesting. He evidently thought so too, because he didn't bother to answer me. He pushed the ground with his feet and his swing began a slow journey back and forth.

"The fog looks spooky," I said after a few minutes. "But kind of pretty, too."

"It looks more pretty than it does spooky," he said, his voice level. I looked at the fog again, letting my eyes take their time.

"Yeah, I guess you're right," I told him.

There was momentary silence. I could hear his breathing: That odd raggedness that had come over it on the day we fell through the table was still audible. He turned his head to the side and looked at me, his eyes half-lidded, pale irises almost glowing in the dim light.

"Sphinx, did you know that I missed you when we moved away?" he said softly. "I wanted to take you with me. They shouldn't have made me leave you behind." He paused, locking eyes with me. "But that doesn't matter anymore. You're here now, until the end."

I nodded my head, unsure of how to respond. And then he smiled. Slowly, the corners of his mouth pulled up, transforming it. The angles rounded out. The brightness of his eyes lit up his face and chased away the signs of illness for a split second. I shivered.

"You should have known I wanted to take you with me, Sphinx," he murmured. "Didn't you miss me too?"

I didn't know whether to lie or tell the truth. All I really knew was that I was in awe of the way he'd turned his voice into velvet and draped it over my shoulders. And my real answer to his question was complicated. No, I hadn't missed him, and yet I had felt the loss of him. I'd been relieved to be safe, without his lies and his mind games and the threat of his presence looming over me anymore, but when he moved away, he took his shining light with him, leaving me alone to fill in the blanks and watch the line on my cheek go from burning red to vague white. And now? I looked away, tearing myself out of his gaze, and focused instead on the way the fog was hovering over Leigh's yard in ripples.

Out of the corner of my eye, I saw him cock his head to the side slowly. Then one of his hands let go of the swing and reached toward me. I flinched away instinctively, but the hand didn't ball into a fist or threaten to do anything harmful; instead, he held my hand, which had been sitting idly in my lap. I stared at him, frozen in anticipation, waiting for him to say something, but he didn't look at me. He just stared straight ahead into the fog, his eyes glowing in the dim light, and squeezed my hand. It was gentle at first, almost as though he was trying to comfort me, but then his grip tightened. Harder and harder and harder, as though he'd never wanted to hold on to anything in this world as much as he wanted to hold on to me. I let out a soft whine. His fingernails were digging into my flesh.

He let go just before I tried to pull my hand away from him, and then he gripped the swing rope again, still staring into the fog. I understood then what he had been trying to do when he had petted Wilbur so hard that he had almost killed him. He had looked at Leigh petting the bird, and he had seen something in her eyes — her affection for the bird, the pleasure that being with the bird gave to her. He had experimented with doing the same thing, but he hadn't understood anything clearer, and so he had petted the bird harder and harder, trying and trying and pushing and pushing, but he had not achieved what he'd seen in his mother's eyes. And just now, when he'd grabbed my hand, and squeezed harder and harder, he had been looking for the same thing, trying to find it in me.

I couldn't help wondering if I could give him the answers he was looking for.

20

The canvas was three-quarters full, the blues reaching ever further toward the other side. I crept up into the attic and stood behind him, holding the digital camera, filming his sweeping strokes, which drew the waves of azure and cerulean toward the end of the empty white expanse. After a few minutes, I turned the camera off, just moments before he lifted the tip of his brush from the canvas. Slowly, he turned and walked over to the shelves where he kept his paint, one thin hand reaching out to select another shade of blue.

"Hey," I said, not wanting him to be startled by seeing me out of the corner of his eye. "I came up here, and then I didn't say anything because I started watching you paint —"

"I know," he said, in a tired, steady voice. "I knew you were there, Sphinx." His fingertips hovered over a tube of sky blue in a moment of indecision before selecting a darker shade instead. I waited for him to chastise me for filming him without asking, but he didn't. *He knew that I came up*, I thought, *but he didn't know that I was filming.*

I watched him unscrew the top of the paint tube and squeeze a generous amount onto his palette. His fingers looked almost translucent now.

"That's a pretty blue," I said, not wanting to just stand there and watch him silently.

"It's not just *blue*," he said. "It's called ultramarine."

"Oh. Cool." I had stepped forward toward him, but now I took a step backward. The giant canvas caught my eye again and I looked at it thoughtfully. "Do you want to be a famous artist someday and have shows in galleries?" As soon as the words left my mouth, I realized how stupid I was for saying them. There would be no *someday*. He had only months left.

"There isn't time enough for that, Sphinx," said Cadence, in a soft, melancholy voice. "And you know that just as well as I do."

I felt a weight settle in my chest. I shouldn't have said that, and it sounded like I'd made him sad. Was that possible? His head was bowed slightly, giving him a sorrowful air.

"I'm sorry," I whispered. "I . . . I wasn't thinking . . ."

He walked back over to stand in front of the canvas again, and let out a sigh as he dipped his brush into the little puddle of ultramarine on his palette.

"Well," he said, "most of the great artists weren't famous until after their deaths." He put the palette down, balanced on the edge of the sink. "Van Gogh, for example." I had studied Van Gogh in school. He had been an amazing painter, but he'd gone mad and taken his own life. Suddenly, I was afraid that Cadence too might turn to suicide as an escape, as a quicker way out instead of waiting for the leukemia to take its course. Or maybe he would feel that he was above that, too sacred to take himself away before his time. He knew that he was sick, but he didn't know that he didn't feel, did he? I wasn't sure how much he understood about what he was missing.

"But tell me, Sphinx," he said, lifting his brush. "What do *you* want to do when you're older?" He drew a thin streak of ultramarine across the canvas and began feathering it out, blending it into the other blues.

"Well," I said slowly. "I'm not really sure yet." It was a classic answer for my least favorite question in the world. Relatives, friends, teachers, even my own parents were all starting to ask me that question with increasing frequency, and it never failed to leave me wishing that I had a real answer for it. A lot of girls at school knew exactly what they wanted to devote their lives to, but I didn't have any idea what college I wanted to go to or what job I wanted to have, and it made me feel immature and dull.

"You mean you can't think of anything," said Cadence, without taking his eyes off the canvas. I felt my entire body tense almost involuntarily, as though I was bracing myself for a physical blow. What did he want me to say? "You can't think of anything to do with your life. And I knew that was going to be your answer, Sphinx. You're the same as you were when we were little, and you always needed me to tell you what games we should play. It was pathetic then, and it still is now. And that is one of the few things that you do know for certain, isn't it?"

I'd been researching sociopathy whenever I could get the chance, in the hopes that if I just kept drilling all the facts into my mind, they might act as a shield and stop me wanting to open myself up to him. Knowledge was power, right? He was beautiful, but he was damaged. It didn't matter what he said as long as I kept remembering that. That was what I tried to tell myself, that was what I wanted to believe. Yet still his words stung me, and his eyes entranced me, and I was never really one step ahead of him — I was always trailing behind, strung along from moments of venom to soft touches of velvet and back again.

I stood there silently, jamming the camera into the back pocket of my jeans and trying not to pay too much attention to what he was saying. *He'll get bored of talking about this in two seconds and become the shining Cadence again,* I was thinking determinedly, trying to reassure myself. *And it doesn't even matter anyway.*

He trailed off, as I had predicted. I expected him to shoo me out of the attic once he'd finished. Instead, he turned around to face me, tapping the handle of his brush thoughtfully against his lips.

"If you found something meaningful to do with your life, would you do it?" His voice was worlds away from the harsh, snippy one he'd been using only moments ago. The edges of his tone had been rounded, vowels drawn out and consonants blurred slightly.

I opened my mouth, and shut it again just as quickly. Was this question another trap? Was he trying to lure me in? If I knew that it could be, then I couldn't really be caught, could I? I decided to answer honestly. After all, there was nothing stopping me from simply leaving the attic or screaming for Leigh if things became too much to handle.

"Yes, I would," I said.

In an instant, Cadence came toward me, stopping barely a foot away. He looked at me, his lips slightly parted, his eyes glimmering with a hint of moisture. Then he tilted his head back slightly, gazing up at the ceiling light, and without meaning to, I noticed a hundred little things about his face. The arch of his eyebrows. The outline of his cheekbones. The way his hair fell across his forehead. The sharp line of his jaw. The precise shade of faint pink that his lips were. The fact that his eyelashes were as blond as his hair. How had I never seen that before? I was captivated. Sometimes, I thought he could do anything to me and I wouldn't care, if it would only make him feel something.

"Sphinxie," he said, and I blinked. He looked away from the ceiling, back into my eyes, and I remembered that I'd never noticed his eyelashes because I wasn't supposed to be looking at him that way, especially not now that I knew his secret. *You were supposed to get married,* said my mother's broken voice in my head, the memory of her crying on my shoulder in our kitchen swimming, unwanted, to the forefront of my mind.

"Sphinxie," Cadence said again, and I blinked again, trying to clear my head.

"Yes?" I said, forcing my voice to be steady.

"Come with me when I go," he said, in a soft whisper.

"Come with you?" I repeated, confused. "Come with you where? I don't know what you —" I stopped short. His eyes were burning underneath the lowered lids, a forest fire beginning beneath a covering of leaves. And suddenly, I understood. My mouth went dry. "You mean you . . . you want me to die too?"

My voice came out higher than usual and cracked slightly. I started shaking my head vaguely, my chest feeling as though it were filling rapidly with ice water. So this was it. This was why he had wanted me, this was why I was here.

"No," I said, shaking my head, trying to make my voice sound firm and strong. "No, I'm not dying with you. I can't do that."

"It would make sense, Sphinx," he said, in that same whisper. "We both know what's going to happen to our mothers' plan. It's only going to break further. It'll break them, Sphinx, when I'm gone and you're still here. You'll be a reminder to both of them of just how wrong everything went. It would be best if you took yourself away, and came with me. Both of us gone, quietly, gently. Our mothers moving on and remembering us how they want to, instead of the way we really are. It's meant to be that way. We were planned for each other, Sphinx, you know that. We were made for each other, meant for each other. And now we have to go together, can't you see that?"

"No," I said, and I heard my voice growing smaller, higher, weaker. "No, that's not —"

"And we'd be dying together," he went on, ignoring my feeble protests and moving still closer to me, only inches away now. "Just think of how we'd look, Sphinx. Imagine us. Lying on my bed, slipping away, as though we were falling asleep. We'd be perfect. It would be art." He reached out with the hand that wasn't still holding the paintbrush and took my hand slowly, gently. "We could even hold hands," he murmured.

My hand was stiff in his, frozen along with the rest of me. But I could imagine us. I could imagine how pale and still we'd be, like statues carved from white marble. Our eyes would be closed and my head would be resting on his shoulder and our hair would be spread out underneath our heads and, yes, we'd be holding hands. My hand started trembling in his grasp, my fingers folding over his, like an invisible force was pushing them down, even though I was fighting it at the same time. My fingertips grazed his flesh and I pulled them back as though they'd been burned, making my hand stiff again. But I could see how we would look, I could see exactly how we would look, a twisted facsimile of Romeo and Juliet.

My heartbeat sped up, feeling as though it were pounding against my rib cage, begging to be saved from the icy ocean in my chest. I felt sick because Cadence was standing so close to me, because of what he'd suggested — because I could see how it was true. The plan *was* only going to break apart further, wasn't it? Our mothers *would* be tormented by my presence after Cadence's death. If we *were* both dead, they would be able to remember us soft and perfect if they wanted to. And I wouldn't be left behind, haunted by the imprint of Cadence and his terrible shining light, like a camera flash that had gone off and stung my eyes and blinded me forever.

We were planned for each other, we were meant for each other, and now we have to go together.

I knew that his words were obviously wrong. They should have been easy to dismiss, they should have sounded crazy, but they weren't. They were starting to make sense, the idea was taking hold inside of my head. I tried to swallow and couldn't. The inside of my throat felt like it was thickening.

But, no. No, no, no. I didn't want to die. I didn't want to kill myself. I would *never* want to do that.

I wanted to protest aloud, but I couldn't anymore. It wasn't an option: My voice had frozen in my throat, the ice in my chest had reached up and caught it there. I just stared at Cadence, at those terrible eyes, at his mouth. I could take my hand out of his at any time. There was nothing really rooting me to the floor underneath my feet. The attic had no locked door to keep me prisoner inside. But what if he tried to take my life if I disagreed, if I didn't do it myself? I had never been so terrified.

But I could see it. I could make sense of it. *Did that mean I could do it?*

"We'll plan it all out," Cadence said. "It has to be art. I'll think of the perfect way for you to do it."

In my head, I was little again. I was in my backyard and the games that Cadence thought up were always the best games in the world, always far better than anything I could have come up with. I was sitting on the floor in his room on the day before the shared birthday party we were going to have. I was looking up at him as he sat perched on his bed and told me that he'd think of the perfect games to play at our party.

Cadence let go of my hand and cocked his head to one side, regarding me thoughtfully. Then he reached out and traced the line of the scar on my cheek, slowly, deliberately.

"Another knife for you, Sphinxie," he said. "Don't you think that would be perfect?"

Click. I felt like I'd been awakened from a state of hypnosis. This was out of hand, I had let him talk to me for far too long. I should have shut him down right at the beginning, run from him. Just because someone knows that there's a steel trap set in the woods doesn't mean that they're safe from walking on top of it. I tore my voice out of my throat, ripping it through the ice.

"No," I said as firmly as I could despite my shaking voice. "No, I won't do that. I'm not killing myself. I'm sorry about what's happening to you, Cadence, but I am not dying with you."

His eyes snapped open wide, no longer soft. He tightened his grasp on my hand, tight enough to make me gasp slightly. Wordlessly, he jerked my hand up and twisted it, turning it so that the underside of my wrist was facing upward.

"Let go of me, Cadence," I said, pulling backward, but his grip was vicious. "I said, let go of me!" He ignored me, and lifted the paintbrush, still soaked with ultramarine. Wordlessly, he painted a line across my wrist and then dropped my hand. I tried to dart backward, but he caught me by the other wrist, twisted it upward, and painted a line on that one, too.

"Let go of me!" I said again, louder and more frantic. He

released my hand as though he were dropping something into the trash and towered over me.

"When I said come with me," he said, his voice reduced to a hoarse growl in his throat, "I meant it, Sphinx."

"When I said I'm not killing myself, I meant it," I retorted, trying to be defiant.

"Why?" he said, challenging. "You don't have anything better to do. No plans for the future, isn't that right? Nothing except this. And there isn't ever going to be anything better for you than this, Sphinx." He turned on his heel and walked back to the canvas. I looked down at the painted lines on my wrists and imagined them changing, ultramarine giving way to dripping red. I felt all the air go out of my lungs, as though I were already dying where I stood.

Then I turned and ran from the attic, sprinting down the stairs fast enough that I tripped and nearly fell. Tears sprang to my eyes as I skidded around the corner into my room, into the en suite bathroom. My hands fumbled with the sink taps. I jerked them on and shoved my wrists underneath the gush of water, scrubbing until there was no trace of the paint, until my skin turned pink from the hot water. Panting, I turned off the water flow and leaned against the bathroom counter, water pooling around my hands, my head down, watching a little tendril of paint snake its way down the sink drain with the water.

I didn't want to kill myself. I would never want to do that. But I wasn't lifting my head to look at myself in the bathroom mirror, and I knew why.

I didn't want to see the person who might take my life.

21

After shakily drying my hands, I went into my room and sat down on the bed. The digital camera was still in the back pocket of my jeans, and it pressed uncomfortably against me when I sat down. I pulled it out and tossed it lightly onto the bed, and then lay down beside it, curling into a ball.

It really felt like my room now, and not a guest room. I had been there for just over a month by then, woken up in that room for more than four weeks. The sheets and pillows had my scent on them; they no longer smelled foreign. And the guest bathroom had my makeup and hairbrushes spread constantly over the sink counter. I no longer bothered to put them away after each use. I had settled in at Leigh's house, snuggled in for the winter.

I shivered and wrapped my arms around my own body; it was a colder winter than I'd expected, and my mind was made of different stuff than I'd thought. People always talk about how when you're young, you feel like you're going to live forever, an evergreen amidst the blizzards. Now I felt my hair fall over my forehead and was reminded of dead leaves — brown, dry, falling, and then covered by a blanket of heavy, icy white.

No. I had to get out. It wasn't time for that, not for me.

I could call my mother. I could tell her everything. I could get a flight. I could make my excuses to Leigh, say that it was too hard for me, that I wasn't strong enough to stay and watch Cadence fade away. I could make myself believe it for a little while, for as long as it took to get out, to safety, to a place where it was still warm.

I had a wild thought in my head all of a sudden: I would stay, but I'd be fine. And when I left, I would take all of Cadence's paintings with me to the United States, show them to somebody at an art gallery, and make them famous. They would hang them up on the pristine walls of the gallery, shine lights down on them from overhead, and charge people to see them. Under them would be a little card with Cadence's name and the title. Did they have titles? I had never heard Cadence call any of his paintings by any particular name, but they had to have titles. He must think of all of them as something. I would find out what they were called, before he died. I would write out all the names on a folded piece of paper and take it back with me, with all the paintings, to some art gallery that would make them famous. And maybe the proceeds from people paying to see the paintings could go to research for the kind of leukemia Cadence had, or research for curing sociopaths . . .

I stopped myself. It sounded like a sappy Chicken Soup for the Soul story: a girl bringing her dead friend's paintings home with her, getting them discovered, donating the money. It was cliché. It was the end of every movie ever conceived on the subject, if any ever were. Besides, whose dream was it to be famous *after* their death? And this was assuming that I ever left Leigh's house. After finding out what was wrong with Cadence, I'd thought that I was protected by my knowledge, untouchable as long as I remembered what he was. I'd thought that as long as I kept telling myself the truth over and over that he wouldn't be able to get inside my head. Now I knew I was wrong. If I stayed, there was a chance I wouldn't be taking anything home with me, that my things might stay spread out in Leigh's guest room forever — or at least until my mother came and packed them away.

And Cadence doesn't believe in God anyway, I thought distractedly. From what I understood of religion, if you didn't believe, you would just disappear after your death. No eternal life. No looking down from the clouds to check and see if you were famous yet. No peering at Earth to check up on how people were remembering you. Would that happen to me too, if I went, when I went? Did I believe enough? My breathing sped up involuntarily: I vaguely remembered hearing something once about how suicides didn't get into heaven. Was that true? No, it couldn't be . . . not if you were a good person, not if you were killing yourself for someone else, not if you were fulfilling an ultimate purpose, not if it meant something . . .

I got up from the bed abruptly. It wasn't good for me to be alone now. I needed distractions, I needed to shake myself awake, I needed to be with someone, anyone. Quickly, I darted out of the room and went downstairs, skidding around the corner at the bottom.

"Leigh!" I said, surprising myself with the urgency of my own voice. She was sitting at the kitchen table, a mug of tea in front of her. I stopped, wondering if she was crying, but when she turned to look at me, she looked only as sad as usual.

"Yeah?" she said, her voice husky. "Something wrong?" Her brow furrowed.

I opened my mouth and shut it just as quickly. *Something wrong?* She'd asked that question so casually. Yes, I was sure that my face looked pale and frightened, that she could hear how fast and odd my breathing was, but she didn't know what was going on. She didn't know what Cadence had said to me, up in the attic, and she didn't know what I had been thinking of, what I was still thinking of.

A sudden burst of mixed anger and horror flared up in me. Leigh didn't know *anything.* She hadn't known what was going to happen the day Cadence cut me, she hadn't known that something was wrong with her son, she hadn't known enough to keep me from being scarred — and even now, with Cadence diagnosed, she still remained unaware of what he was doing to me. And my mother — my mother knew even less. My mother was probably standing in our kitchen back at home right now, doing something trivial like rinsing dishes in the sink, completely unaware of what was happening to me. Why didn't they know? They were adults, they were *mothers*. It was their job to know what I couldn't tell them.

"No," I said, forcing myself to speak in a level tone. "No, I'm fine." I looked around, making sure that Cadence hadn't snuck up behind me. "But, Leigh, I was just upstairs watching Cadence paint, and he was talking —" I paused, reining in the words that were on the verge of tumbling out of my mouth. I could not tell Leigh what Cadence had said to me. She would react in horror, she would march upstairs and speak to him about it, and he would be angry with her — with me. What would he do, if I were to tell Leigh what he had said to me? I thought of the blue painted lines on my wrists; they were still there in my head even though I had washed them off, phantom reminders.

"He was talking about how most artists were only famous after their deaths," I said haltingly. "I think . . . I think he thinks that's what's going to happen to him. I was wondering, maybe could we fix it so that he has some kind of an art show somewhere, like, in a real gallery?"

Leigh's eyes lit up, and I knew that she had just forgotten whatever white-faced expression I'd had on when I'd come downstairs. It had been put entirely out of her mind by the suggestion of something else she could try, another chance to wake her child up inside.

"I can't believe I never thought of that myself," she said, stammering slightly. "It's just that he's always kept his art so secretive . . . always hidden up there in that attic . . . but I'm sure he'd love that . . ." Her voice was already tinged with hope. Hope, as her kitchen floor turned to quicksand underneath my feet, my hand gripping the edge of her kitchen counter, white-knuckled. And she didn't know.

"Do you have any local art galleries?" I said, and marveled at how convincingly calm I sounded. "We could call them and tell them the situation, I'm sure they'd let us have one of their rooms to put up Cadence's stuff, it'd be so great . . ." I trailed off. What was I doing? What had come over me that made me think I couldn't ask for help, that made me think I had to cover up my terror and deal with this on my own, as though there were no one else in the house? Of course I had to tell Leigh, I had to tell her everything. It was a simple, horrific fact of life that mothers did not always know what was happening to their children; I could not rely on Leigh's being able to read my mind to save me. And keeping secrets when my life was at risk was stupid, I was old enough to know better.

I suddenly recalled sitting on the airplane before takeoff, when my journey here had begun, listening to the flight attendant explaining the oxygen masks. *If there is a loss in cabin pressure, yellow oxygen masks will deploy from the ceiling compartment located above you.*

"Yes, I'm sure they would," Leigh went on. She had gotten up from her seat and starting pulling open drawers, looking for a phone book. I sensed that she was holding back tears, but pushing all of her emotion into looking for that phone book, and then into rapidly flipping through the pages. Her eyes were a mother's eyes, hungrily drinking in the sight of the phone numbers, searching for that one art gallery that would give her one more chance to make her kid smile. *To secure, pull the mask toward you, and fasten it so that it covers your mouth and nose,* said the flight attendant in my memory, holding up the example mask and stretching out the elastic band to demonstrate how it worked. *Please make sure to secure your own mask before assisting others.*

"Wait!" I said suddenly.

She turned to look at me, her eyes full with her desperation. And I was trapped again. I thought it would destroy her to know what Cadence wanted me to do . . . to know he was able to say it beautifully enough that I wasn't sure if I was going to leave her house alive. And this woman must have been destroyed countless times already: when Cadence had cut me, when he'd been diagnosed as unsaveable, both in mind and body. Would she finally crack if she found out what he had done now? I envisioned her committing him to some kind of a mental hospital, finally too overwhelmed to care for him anymore. That would be unacceptable; he couldn't spend his last days locked away because of something I'd told his mother.

"Leigh," I said, and my voice was calmer than it had been before, sounding foreign to my own ears. I licked my lips, trying to bring some moisture back into my mouth. "Leigh, I don't want it to be just because he's sick. He's a really, really good artist. Can't we get him discovered, or something? Can't we find someone who'll want his paintings before they know he's got leukemia?"

Her eyes dulled. She was thinking now, of the difference between a real achievement and the result of a stranger's pity. We both knew Cadence would hate that. Only one of us knew everything else. And I was getting better and better at producing that calm voice. With every moment that went by, more hiding layers were forming over the top of me, like a shroud. I had to tell her before I became unable to, before I disappeared entirely.

But I wouldn't tell her. I knew I wouldn't. The flight attendant was gone out of my head, taking her oxygen mask with her.

"I don't know if —" Leigh started to say something, but left her sentence hanging, an unfinished thread in the air. "I don't know if we have enough time." No, we didn't have enough time. I didn't have enough time. There would never be enough time for what was happening to me. But Leigh was talking about art galleries, about paint on canvases, not the paint on my wrists. I wished that I hadn't washed it frantically away. I should have left it there so that she could have asked me about it, perhaps pressured me into explaining it to her. Now there was no evidence of what had happened. She was never going to ask me anything.

The pages of the phone book relaxed, floating down to rest, slightly bent after her frenzied flip through them. And then suddenly, angrily, she crumpled the pages under her fingers, balling up them in her fists. When she let go, they stuck up stiffly from the rest of the phone book, wrinkled and torn in places. She looked at them for a moment, and then seized the book, raised it above her head, and threw it. It landed with a loud thump on the floor at our feet.

"Are you okay, Leigh?" I asked timidly.

She looked at me as though she had forgotten I was there. I knew there were dark circles underneath her bloodshot eyes even though she had makeup on to cover them up. She was staring at me, and I stared back, making direct eye contact with her. *Talk to me. You know what's wrong with Cadence. Can't you see what's happening to me, Leigh?*

Shakily, she leaned over to pick up the phone book. The look of a child was framed in her eyes, a child too old to have a temper tantrum, who was embarrassed that she had let go and had one anyway. No, she couldn't see what was happening to me, not at all.

"I'm sorry, Sphinxie," she said, and her voice was crackling in her throat like dry leaves, blowing away in a cold November wind, while her mouth trembled at the edges.

I forgive you, I thought, my throat stinging with a sudden lump. She was apologizing for throwing the book on the ground, not for being blind, not for hiding the truth. But it was easier if I pretended she knew what she should be sorry for. And if I thought *I forgive you,* over and over, maybe it too would become believable, like the calmness in my voice. I would be able to swallow it.

"I just . . . I can't believe I have to say that, no one should have to say that about their own child," Leigh continued, putting the phone book down on the counter. "That there isn't enough time. There should be enough time for everyone, you know?"

"Yeah," I said, so quietly I almost couldn't hear myself. "Yeah, there should be."

Awkwardly, I moved to hug her; I wanted to comfort her, and I wanted a mother to hold me, even if she didn't understand what was happening. She was an awful lot taller than me, making me feel more babyish than I should have. I felt like I was intruding into her private space, and I looked up at her, trying to discern if this hug was making things worse or better for the two of us. Her soft, moist blue eyes locked onto mine.

"See, it's that," she said, shaking her head back and forth. "It's that. I keep thinking if I had more time, I might see that in him."

"What do you mean?" I asked, confused.

"Just your eyes," she said, still shaking her head. "You're looking at me, and I'm looking at your eyes, and I can see that you know that I'm upset, and you understand, and you can feel what I'm feeling . . . you understand, because you can feel it too." She took a ragged breath, wiped her eyes on the back of her hand, and patted my back lamely, in an effort to resume her position as the grown-up — more collected, in control. The control only lasted a moment before she fell again.

"Sixteen years have gone by," she whispered. "And I don't think I've ever seen that with Cadence. Your mother sees it every day in you, but I've never seen that and now there's no time."

My confusion had left me. I understood her pain now. She had never gotten anything in return; her relationship with her child was one-sided. He may have run to her when he was scared, or sick, or wanted something from her, but he had never gone just because she was Mom, just because hugging was something mothers and kids did with each other to show that they loved. Leigh had raised an empty vessel.

Her arms unfolded from around me and I stepped back, taking it as the signal to end the embrace. Then she looked at me for a moment, paler than she'd been a few minutes ago, as though trying to discern whether she'd given away too much. And I averted my gaze, thinking to myself, *I already know. You could have told me, but I already know. I forgive you, I guess. I forgive you.*

Unknowing, she started trying to smooth the pages out in the phone book, to undo the damage that had been done, but it was obvious that the pages would never lie flat again. I watched as she returned to looking for an art gallery's number.

"Thank you," she said thickly, "for suggesting the art gallery thing." Her voice seemed ungainly, unsure of itself after pouring out such an unexpected wave of emotions. "I'm going to work on that, I'll have Vivienne help me, we'll try to get something done."

"Okay," I said. So this was what she'd do now. She'd become obsessed with this, she'd focus in on this, and block out everything else. And I was on my own, out in an ice storm without a coat.

Across from me, Leigh looked down at the phone book again. She ran her hands over the crumpled pages one more time and took one last shaky breath, recovering herself and recharging, ready for another try. Maybe an art gallery would let Cadence in, and maybe she would drive him to his show and at one point, he would turn around and see her and she would finally see it. Shining, warm instead of cold.

And maybe I would be able to remember that there was a world outside Leigh's house, outside Cadence's icy eyes, outside this situation that I was entangled in the middle of. I knew there was, but it didn't feel like it had anything to do with me. As it was, there were only the walls of Leigh's house and what went on inside them, what went on inside my head. But maybe.

Maybe there was enough time.

22

The director at the art gallery Leigh ended up calling said that it wasn't really their policy to look at art from a random source, especially from a teenager. Leigh had bitten her lip while she was on the phone with him, and I knew she was struggling inside, on whether to mention that this particular teenager had terminal leukemia or not. Part of her wanted to, just to make it happen, to shock the gallery director into saying yes right away. But the rest of her was a mother who knew her child. He would hate it if he found out that he had been given something because he was dying — and, oh, but he would find out. And really, was she doing this for him or for herself, for that chance that he might turn around and suddenly love her? For a distraction from the inevitable, so that she could believe for a little while that as long as she was searching and trying, Cadence would still be here to search and try for?

"What if I just emailed you some pictures?" she'd said, her voice rising higher. "Just three or four. Just take a quick look and tell me what you think. Please, if anything, it'll just be a nice experience for my son to get some feedback on his art."

Leigh drew out the conversation, babbling on and on, and struggled still. I knew she wanted so badly to just tell him that Cadence was sick — but she didn't. Instead, she got off the phone.

"He said that I could email him some of the paintings," she said, putting the phone down with a shaking hand. "He'll try to take a look at them if he's not too busy." She rubbed her eyes like a tired toddler, and added, in a much smaller voice, "I hope that I did the right thing by not mentioning that Cadence is . . ." She trailed off.

"You're his mom," I told her. "You know." *But you don't know anything.*

I felt she and I were switching roles; I was quickly turning into the adult, and her age seemed to be dwindling just as rapidly. Maybe I was imagining it, but it seemed like Leigh kept looking at me, almost as though for guidance, a light through the storm. I kept averting my eyes. Yes, I wanted to be there for her, but I didn't know if I could really do it anymore, not now. I wasn't strong, I was a leaning building in a great wind. I was standing on the edge of a precipice. I had a knife to my wrists, tracing the places where the blue lines had been, about to throw up because of the sight of my own blood. I could see Cadence and me lying motionless in his room . . .

You are *strong, though,* a voice in my head told me. *You have been here all this time.* And I knew that it was true. I had wanted to stay, I had put myself in a position where I knew I would be broken in some way, fighting it and wanting it all at the same time. I had been scared, and sad, and I had felt so small most of the time, but I had been there. I was there, just as I had always been, from the moment my mother was born, when she planned out her life in the fort in her backyard. I had been there all of those years, through the day that Cadence cut my face until now, and I was still here, and I would continue to be here. I was stronger than I thought.

But I didn't know what that meant. Stronger than *what?* Strong enough to take the abuse? Strong enough to sacrifice myself? Strong enough to live? Living, surviving, overcoming: That was strength, that was meaning and purpose. But walking willingly into death was strong too. Living, surviving; sacrificing, dying. At that moment, they were horrifically indistinguishable from one another.

During dinner that day, Leigh told Cadence that she had spoken with the director of an art gallery. "I asked him if I could send him some of your work, so that he could take a look," she said eagerly. "You'd like that, wouldn't you?"

"That would be fine," said Cadence. He reached into his water glass, extracted an ice cube, and put it into his mouth, sucking on it. Blank. He smiled, but there was nothing behind it. There was never anything behind his smiles except very occasionally, when I would think that I saw something shining with real warmth — but those times were never caused by Leigh. They were only when he was with me. Across the dinner table from me, Leigh drooped slightly, almost unnoticeably. She wasn't me. It had happened to her again.

And Cadence looked at me knowingly. I was rearranging my food on my plate, my appetite ruined by the sick feeling in my stomach. I met his gaze, trying to harden my own. *Don't let yourself be seduced,* I told myself. *I want to help him but I don't want to die. I don't.*

He bit down on the ice cube in his mouth, crunching on it. When he'd swallowed it, he fixed me with one of his dazzling smiles and pushed a stray hair away from his forehead, widening his eyes.

"You know," he said, "I am so glad that you're here, Sphinx." His eyes darted toward Leigh. "Aren't *you* glad that Sphinx is here?"

Leigh brightened, beaming at me. "Yes," she said at once, her eyes moistening slightly. "I'm very glad that Sphinx is here." I reached for my water glass and took a drink to alleviate the sudden dryness that had come into my mouth.

"I'm . . . I'm glad too," I said, and took another drink of water. *I made him smile. My presence had made him smile. I could do it. For him. For us.* I put my glass down, listened to the soft clink as it touched down on the dining-room table. *I could do it.*

Across the table from me, Cadence nudged his plate away with his forefinger and blinked, the persuasive smile still glowing on his face. And Leigh was still happy, still running on her momentary high from Cadence's being apparently glad about something. I reached down and gripped the sides of my chair, as though I would float off it if I didn't anchor myself. *I'm slipping,* I thought, and avoided Cadence's gaze for the rest of the meal.

Over the next few days, I tried to keep my mind occupied by thinking about the art gallery, and it became my go-to distraction from my scattered thoughts about Cadence's words and the blue paint on my skin. I wondered constantly if the director at that art gallery had finished his real work, found a few minutes of time in the office, and sat down at the computer to open his email. I pictured him putting a pair of persnickety glasses on the bridge of his nose, leaning forward in his wheeled office chair, his eyes roving over Cadence's paintings. I knew he'd see what a genius Cadence was, if he'd just take the time and look at the paintings, just like I saw it in my head. He'd snatch up the phone immediately to call Leigh, and Cadence would have his art show. And it wouldn't matter that he was sick. It wouldn't matter at all.

The only threat, the only thing that could make this fail to work, was time. The same thing that hurt Leigh every day, that made us all a little older, a little closer, as every clock in the world spun around day after day. I hoped that the art director would find the time, *make* the time, and just have one look. One look, that was all. Just enough time for one look. If he had the time for that, then maybe I had enough time to understand what I was supposed to do with myself.

The art gallery was the last thing Leigh could do. Before Cadence and I had gone through the coffee table, she had taken us out to do something almost every day, to fill our minds with something interesting and new and fun. Every single day, something to take our minds off the inevitable and fill the last days — the remaining time — with a better emotion. But we didn't go out anymore. Cadence was tired now. His cuts were still having trouble healing, his fractured rib not setting itself. His world had shrunk to include only Leigh's house and the few things that he did within it. He painted and played the piano and slept, and when he woke, I talked to him, letting him fill my ears with words that made my chest tighten and hurt.

Even though I was frightened, I was determined not to hide from him. I still needed to be there for him — that, at least, was something that I firmly felt I was supposed to do. Day after day, I went up into the attic, or into the room with the piano, right to his side. For the majority of the time, he ignored me, as though I were nothing more than another piece of furniture in whatever room we happened to be in. I'd stare at his back, noticing how elegantly he carried himself. Then I'd try to talk to him and receive nothing but silence in return. After his long speech to me up in the attic, this silence was unbearable. He was the only person who knew what was going on behind the veil of calm that I had donned to hide from Leigh. He had told me to give myself away for the sake of meaning and purpose and plans, for him, so that he wouldn't be dying alone. And yet he wasn't speaking to me. *You are the only one who understands! I need to talk to you!* Sometimes I wanted to scream, but I didn't have it in me.

One day, finally, after what seemed like years of agonizing quiet, I couldn't bear it any longer.

"Why aren't you talking to me?" I asked. I was sitting in my usual place, listening while he played Beethoven's *Moonlight* Sonata over and over again, and hugging my own knees to my chest for comfort and security.

"You know," he said, without ceasing his playing, "a lot of people lose their minds a little bit when they hear that someone's dying young, because children are always expected to live to see adulthood, or whatever. But I've decided that if you're smart enough, you can grow up whenever you want to. Some people are infants, Sphinx, infants forever. But not me. I'm not dying young." His voice took on a hardened edge. "I'm older than everyone."

"Oh," I said, trying to form a coherent response. "That's —"

He cut me off. "The reason I'm not speaking to you is because you need quiet to think," he said gently, rounding the edge to his voice in an instant. "You need to think about what you want to be when you grow up." He finished playing the piece, the last notes fading away into the open air of the room. "Oh, and I have a knife for you," he said, just as casually as if he was discussing the weather. "It's in the top drawer of my desk, in my bedroom. I'll tell you when to get it."

"No," I said, but the word felt flimsy and artificial as it came out of my mouth.

"It'll be soon," he said, through suddenly gritted teeth, and let the cover fall down over the piano keys, making me jump. Then suddenly he left the room, leaving the echo of the piano cover coming down ringing in my ears. I was still hugging my knees to my chest, tighter, tighter. *It'll be soon.*

I'd known that already, of course. I could tell that Cadence's life was coming to a close. Every day he was paler, every day he went to bed earlier, every day he moved slower. The hollows in his face deepened further. He could see the signs, feel them. And it was making him bitter, and frightened, and jumpy. He was clawing at the air, trying to find a foothold, trying to make sure that everything would be as he wanted it to be. Yes, he was resigned to his death, yes, he understood that it was coming, but he still didn't want it, he was still fighting. And in a way, it was the same for me.

But you have a choice, I tried to remind myself that night, after I had gotten into bed and turned out the lights.

Yes, I have a choice, I answered myself, curling into a smaller ball underneath the sheets and blankets. *I don't have to wait to grow up, to see if I ever get a boyfriend, to see if my mom and Leigh ever get over what happened to the plan, to see if I ever do anything else with my life, to see if anyone wants me with this scar on my face. I have a choice.* I pulled the blankets up halfway over my head and closed my eyes, but I was wide awake.

I heard Cadence throwing things in his room later that night; whatever they were, they thumped against his walls and fell to the floor with resounding thuds. I sat up straight in bed, my ears seemingly tuned to every sound that issued from his room, and listened. I could almost feel the frustration and anger floating on the air, emanating out of his room and hissing slowly down the hallway until it surrounded me in mine. There was a crash, larger than any of the previous ones, and I jumped. The sound was rippling over the skin on the back of my neck, giving me goose bumps.

Outside in the hall, Leigh's door swung open, and when she hurried past my room, her shadow stretched out in the light from the hall, tall and mutant.

"What are you doing?" she asked, her voice a loud whisper. She flung open his bedroom door, and I could almost picture her rushing in, anxious and eager. "Are you all right? Cay?" I got scared then, because I thought that the last crash might have been him, fallen.

"Get out of my room!" he shrieked, splitting the brief silence like a cracked piece of china. "Get out, get out, get out!" I pictured Leigh backing out reluctantly in my head, Cadence leaning forward aggressively, his eyes slits of burning blue in his head.

"Okay, okay," she said softly, trying to calm him down. "But please . . . please don't throw your things, okay? Please don't."

There was a pause, and then he exploded.

"Don't you dare try to tell me what I can't do!" he screamed, and I knew exactly how he was standing, so terribly ramrod straight, and trembling slightly, from head to foot. "Don't you dare!" He stopped and breathed, loud and hard and raggedy, making me wince. "I can do anything!" he went on, still panting. "Anything! Now get out!"

"Okay," Leigh said, trying to keep her voice soft and patient. She wanted to cry, and she wanted to be a normal mother and punish him, but neither would do her any good. "Okay, Cadence," she repeated, still soft.

There was another moment of silence, and I thought she had walked away, and I had simply missed seeing her shadow pass.

Then Cadence screamed again, wordlessly this time, just a long, high sound of twisted emotion that I couldn't even begin to interpret. And Leigh made a noise too, a yelp of pain, and something fell on the floor in the hall, something heavy and thick.

I dug my fingernails into the comforter on the bed and tried to chase the images out of my head. Why is it that your mind always imagines the worst-possible scenario to go with sounds? A moment later, Leigh went back into her bedroom, and I heard Cadence's door slam. And then the water running in Leigh's bathroom, trickling down into the sink and gurgling down into the pipes below it.

When I woke up the next morning and went out into the hall, there was a thick book on the floor in front of Cadence's room. The door to his room was tightly closed, no crack left open this time. I left the book on the floor, unsure of whether they wanted it moved or not, and went downstairs.

Leigh was standing in the kitchen, looking out the window over the sink. Her back was to me, and she was illuminated by the morning sun, the flyaways from her uncombed hair glowing in the light. When she turned around to greet me, she had a cup of steaming tea in her hands, and a gash on her forehead, red around the edges and scabbing over in the middle. I looked around, making sure that Cadence wasn't yet downstairs. He had been sleeping later recently, not rising at the crack of dawn as he had when I'd first arrived.

"Did he throw that book at you last night?" I asked, referring to the volume that had been left out in the hall.

"Yeah," she said, and her voice was just as it sounded in the night: soft and controlled, but defeated. Something missing from it. "Yeah, he did. I'm sorry if we woke you up, Sphinx."

"Oh, that's okay," I said. "I was actually awake. Anyway, I just hope you're all right."

"I'm fine," she said, shaking her head dismissively. One of her hands left the cup of tea and went up to her head, gingerly touching the wound. An odd look appeared in her eyes and I wondered if she was hoping that it would leave a scar, a mark to remember him by. Cadence couldn't give back to her emotionally; perhaps she wanted a physical effect, a piece of proof displayed forever that would keep telling her, *He was real, he was yours, you had a son.*

The memory of my first day at Leigh's house, of Cadence and me out on the swings, came back to me immediately. He had yelled at me for hiding my scar with concealer and asked me that question, the one that would ring in my ears for the days to come: *Don't you know that you have been touched by an angel?* Perhaps it was true for Leigh. He was her baby, her broken, fallen angel. Perhaps she wanted any touch he could find it within himself to give her, even if it was a scar. And perhaps Leigh and I were more alike than I'd ever thought.

All of a sudden, I realized I didn't know what I would leave behind for my own mother if I were to die. Just my clothes, my things in Leigh's house? The little painting of the crooked table that I had done up in the attic that day when we all painted together? Or would the countless pictures she had of me suffice? *Stop it,* I told myself.

Cadence came downstairs a moment later, breezed into the kitchen as though there were nothing wrong, as though nothing had happened in the night. His eyes studied the cut on Leigh's forehead for a few seconds, but quickly moved on. He stood leaning against the kitchen counter, the sunlight from the window throwing shadows into the hollows of his face; he had his painting shirt on, a rainbow of colors smeared over the fabric.

"I see you're planning on painting today," Leigh said, in that soft, soft voice.

"Yes, that's right," he answered casually.

"Are you almost done with that big blue canvas?" I asked him.

"No," he said.

"But there's only a little bit of white left," I said, remembering how far he had pulled the blue across the last time I had been up there. He tossed his head, flinging a few stray waves of hair out of his eyes.

"I know," he said, and strode out of the kitchen.

"Don't you want breakfast?" Leigh called after him, but he was already gone.

"Did the art gallery guy call you, by any chance?" I asked Leigh as she slumped back against the counter, gripping her tea with both hands. She shook her head, her lips flattening out thin as she did so. "Oh," I said. "Well, I bet he will, soon." I was trying to keep things positive in front of her, to make it easier for her. I didn't want Cadence to bring her down with him, and I didn't want to bring her down with me, either.

The phone rang while I was helping Leigh make breakfast:

homemade waffles on her old, heavy griddle. I went to check it and recognized my home phone number on the caller ID. Reluctantly, I picked it up, dreading what was to come.

"Sphinxie," came my father's voice when I put the phone to my ear. He hardly waited for me to greet him back before bursting out, "I know you want to stay, but you've dragged this out long enough. I want you home. You've already fallen through a glass table, and I'm afraid something else will happen. Put Leigh on the phone, I want to tell her to make flight plans for you tomorrow."

This was it. This was my chance to escape, to leave, to live. My dad wanted to make flight plans for me tomorrow, the very next day. I would be home and safe and there would be no more of these thoughts that I was having. I would go back to school. I would decide, eventually, on a college and a career and countless other things that I wanted to do . . .

But I was supposed to stay, until the end. I had told my mother that. This was the new plan. I was meant to be here.

"Okay, Dad," I said shakily. "Okay, but can I . . . can I talk to Mom quick?"

He sighed. Then I heard the phone being passed from hand to hand.

"Mom," I began when she got on the line. My voice was caught in my throat. "Please, Mom." I didn't know what I was saying *please* for. I was asking her to take me home and I was asking her to leave me where I was, all at the same time. And I expected her to understand what I had to do. She would have done the same for Leigh, after all.

"I know it's going to be hard for you to leave," she told me. "I know what you wanted to do. But your father wants you home, and I want you home. We've had a lot of discussions about this, and we've made our final decision on the matter. That's all." I was silent, biting my lip, feeling a lump grow in my throat. I didn't want to cry. I didn't want to die. The tiny little girl who would always be there inside me wanted her mother to save her.

"I love you," my mother said gently. She didn't even know what was happening to me, but she'd said *I love you* in a way that made me feel like she did. I swallowed the lump in my throat.

"Yeah, I love you too," I managed to say. Slowly, slowly, I handed the phone to Leigh. I was painfully aware of it slipping out of my hand, of my fingertips brushing against it as Leigh took it away and raised it to her own ear.

It felt like there was a crushing weight on my back as I went over to pry the waffles out of the griddle before they burned, as I heard Leigh move away from me and try to plead for me, as I heard her voice grow softer, her sentiments changing from protest to reluctant agreement. She went into the living room and turned on her laptop, beginning the process of purchasing a plane ticket for me, still talking to my mother as she did so. And I stood in the kitchen with a plate of new waffles in my hands, feeling like I might crumple to the floor.

I needed to stay. Cadence needed me, he was coming so close, it was coming so fast. We had called the art director, he might call back, and I needed to be here and go to the art show if he did. Leigh wasn't taking care of the budgie anymore, I was doing that.

And time was going, and I was going to have to make my decision. I was going to do something meaningful here. I was trying to make a choice, to decide what was going to happen to me, what being strong meant, what my life meant. But now my flight was booked.

Suddenly there was no choice, no time.

23

When Leigh hung up with my mother, she thanked me for staying as long as I had. She hugged me and took the plate of waffles from me, put the biggest one on a plate for me, asked me if I wanted syrup. I nodded and she drizzled it over, and it glistened like wet amber on a tree trunk in the morning sunlight. She perched a fork on the edge of my plate and began to get a plate ready for herself.

"I'm going to take my breakfast up to the attic," I said. "I want to see if Cadence will let me eat up there with him. Is that okay?" I thought maybe she might need me to stay with her. Maybe she needed to cry to someone again, just one more time. Soon I would leave and she wouldn't have anyone to be with her — well, except for Vivienne, I remembered. Even so, I didn't want to abandon her. With only one day left, I knew I should probably focus more on Leigh than on Cadence. She was the one who would truly miss my presence in the house, after all.

"That's totally fine, Sphinxie," she said reassuringly. "You go right ahead."

"Okay." I took my plate and walked upstairs, past the book in the hallway, still lying on the floor like a permanent tribute to what had occurred there. And then, up the attic steps I went — halfway, because suddenly I remembered the digital camera, and realized this was my last day to film Cadence. I went and got it out of my room before I went to the attic, shaking slightly.

I didn't know what he was going to do when he heard that I was leaving him, that I wouldn't be there to get that knife out of his desk. I wondered if he would give me some sort of grace because it was not my own choice anymore, because it was my mother who was taking me home. But that was silly; Cadence didn't do things like that. I felt a tremendous sense of apprehension building in my chest as I ascended the attic staircase. I wasn't crying, but my eyes were stinging, moisture forming at the corners.

Cadence hadn't yet started painting when I entered the attic; he was standing in front of the shelves of paint, mixing this blue and that one. The huge canvas was even fuller than the last time I'd seen it: Only a thin strip of white about four inches wide was left, the rest dominated by those familiar blue swirls, an ocean of nothing. I sat down near to the stairway and put my plate down next to me, softly, so that it wouldn't make a sound. Then I took the camera out of its case and turned it on, pressing the button to begin filming. I watched him through the little screen, choosing his colors, with a terrible sadness in my chest.

There was no way I could leave tomorrow, it simply wasn't possible. I had to be here. I had to see this through to completion. And if that meant dying along with him, then that was what would happen to me. We would be in his bedroom, white and still, surrounded by his art — art in and of ourselves. Our mothers would heal eventually, they would see us in sunsets and trees and blue skies and old videotapes and crumpled photographs, they would move on. The plan was out of their hands. It was our plan now, Cadence's and mine, and only we could decide what we were meant to do.

And yet the decision had been made for me, stolen from me. I was going home. I didn't have to die. My parents were insisting and my flight was booked for tomorrow.

I turned off the camera before he stopped selecting and mixing, not wanting to get caught filming. I put it back into its case and set it down behind my back, out of sight. And he turned around, the palette balanced delicately in his hand, a paintbrush held like a cigarette between his middle and forefingers.

"Hey," I said. "Sorry for not telling you I came in."

"I knew you were there," he said dismissively. "You can't startle me, Sphinxie." He walked over and stood in front of the canvas, his head tilted to one side. Slowly, he dipped his brush into one of the blobs of blue. His hand was shaking slightly, I noticed, like my grandpa's hands had before he died of a heart attack. I cut my waffle up and took a bite, and Cadence touched his brush to the canvas, lightly, gracefully, drawing out a string of ocean blue.

"I'm leaving tomorrow," I said, forcing the words out. "I have to go home. My dad's insisting this time, and my mother agrees with him." My waffle was stuck suddenly, somewhere deep inside me.

"Oh," he said, and I was sure that he hadn't really heard me, that he was too absorbed in the painting. It was more of a grunt than an *oh*, in any case. He was too busy drawing out those strands of blue, pulling them out longer and wider, covering the remaining white of that canvas.

I took a few more bites of my waffle and then set it aside, feeling the furthest from hungry that I'd ever been. I took the camera out from behind my back and started filming again, even though I already had a clip of him painting. His hand was still shaking, even though he managed to make all his brushstrokes smooth and flawless, flowing as perfectly as all the rest. All of a sudden, his entire body seemed to waver, and I leaned forward slightly, half expecting him to fall over backward, for his legs to give out from under him.

"You okay?" I asked, hoping both that he was fine and also that he wouldn't turn around and see me filming. He moved his feet, spreading them wider apart, as though to stabilize himself more. His head shook slightly from side to side, like he was chasing a wave of dizziness from his vision, and then he lifted the brush again.

Across the white it went, bringing a new blue with it. Mixing and blurring with the others that he'd already put down, reaching out further and further. I held the camera steady, but his hands were trembling, the palette wobbling, the brush dipping up and down. He was practiced, though, and he didn't falter. I edged slightly to the side, moving around so that I could get a view of his face, and slowly his profile came into view. I was taking a risk, filming in the corner of his eye, but he was focused completely on the painting. I moved the camera, following the arcs and lines, following the quivering hand, the slender, bony fingers.

And then suddenly I saw every line as a lifeline, a mark for everything that had happened to him, everything that he had been. A line for when he had woken up this morning. A line for looking in the mirror and seeing the bruises spread over his body, his white skin, his hollow face, bones pressing outward in protest. A heavy line for screaming, for anger, for confusion, for throwing the book at Leigh and then slamming the door. One for every time he had ever looked at the clock, at the calendar, and realized he was that much closer. One for when he had petted the bird so viciously, trying so hard to find what he could never grasp — that line started out thin and eager, and then exploded into a thicker swirl, for when he had gotten angry, for when we had fallen through the table.

A line for that day when he had asked me, if there was something meaningful to do with my life, would I do it? A line for when he had walked across the room and spoken so softly to me, and filled my mind with all of the terrible, beautiful images of what he wanted to come. Two lines to match the ones he had painted on my wrists, warnings, orders, vanishing scars, didn't I know I'd been touched by an angel?

There was a line for the day we saw my mother off at the airport, for when he had tried to bring a knife through the security checkpoint. A line for watching the raindrops course down the window in the restaurant. A line for pushing me down when he caught me in the attic alone, a line for us out on the swings, him whispering into my ear, and me remembering that we were supposed to be married. A line for the things he had left in the car, the brown shoes and the scarf and *The Metamorphosis*. And the blue spread out, and out.

A line for the pictures of him at my house, the one of him in front of the *Mona Lisa*, the blurred Christmas tree one that my friends had seen. A line for the phone calls Leigh had made about him, a line for the fancy private school and the teachers and the headmaster, and the doctors who had told Cadence that he was a monster for life, incurable, a sociopath.

His hand shook, and something behind his concentrated eyes clenched. He dropped the brush on the floor, and it rolled a few feet away from him, spattering thin drips of blue over the floor. Carefully, with decision, he dipped his forefinger into the paint on the palette and used it instead of the brush, finger-painting.

Lines for his childhood appeared, for the innocence lost, for the times he yelled at me and used me and lied, over and over again. A line for when we were outside with my father and the butterfly, and the second it was crushed between Cadence's little palms. A line for the switchblade in the desk in his room, a line in the shape of the scar on my face. A line for the sound that echoed in the room. *Click, click, click.* The blue went on, bigger and bigger. There was only a small space left now.

A line for when he was a baby, for when nothing was wrong with him yet. A line for him crying, for food, for warmth, for a new toy, like an ordinary child. A line for the first glimpses of shining talent, of the mask of good and perfect and beautiful. And then one for being new and formed and growing in the womb, floating upside down in a warm, mysterious ocean, while at the same time I too was floating, growing, elsewhere.

A line for the eggs underneath the fort in the backyard. For the plan.

There was a line for everything that had happened to him, everything that he'd done — and my presence was interwoven through each one. I felt tears stinging my eyes. It was impossible to tell the story of his life without telling mine too, so how could it be possible for my life to continue onward without him?

My own hands were shaking now, making the camera screen shiver and blur for a split second. And I looked over it, past it, at the full blueness of the canvas. There was no more white. *Beep.* I looked back down at the camera. A little black box had appeared over the screen, cutting off my video. *Memory card full.*

In front of me, he dropped the palette, and amazingly, it landed paint side up. He stood there for a moment, his blue-stained hands hanging limply at his sides, dripping paint onto his fitted jeans. The canvas seemed taller and bigger now that it was completely full of blue, and it surrounded him like a body of water. He was framed there by the blues, by the emptiness, by the nothing, and by the lines that represented everything, a paradox.

And then he fell, crumpling to the floor like a doll, carelessly thrown, a puppet whose strings had been cut.

There, done.

24

Leigh flew up the stairs when I screamed; in an instant, she was there in the attic, and the footsteps echoing on the second floor told me that Vivienne had arrived for the day and was close behind. I sat where I was on the attic floor as they rushed past me, knelt on the floor next to Cadence, as Leigh put her hand on his head and shook him. The digital camera was still in my hands, the little black box still proclaiming that there was no space left in the camera, that the memory was gone. I wanted to get up and run over to the rest of them, to see if there was anything I could do to help, but I was frozen within my own body. It was as though what I was watching wasn't even real, and went on before my eyes in stop-motion; I gripped the camera and blinked stupidly, feeling helpless.

For a moment, I thought he had died in front of me. Left without me. I thought I was safe, and at the same time, my throat was constricting because it meant I had not gone with him, I had not done what he asked of me. My hand was aching because of how hard I was squeezing the camera. I didn't know what I was supposed to do.

In front of me, Leigh kept shaking him, trying to wake him. She grabbed his hands, covering her own with smears of blue paint in the process, and it almost made me nauseous, as though they were smears of blood instead of paint, as though they were linked to those lines that had been on my wrists. *Leigh's never going to get that off,* I thought distractedly. I had momentarily forgotten that you could wash paint off; it all seemed permanent.

"Sphinxie, go get the phone," Vivienne said, and her voice was quiet and serious. It was more frightening than if she had yelled for me to get it. I turned the camera off and ran down the attic stairs with it flopping from my wrist by the strap, slapping against my hip.

Vivienne stayed home with me while Leigh went to the hospital with Cadence. They wouldn't let her in the ambulance; she had to follow behind in her own car, and I imagined her driving after them, blind to the speed limits, her knuckles white as she gripped the steering wheel, the color gone from her face. For some reason, I desperately wanted to know what was playing on her car radio, if she had it on at all. And did they have radios playing in ambulances? *They should,* I thought, *they definitely should.* If someone was slipping away in the back of an ambulance, there should be music playing, any music, just something to send them off. Something for their semiconscious being to concentrate on before they fell away into darkness.

I sat down woodenly on the sofa in Leigh's living room, the camera still clutched in my hand. Would Cadence want me to go off my own and get the knife and lock myself in the guest room, instead of sitting here? Was that what I was meant to do? But I didn't know if he was slipping away in the back of the ambulance, I couldn't know that. Perhaps it wasn't time. And what was I thinking anyway? I was going home tomorrow. A plane ticket had been paid for already.

I turned the television on to distract myself, and Vivienne sat on the sofa with me, watching a British game show without really paying attention to it. I couldn't sit still; every second, my eyes darted toward the phone, waiting for Leigh to call us and tell us what was going on. I hoped with all my heart that Cadence hadn't died in the ambulance, or in a white, white room at the hospital. He hadn't wanted hospitals, he wanted to go at home. They needed to send him home.

An hour later the phone rang. Vivienne leaped for it, and by the words she spoke when she picked it up, by the way she pressed the receiver to her ear, I knew that it was Leigh. I turned off the television so that Vivienne wouldn't have trouble hearing her.

"Oh, he did?" she said, sounding relieved. "I bet he was." She laughed weakly. "Well, we're right here waiting for you." She paused, tapping her fingernails against the kitchen counter. "I know. I'm sorry." I stopped listening then, some of the worry lifting from my chest. He hadn't died; they were sending him home after all. I heard the click of Vivienne settling the phone back into its base.

"Cadence woke up in the ambulance," she told me. "He was angry," she added after a moment's pause. "He wanted them to turn around and bring him back home, but they insisted on at least checking for any problems that might have been caused by his hitting his head on the floor when he passed out."

"Well, that's good," I said, feeling like there was more to come.

"Yes," she said slowly. And then, "They told Leigh we're very close."

"Okay," I said, nodding my head and staring at the floor for no reason that I could fathom. "Okay, so . . . okay." I stopped myself before I could say something stupid. There was nothing I could say to change it. We were almost done.

And I was going home tomorrow. The feeling in my chest could only have been described as the desire to throw a tantrum on the floor, to be little again and vent what I was feeling, to scream to everyone that I was on the verge of something tremendous and meaningful. I was here to fulfill something. And he was almost gone, and I was going home tomorrow.

"Hey, Vivienne, can I use the phone?" I asked, my voice quivering.

"Sure, honey," she said, in a motherly kind of way.

I took the phone out of the kitchen and into the room with the piano, and I sat on the piano bench as I dialed my own home phone number. Outside, a cloud had covered the sun, and there was a flock of birds just outside the window, rustling through the trees. As I looked at the piano, listening to the dial tone and waiting for my mother to pick up, I could see a reflection of the window and tree branches outside on the shiny black surface.

"Hi, Mom," I said when I heard her voice on the other end at last.

"Hi, sweetie!" she said, bright and happy. "How are you? Your dad and I are looking forward to seeing you tomorrow! We've really missed you."

"Mom, I really miss you too, and I love you, but I can't come home tomorrow." My voice was wobbling all over the place, cracking and breaking like a crumbly ceramic vase. "Cadence passed out today, Mom, right in front of me, and they took him to the hospital. They're sending him home, but the doctors said this is it, Mom. I can't come home. This is it." I was pleading now, high and almost whiny. The sound of myself would have annoyed me under any other circumstances, but I needed to let myself sound like this. I needed to be a little girl talking to her mother. Maybe this was the last time that I would ever be such a thing.

"Mom, you have to understand. I have been here for so long, I've been through so much, I've gotta see it through . . . I just have to . . . please . . ." I was too busy talking to hear anything she had to say, to notice that she was silent on the other end.

"Sphinx," she said, and I didn't really hear her voice. I interpreted it as her trying to gain control of the conversation, to begin explaining to me why I had to leave tomorrow. I started talking again.

"I have to stay! All this time I've been here, I've been thinking about lots of things, like life and God and feelings and being alive, and being lucky and thankful and just being, and death and how" — I faltered, tears springing to my eyes and spilling down over my cheeks — "how not to be afraid of death, because it's a terrible thing but it's beautiful too, Mom, it can be an art just like life can, like everything can . . . and, Mom, you have to let me stay, because this *is* the plan. I don't know why it didn't turn out like you and Leigh planned, I don't know why it is how it is, but this is it. Our plans don't mean anything, Mom, because there's a bigger one, and we're all a part of it. This is the plan, I have to do this, I'm supposed to do this." I gasped for breath; I'd forgotten to breathe in between my words.

"Do you understand?" I finished, still panting. "Do you —"

"Yes," she said, in such a soft voice. "I know, Sphinxie."

For a minute, neither of us said anything. It gave me the sensation of hugging through the phone, that we were simply being together without actually touching one another. I heard her breathing. I wished I were really in her arms. I wished I could breathe in and smell her — her bodywash, her shampoo, the scent of our house.

"Dad and I will fly up there to get you, when it's over," she said finally. "We want to be there for Leigh, at the funeral." I nodded my head, and then realized she couldn't see me. And she wanted to come get me, when it was over, but I wasn't sure that I would be here to get. I stared down at the reflection of the window and the trees on the piano and watched it blur through my tears, swirling into nothing.

"Okay," I said, still nodding as I tried to blink the tears from my eyes, as I tried to convince myself about everything and nothing at once. "Okay, you'll . . . you'll get me then."

For a minute longer, there was more silence. I wondered if she was consciously listening to me breathe, as I was listening to her. I imagined her standing in the kitchen back home and was immediately hit with a wave of homesickness and a longing to be safe with my family, but I forced it back out of my head. I was staying, and that was all there was to it.

"I'm going to call you again, okay?" I blurted out, breaking the silence. "I'm probably . . . I'm probably going to try to call every night, from now on, okay?" I hadn't been talking to my parents on a regular basis since my mother had left to go home, but now I felt the need to start. I couldn't let this fragile, shaky conversation be the last one I might ever have. If there was going to be a last time, I wanted to sound strong and happy for her.

"We'll be here to answer," my mother said softly. "We're always here for you, Sphinxie."

"Thanks, Mom," I whispered, gripping the phone as though it were her hand.

Deep down inside, I felt like I had known what was going to happen. From the moment that Cadence had asked to see me, everything had been set into motion. He had wanted me here for a reason, had wanted to take me with him for a reason. I was the first playmate, the one he had first told what to do. I was the one whom he had learned to cry from, when the butterfly died, when things went wrong and people were supposed to feel bad. It was me.

His intelligence, his talent, his artistry? That was all his. But the semblance of normalcy, the fake smiles, the laughs, the tears that he forced out of his eyes, the emotions that he had learned to fabricate even though he would never understand them? He had copied them from me when we were very small, carried them with him all of his life, used them as a sturdy base for the rest of his illusion. I put a hand over my mouth, feeling a ragged sob rising in my throat. *I was Cadence's mask.* That was why he wanted me to die with him.

Leigh and Cadence came home not very long after I got off the phone with my mother. Vivienne and I went out and met them in the garage. There were dark circles showing under Leigh's eyes, making her look as though it were late at night even though it was only midday. And Cadence was weak and strange; he was shaky on his feet, but he didn't want any of us to touch him or support him. Vivienne tried to put an arm around him to steady him, and he bit her on her forearm, like a dog. No one even said anything; there was nothing to say. When we finally got him inside the house, he lay down on the sofa and stared at the ceiling, trying to fight the obvious urge to fall asleep. His eyes kept almost closing, but he always forced them back open, returning to glaring upward.

I wondered if he was afraid of falling asleep and never waking up again. He was certainly aware of the possibility, even if there was no fear attached to the concept. And he was looking so hard at the ceiling, almost as if he was seeing something other than what was there. Did he look up and see his life, his memories? Did he see his canvas of blues, stretching out and out? Or perhaps it was just the ceiling, and nothing more. Nothing beautiful, nothing profound. Just the ceiling and a stubborn child below it, clinging to any string he could find that looked like it was attached to life. He was such a fighter. He would go down throwing knives at his unbeatable opponent.

And me? I couldn't tell if I was fighting or surrendering. It was as though I were in a pool of deep water, deep enough that the light was blocked out, that I couldn't tell which way was up toward the surface. Deep enough that my fingers would not reach past the water and into the air if I lifted my arms up and searched for it. Searching, searching.

I sat on the sofa opposite from him and asked him how he was feeling.

"Fantastic," he said, giving me a wry smile. Then he touched his chest and said, in a more detached voice, "My rib hurts. Go get me some Tylenol."

Leigh got him the pills and a glass of water. He swallowed them and poured the rest of the water on the floor — just let his wrist fall limp and the glass turn over, as though he hadn't a care in the world. I stared at the puddle on the floor as Vivienne came over with a hand towel and began mopping it up, stepping on it to draw the moisture out of Leigh's living-room rug.

"Why'd you do that?" I asked.

"I can," he answered. "I can do it, and so I did. It was an experiment."

I didn't know what the point of the experiment was, but if it had been me, I supposed it would have been to see if anything would happen to me. If somehow the universe would shift if I just did something different like pouring my water all over the floor. Maybe doing something would stave off the inevitable, shock time into stopping for a minute to see what was happening here, to stare at the boy who was slipping away right in front of me. Beautiful and terrible and still stunning me, even now.

I used Leigh's laptop again that night, taking it up to my room with hands that felt colder than the rest of my body. I set it down on the bed in my room and climbed up in front of it, opening it and pressing the start button. The screen illuminated and came to life, icons popping up on the left-hand side, that picture of Cadence at the piano dominating the desktop. I shivered.

My cold hands trembling, I took the little blue plastic memory card out of the digital camera and plugged it into the USB port at the back of the laptop. A window came up on the computer screen, asking me if I wanted to upload the contents to an existing folder or create a new one instead. I created a new one.

The movies that I'd taken of Cadence, all the candid moments and short clips, little bits and pieces of an extraordinary life that was slipping away — they all came up on the computer screen, filling the empty folder that I'd labeled with his name. Each one was a little box, with a still frame in it: him at the piano, him painting, him, him, him. When I clicked on the first one, it grew and filled the screen, playing out for me. I adjusted the volume so that it wasn't too loud, and watched. I watched them all, there in my guest room. And when I was finished, the first thing I thought was of the blue canvas, finally filled, and the black box on the camera, beeping. *Memory card full.*

It struck me that I was never seen in any of the videos. In all of them, I was merely an offscreen presence, a silent camera operator. Now I wished that I had filmed them differently, so that I was visible in them too. So that if I did take my life, my mother would have films of me to look at, just like Leigh would.

I took a deep breath and saved the folder, once, twice, three times, making absolutely sure that it was stored in Leigh's computer. And then I closed the window, and turned off the laptop, and brought it back downstairs, my mission almost accomplished.

On the sofa, Cadence's hand moved slightly, the fingers stretching out, reaching and reaching for a split second before becoming still again.

25

They had a children's hospice nurse come to Leigh's house. I was the one who answered the door when she knocked for the first time. She was a short woman with red, frizzy hair pulled back into a bun, and a gold heart-shaped locket hanging from a chain around her neck. It looked like the kind of necklace every eight-year-old girl wanted, out of place on a grown woman's neck. She looked like a kind woman, but in my eyes, she was not a welcome presence: She was a harbinger, an omen of death to come, and when I saw her standing there on Leigh's doorstep, I felt nauseous. I couldn't bring myself to greet her politely because I was afraid of what might happen if I opened my mouth, and so I looked down at my feet and stepped silently aside from the doorway to let her in.

Moments later, I was sitting down in the living room, just feet away from her, still looking at my shoes, feeling embarrassed for not mustering a hello. She was perched on the edge of Leigh's sofa as she talked to us, her legs crossed primly at the ankles. On the sofa opposite, Leigh was leaning forward to listen, looking over every so often at Cadence, who was sunk into the sofa cushions beside her.

The nurse asked if we wanted to have a hospital bed installed in the house; it would make things easier, she told us. Cadence refused. He did not want to die in a hospital bed, he said, and forcing him to do so would leave him completely without dignity. The nurse shrank slightly under his burning eyes, lacing her fingers together in her lap. She looked stiff, sitting there on the sofa like a little stuffed bird.

"All right," she said. "We won't do that, then." Her voice was high, like a little girl's. I thought they should have sent a different nurse, one who was stronger and more fit for dealing with someone like Cadence. Then I thought that perhaps they had sent a doormat on purpose, to avoid any power struggles between nurse and patient. Perhaps she was the best choice after all.

She brought up IVs, fluids, and nutrients, moving her hands around in little gestures as she explained different choices and processes to us. Cadence watched her like a hawk, as though he were looking down from above at a smaller animal. In his head, he was standing on a pedestal, on his sacred ground; the nurse, of course, was removed from that, just like everyone else.

"No," he told her. "You can give me something for pain. You can give me something when I tell you I can't sleep. I don't want anything else. The only other thing I need is Sphinx." His eyes were glaring out from dark hollows in his head, shining, angry, icy, blue. "I am not prolonging this," he said, baring his teeth slightly. And the nurse shrank again.

Whether she was intimidated or frightened or simply saddened, I couldn't tell; she had seen a teenager — a child — who was dying, and who was accepting of it, urging it to come forward and take him on. No hospital bed, no fluids. Take him on. I wondered if she was just put off by the morbidity of the situation, or if she was thinking that he was something stunning, something shining. *Such a fighter.* She didn't know about the paintings, I realized. I thought she needed to go up to the attic and see the paintings.

Before she rose from the sofa and left, she reached over and gave me a comforting squeeze on the knee. I stared at her. She was smiling at me, and there was a dimple in her right cheek, and she thought that there was only one dying person in the house.

You don't have to die, I thought to myself reflexively.

"Make sure you take care of yourself," she said. Her little hand, a wedding ring glimmering on the ring finger, lifted away and she stood up.

"I will," I mumbled. I didn't know what my answer meant. The nurse's kitten heels were clicking away on the hardwood floors as Leigh showed her to the door, and then suddenly the coppery taste of blood was blossoming over my tongue, sharp and bitter. For a moment, I thought I was imagining it. I put a hand to my mouth.

"Did you hurt yourself, Sphinxie?" said Cadence softly. "You were chewing your lip the whole time that idiot was here." He raised an eyebrow. "See how easy it is to bleed? You don't even *notice* it."

Abruptly, I got up from the sofa and went to the bathroom to wash out my mouth with cold water.

Within the next few days, a morning came when Cadence didn't get up at all, and from then on he stayed there, in the bed that had nothing to do with a hospital, surrounded by the paintings on the walls, the fish swimming above his head. Leigh and I sat in his room in chairs pressed up against the wall, feeling like people in a waiting room. And he paid us no mind, he just read, and read, and read. Every classic he could think of, he read it, even if he had already done so. The books piled up on his desk in little leaning towers, the titles facing us, and I checked them off in my head. *The Metamorphosis*, the same copy that I had picked up off the floor of Leigh's car, was in the middle of one of the piles. I took it out one day and tried to read it, to gain new meaning from it, but I couldn't. I got through the first three pages and closed the book, placing it down on the floor underneath my chair.

Leigh didn't want to leave her chair, didn't want to let her eyes close. It was a struggle to convince her even to get up and go to the bathroom, and when she did, she raced out of the room and back in, her entire body shaking. She would return to her chair and sit down with relief written all over her features when she saw that she hadn't missed something, and her hand would stretch out, trying to hold Cadence's. And he always pulled his hand away, a hint of a smile tugging at the corners of his bright eyes, that smile that came over him when he was gaining amusement from someone else's pain.

"Please," I heard her beg once. "Let me hold your hand, Cay, please."

"No," he said, his emotionless voice sounding like something lost in the wind.

"Why? Does it hurt?" she asked, her mouth quivering.

"No," he said flatly. Then he turned his head to look toward me, his eyes burning.

I knew instantly that he wanted my hand, not Leigh's. His eyes were demanding it. When I shakily moved my chair closer to his bedside and extended my hand, he gripped it so tightly that I had to grit my teeth to avoid crying out in pain. It was the same thing he'd done to me out on the swings, looking for that feeling that was out of his reach, that feeling of attachment to another person. Now he was looking twice as hard. My fingers felt like they were being crushed, but I forced myself not to protest, to just let him squeeze. When he finally let me go, my hand was red, imprints of his fingers bruising on my skin.

Then he turned his head away from me, leaving me hurting and wondering what would have happened if he hadn't let go, just like I'd wondered what was going to happen all those years ago when he'd cut me. If he'd only held on longer, searched a little longer, would he have felt anything? If he'd kept on squeezing until my bones broke, would the wall inside his head break down with them? I stared down at my hand, the skin still marked red. The lingering pain was haunting me, making it feel as though Cadence were still holding on to me. The nurse came an hour afterward and gave him a shot of something for pain, making him out of touch. Leigh was quivering in her chair next to me.

I was thankful that she refused to leave the room. It meant he couldn't get me alone anymore. There were no more moments up in the attic or out on the swings or in any other places where Leigh's watchful eye couldn't see what he did to me. The only thing he could do was stare at me, and so that was what he did. Sometimes he looked at me for hours on end. I hid behind books and magazines and pretended to be reading them, but I wasn't. I couldn't. I couldn't think of anything else except that he needed me. But how were we going to do it if Leigh was always in the room? I was aware of my teeth sinking into my lower lip; it was becoming my new nervous habit.

You aren't going to do it, that's how, I thought, and stopped myself before I bit down. But hours later, after talking to my mother on the phone and flipping through a fashion magazine without really seeing anything that was printed in it, I tasted blood. Again, I'd hurt myself without meaning to.

On Friday, Leigh was asleep in her chair early in the morning when the light began to come through the windows. I crept in from my room to take my place in the seat next to her and found her head lolling down, her chin touching her chest. In her lap, she was holding her own hand; under her eyelids, her eyes were moving back and forth. I wondered if she was dreaming. I was about to pull up the shades over Cadence's window when she stirred and opened her eyes.

"Hey," I said softly.

Leigh mustered a weak smile. "Did you just wake up?" she asked, putting a hand to her face as though she could wipe away her exhaustion that way.

"Yeah." I sat down in the chair next to her. For a moment, we were silent.

"Sphinxie," she said hoarsely, "I think I need to lie down in my room. Just for a little while." Her voice quivered and she added, "But I don't know if I should. I don't want to be out of the room if . . ." She trailed off and put her hands to her face again, then ran her fingers back through her unbrushed hair. I had never seen anyone look so drained before.

Don't leave me here, I thought.

"Go on" was what I said. "I promise I will call you if . . ." I felt my own voice dissolving into dust in my throat. I had to pause and concentrate before I managed to finish. "If anything happens."

"Thank you," she said. "I'll just be a little while. A very little while."

Her eyes were red-rimmed from lack of proper sleep. As she rose from her seat and started walking toward the door, I found myself repressing an urge to reach out and grab the sleeve of her shirt, like a little kid looking for something to cling to. Instead, I grabbed the edge of my seat. And Leigh drifted out of the door, and disappeared into the hall.

And I sat in the dim room, perched on the edge of my chair with my knees drawn together, and listened to the sound of

Cadence's breathing. It was raspy and hoarse, as though something was caught at the back of his throat.

His eyes opened slowly, and stared at the painted fish on the ceiling; they moved back and forth as though tracing actual movement. He turned his head to look at me, and I jumped slightly, startled for some inexplicable reason. And he stared.

"Hey," I said quietly when he didn't say anything. "Good morning."

He nodded in acknowledgment, a vague twitch of his head. I saw his chest moving up and down shallowly, in and out, rasping. He clenched and unclenched his hand.

"You want me to call the nurse to come over? Do you need more medicine?" I asked, thinking for a second that he had lost the ability to speak, that he was in pain and trying to tell me with that clench of his hand.

"No," he said hoarsely, in a vestige of his old slick-as-oil voice.

"Oh, okay," I said. My heart was suddenly pounding in my chest.

He was silent for a moment, clenching his hand again. Then he licked his lips, and said, "Your mother told you the story, didn't she?"

I fidgeted slightly in my chair, feeling like a suspect in an interrogation room, and thought, *No, no, no. Not now.* I looked toward the door. I imagined myself running out into the hall, calling for Leigh, but I couldn't. My hands were stuck to the seat of my chair, fingers gripping the edge so hard that my knuckles turned white.

"You mean about the plan? Yeah," I said.

He laughed, a dry croak, and reached a hand up to push his hair out of his eyes. And I thought of the plan, and of what he and I were supposed to do. Boyfriend and girlfriend, engaged, married, children, grandchildren running around the feet of my mother and Leigh on Thanksgiving. And I remembered Cadence and me out on the swings on that first day, and how his hand had felt on my skin, warm and human and all there, touching me.

"I suppose we won't be getting married now," he said, and laughed again.

"Yeah," I said, biting my tongue in an effort to keep myself from crying.

"Imagine," he said, his eyes wide and haunted. "Imagine what it'd be like." And he laughed again, for the last time. "You couldn't raise my children, Sphinxie, I know you couldn't. That wasn't what we were supposed to do." He took a shallow breath and explained, "*This* is what we're supposed to do, you and I. We're meant to end this way. We always have been."

I imagined a little blond boy or girl in my arms, one with icy blue eyes, one who was nothing like me, one who was shining and smart and terrible. *But maybe we would've had one like me,* I thought, and immediately stopped myself. I couldn't think like that, especially not now. I gripped the side of the chair tighter and concentrated on driving all thoughts of the broken plan, of what was supposed to be, out of my head.

"Sphinxie," he said, tearing me away from my thoughts.

"Yeah?" Cadence was looking at me as though I were the only thing he could see, and I was thinking, *No, no, no.* My hands were freezing.

"I want to hold the bird," he stated.

"The bird," I repeated. I felt as though someone had removed a gun that had been pressed against my head. He just wanted the budgie right now. That was all.

"Yes, that's what I said," he told me impatiently. "Go and get the budgie, Sphinx."

I rose from my chair and went downstairs, my footsteps sounding louder than usual through the quiet downstairs part of the house. Inside his cage, Wilbur was fluttering around, singing in celebration of the morning. I hesitated after opening the cage door, but then a grown-up part of me insisted that people were more important than budgies, and I took the bird out, holding him with both hands so that he wouldn't flap away. He chirped and nibbled at my fingers with his blunt little beak, and I carried him back upstairs with me.

"Here he is," I said as I came through the door into the bedroom. I brought him over to the bed and put him down near Cadence's hand, which lay idly on the bed at his side, clenching and unclenching. The budgie swiveled his head around curiously, and climbed up on top of Cadence's hand, pecking absentmindedly at his thumbnail. "There you go."

"Thank you," said Cadence primly, and fixed his eyes on the bird's little head. He watched him for a moment, his eyes seeming to grow wider by the moment, and then he said, "Sphinxie, I need some water."

"Oh? Sure," I said, hopping up from my chair again. When I left the room, a part of me knew perfectly well what was going to happen, even though I didn't fully realize it. And as I went downstairs, as I got a glass out of Leigh's kitchen cabinet and filled it with water from a pitcher in the fridge, as I carried the glass back upstairs, I was preparing myself, thinking about what I would do when I went back into the room.

And when I did go back, with that glass in my hand, I saw exactly what I knew I was going to see. The budgie was lying next to Cadence's hand, the little feathery neck at an odd angle, one wing splayed out limply.

A last-ditch effort to feel something.

I set the water down on his bedside table. He hadn't really wanted a drink, I knew. He had just wanted me to get out of the room while he was with the bird, while he was breaking it between his hands. While he was trying, so hard and in the most broken way, to feel alive for just a second, to feel something other than a stony mask.

I sat back down in my chair, feeling so terribly small. Cadence withdrew his fingertips from the bird's body and closed his eyes briefly before opening them again. He looked tired, awfully tired. And who wouldn't be, after sixteen years of trying so hard?

Then he hissed, "Go to my desk and open the top drawer."

Suddenly, the gun was pressed against my head again. I shook my head wordlessly, and felt hot tears burning against my cheeks.

I was still shaking my head as I went to the desk and did as he said, reaching out, sliding the top drawer open with a soft scraping sound of wood against wood.

Lying on the top of a mess of papers and old notebooks was a run-of-the-mill kitchen knife, probably stolen away late at night when there was no Leigh or Vivienne bustling around cooking something or making tea. I reached out a shaking hand and picked it up, gripping it. For a split second, I could see my reflection in the blade: my wide eyes, my twisted mouth, my mouse-brown hair tangled around my face.

I turned back to face Cadence and he gave me an unreadable look, his eyes fixed on me as though I were the only person left on the face of the earth.

"Sphinx, you shouldn't be crying," he said. I hadn't realized that I was until he said it. "Not when you're about to do something meaningful."

The knife quivered in my hand. I willed my fingers not to betray me, to hold on to the hilt. He stared at me, his eyes hardening, and leaned forward, raising himself up from the bed as far as his weakened body would allow him to go. And I stood in front of him, shaking, thinking about his fist in my hair when we were little, holding me as he drew the blade across my cheek. About Wilbur, and how he had been alive just a minute ago, only a minute ago. About all the times I had ever looked in the mirror and wondered what I was supposed to do with myself, what I was meant to do.

All of it was swirling in my head, faster and faster. Slowly, my hand trembling, I lifted the knife, holding it poised over one of my wrists, right over the place where one of those terrible blue lines of paint had once been. And for a split second, my sobs quieted, as though my chest had been frozen, a premonition of last breaths to come.

"There," Cadence whispered. "Go on, Sphinx."

But I don't want to die, I thought, and a fresh sob ripped from my throat, rough and painful.

"Why are you *crying* again?" Cadence said, spitting out the words like a schoolyard bully calling someone a name. His voice was laced with sudden scorn, his burning eyes narrowed. I couldn't answer him, I couldn't speak. I stared back at him and tried to convey what I was thinking through my eyes: *I care about you, I care about you, I don't want you to die, I don't want either of us to die . . .*

"Why the hell are you crying?" he demanded. "Do it, Sphinx!" His voice was higher now; it was still scornful, but underneath there was something raw and soft, like an insect that has just shed its skin, not yet hardened. "You're supposed to do it!" he said, his voice breaking. "Stop crying and do it!" And I stared at him, and felt the hot tears running down my cheeks. *I care about you, really, you were part of my plan, I don't want you to die, I don't want either of us to die . . .*

It took strength to die, yes, that was something I was certain of. And Cadence was strong enough to die, strong enough to live as an illusion for sixteen years, strong enough to leave a world filled with unanswered questions and things he could never have behind.

But me? I was not an illusion, I was not a mask. There were people I loved here, and loved fiercely; I always had. The questions that I wanted to answer, questions of life and growing up and how to be a person — the answers were in my reach, my hands were open and ready to receive. And I realized, standing there in his room, the hilt of the knife like ice in my palm, that I wasn't strong enough to follow the plan, I wasn't strong enough to belong to someone like Cadence. I wasn't strong enough to die.

I was strong enough to live.

"I can't die with you," I whispered. "But I love you. I love you."

His eyes widened. Everything about him seemed to be searching, computing, trying, trying, but coming up with nothing. His fingers were moving as though preparing to grasp something physical, but they came up short, and he dug his nails into the bedspread.

"I love you," I choked out again.

"Why?" he asked. For an instant, some of the ice softened, his eyes opening themselves at the iris, trying desperately to let something in, past the wall. He reached for the budgie, long, pale fingers lengthening, his heartbeat pressing in his eyes. And he was a genius in front of his canvas, and in the school, and a living statue everywhere else.

And then he was gone, lying there in that bed underneath the ceiling fish, with the dim morning light filling up the corners and his blond hair tangled. And his eyes, his blue, searching, beautiful eyes, no light behind them anymore, finally human.

The knife dropped out of my hand, and just like that, we were both free.

Click.

26

Leigh came back in a moment later, as though some part of her could sense that her child had left the room. She froze in the doorway and looked at me first, me standing there with my shaking hands at my sides, my eyes like miniature waterfalls. And then she ran forward.

Almost without thinking, I kicked the knife and it spun, flying underneath Cadence's bed and out of sight. Leigh was a blur in front of me, checking his breathing, but it had stopped. And then she was up on the bed, touching his hands, his face. Holding him. Crying silently, with her lips just barely parted. And I simply stood there, numbly thinking. Cadence, this boy whom I had once known, who had once cut me, who had once marked me. He was gone, and I was alive. *Didn't I know that I had been touched by an angel?*

I couldn't stop looking at his eyes, open and staring and bare now, the ice melted, gone with his life. They were just blue eyes now; there was no fire burning, not anymore. Ordinary blue eyes — you might have seen them in anyone's head. Somewhere, was Cadence awakening, feeling peaceful and normal at last? Somewhere, was he standing on ground that was truly sacred? Would I know someday?

I stumbled backward and sat down in my chair. I wrapped my arms around my legs, hugging my knees to my chest, and closed my eyes. Floating behind the blackness of my eyelids, I could still see him looking at me.

I took a deep breath in through my nose and let it out through my mouth, shuddering. *Alive.*

Alive out of my own choice. Not because of my mother's plan, not because of Leigh, not because of anything except for me, and what had happened to me. This was what was really meant to be; this was my strength, my purpose. Alive.

My mother flew in the next day, and Vivienne met her at the airport. She came through the front door of Leigh's house and entered into a world of chaos: Leigh was trying to make arrangements, but she was scatterbrained and grieving, unable to do anything properly; the entire house was a mess, no one knew where anything was, and there was no food in the fridge. I kept expecting the doorbell to ring, neighbors to come over with food. Wasn't that what was supposed to happen? There were no neighbors, though, what with Leigh living in a field in the middle of nowhere. And I was slowly realizing that she had withdrawn herself and her son from the outside world, secluded both of them in a safe haven where no one could get hurt but themselves.

When my mother arrived, I was out in the backyard, burying the budgie. I had walked all the way out to the edge of the forest, at the very back of Leigh's yard, and dug a little grave underneath a tall tree. Carefully I laid the little body in the bottom of the hole, wrapped in a tissue, and covered it up with dirt, patting the pile with the trowel I'd brought to make it flat. There was a small stone on the ground, nestled between some of the tree's roots, and I placed it on top of the grave, a marker. I had really liked that little bird, I realized. I'd always imagined, in the back of my head, that I would take the bird with me when I went back home if I was still around to do so. That wasn't going to happen now. I could feel a sob wedged in between my lungs, putting pressure on my insides, but I didn't cry. I was dried out from the day before.

I went back into the house, carrying the trowel limply in one hand, and found my mother and Leigh sitting on the floor of the kitchen, with Leigh's laptop lying on its side on the floor next to them. Leigh was crying loudly into my mother's shoulder, like a little, angry toddler; looking at her made me feel as though I was watching something I shouldn't, something not appropriate. Vivienne was standing awkwardly next to them. After a few moments, she leaned down and picked up the laptop, putting it right side up on the kitchen counter. I looked at the screen and saw the clip of Cadence playing the piano paused, frozen in its little gray window. And behind it, an Internet window. Vivienne clicked on the Internet window to bring it to the front, so that she could exit it, and in the brief second that it was up and readable, I saw that it was an email: the art gallery director's reply.

My mother and Leigh separated; Leigh remained hunched on the floor as my mother pulled me into a tight hug.

"Dad's coming," she said. "He couldn't leave with me because of work. He'll be here tomorrow."

"Great," I said, feeling so, so strange. My mother was talking to me so casually. In her mind, she was greeting me at the end of a short time apart. She didn't know what she'd almost lost. I buried my face in her neck.

"I've really been missing you," she said into the top of my head.

"Yeah, I've missed you too," I whispered. My mother's clothes smelled like my bedroom at home, like her lavender bodywash. Someday, I would tell her everything. I would tell her what had almost happened. Someday, I would explain to her exactly why I had held her so hard, exactly why I would live from this point onward with my head held higher and my voice louder. I dug my fingernails into the back of her shirt and clung to her.

Then I looked up over her shoulder and saw Leigh, still down on the floor, with Vivienne kneeling in front of her, saying something I couldn't hear, her lips moving slowly. Reluctantly, I let go of my mother and left her to help Leigh, to talk about adult things and try not to cry, and I went upstairs to clean up the bedroom I had been staying in. The stairs felt hollow under my feet as I climbed them, like a ghost of something solid. The fact that Cadence was gone, the fact that I was not — none of it had quite sunk in yet.

In a fog, I cleaned all my makeup out of the guest bathroom, scrubbed the sink, shook out the towels and hung them up, wiped out the shower. When I left the bathroom with all my stuff bundled in my arms, there was no trace of my having been there. I had erased my presence, like a good houseguest. I dumped all my makeup on the bed and dragged my suitcase out from the closet, laid it out open next to the makeup, and went to work. Folding my shirts, my pants, deciding which shoes to wear and which to pack in the bottom of the suitcase. I filled and zipped up all the little compartments, and then went into the closet and made sure I hadn't forgotten anything. I hadn't, I was packed. I put the full suitcase back down on the floor, leaning against the wall, and made up the bed. I didn't have anything to wear to a funeral, I realized.

The digital camera was the only thing in the room that hadn't been there before I came, and that wasn't mine. I picked it up and sat gingerly on the edge of the newly made bed, turning it over and over in my hands. Slowly, I opened the case and took out the camera, my fingers hovering over the button to turn it on. Did I want to watch the clips, or was it too soon? Yes, I did, I did want to see them. I pressed the button and the little screen lit up.

When I went into the camera's memory, I expected the first clip to be the most recent: the last film of Cadence, completing the blue canvas. Instead, it was a shot of Cadence, sitting in the chair in front of the desk in his bedroom. It was framed harshly around his face, and I assumed the camera had been propped up on a stack of books. When I pressed down on the button to start playing, the first movement was his hand moving away from the camera, having just started filming.

"Sphinxie," he said, and the urge to reply, to acknowledge him somehow, was on the tip of my tongue. "I always know." I shivered, feeling as though he were right there, not really gone yet. "This was my old camera. You've done exactly what I wanted you to do." And I could see him in my head: getting his old camera out, inserting a new memory card, placing it on the table in the piano room, somehow knowing what I would do when I saw it there. He wanted me to film him. And, like a twisted prophet, he knew I would do it.

He laughed, and the camera screen blurred for me, somehow softened.

"You're a good girl, Sphinx," he said, in that cheerfully mocking way, and leaned back in the chair, looking satisfied, his eyes glowing. He shook his head, looking at the camera screen for a moment, a vague hint of a smile playing around his mouth. "And you're *different* now." His hand reached out to press the button on the camera, to end the movie, but stopped.

"Cremate me," he said decidedly, and his hand came forward. The clip ended.

Only five people were present at the service. Near to the end, Cadence's father arrived and joined Leigh, my mother and father, Vivienne, and me. Leigh didn't look at him, and he didn't look at her. Instead, they looked out at the ocean, where the ashes were, where the human being was whom they had once created together. I stood back from the group, wearing a dress my mother had brought along in her suitcase. It was simple, black, conventional. Once again, I was the ordinary one.

In front of me, the ocean reached out in every direction, rolling and changing, like the blue canvas.

We drove back to the house in a rental; there wasn't enough space for my family plus Vivienne in Leigh's little car. We were only going to stay a night or two, depending on what Leigh wanted us to do, and then we would be gone, sitting on a plane, flying over that expanse of blue. In the backseat of the car, I let my head rest against the window, and it was cold against my skin. It was so strange that everything was over, that Cadence was gone, that soon I would really go back home, and I had no reason to try and lengthen the visit anymore.

There was no one in the house who rose at the crack of dawn, who read books that made my head spin, who played the piano when the sun came in the window, who held his head high, whose eyes burned like flames behind ice, who was such a genius when he painted.

I licked my finger and rubbed the concealer off my cheek, exposing the scar. I straightened up and looked at my reflection in the car's rearview mirror, at the thin white line on my upper cheek. Perhaps I hadn't been touched by an angel, but I had been touched by something. Once, I had been marked by someone who shone so brightly, and who lived in the dark. Once, there had been a plan for our lives.

Outside the car window, a woman was coming out of her house, a handbag slung over her arm, holding hands with a little girl. I watched them walk down the front steps from their house, toward the car in their driveway. And I remembered: all the eggs, all the children a woman will ever have, are with her, inside her, from the moment of her birth.

A child I was supposed to have, my own end of the plan, the future of the world. A little girl or boy of my own, who would someday look up at me and ask me why there was a mark on my cheek, why I had a scar. I would tell a child the reason, someday, and that child was with me now, had been with me when I received the mark, when I made my decisions, when I was out on the swings, when Cadence had touched me, when I watched him paint his life away on the canvas of blue, up there in the empty attic. At the end, when his eyes were so bright, when he looked at me like I was the only one in the room, when I lived. My child was there with me, dormant, sleeping, one egg out of millions.

My child was there.

Acknowledgments

My utmost thanks go out to the following beings:

* To my God, Who first showed me the future and told me to write when I was very young.

* To Barry Cunningham and Imogen Cooper, without whom this book would not be here today.

* To my mother, who has answered the question "What did I do good today?" a thousand times over.

* To my father, who took me walking on the bridge when I asked him to.

* To my sisters, both blood and adopted, who strengthen me, inspire me, and stand by me as the very best of friends.

* To my soul twin who sat on her porch at night with me, and to our old black sheep man in another universe.

* To all of the dear friends who have been readers, listeners, laughers, and sparklers.

* To the lost little girl from my childhood, who knows not what she did for me.

* And to my shining girl, in the light — endlessly.

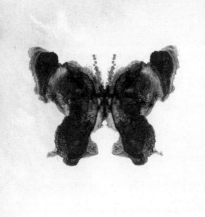